This book is a word of fiction. Names, characters, places, and incidents are the product of the author's imagination or are used factitiously. Any resemblance to actual events, locales, or persons living or dead, is coincidental.

PROLOGUE

Once upon a time, in a far-off land called New Orleans, a beautiful princess met the love of her life. Nothing bad ever happened, and they lived happily ever after....

Kidding!

If only it were that simple, right?

The true story—much like *real* fairy tales—is far grimmer. Death, deceit, decapitation, all our favorite D-words. Not to mention non-marital sex. Gasp! I know.

For those who missed everything, allow me to fill in those pesky little details. First, I'm the aforementioned princess. Second, I'm not an *actual* princess. And third, I really did meet the love of my life. Not that he knows how I truly feel about him. Yet.

As for the finer minutia....

The death was mine—I'm now a vampire.

The deceit was personal—a so-called ally handed me over to a nasty enemy who tried to burn me alive.

The decapitations were well-deserved—the love of my life (aka Dracula, aka Vlad) punished our betraitor, and a local werewolf cut off my enemy's head to save me.

As for the non-marital sex? Well, that's pretty damn self-explanatory. Dracula and I did the nasty, and it was *awesome*. We're already doomed, considering we're vampires, so what's a little sinful lurvemaking on top of that? Completely worth eternal damnation, believe me. Vlad is over five-hundred years old. Meaning his sexual prowess is off the charts.

Unfortunately, even after all the decapitations, there's still no happily ever after in sight. And that's because of our Vampire Queen Genevieve, Miss Formerly-Known-As-Marie-Antoinette. Apparently, she hates me. Why, you ask? Well, that enemy I mentioned? He was her sire—*was* being the operative word. Even vampires can't live without heads.

I doubt word of his death has reached the queen yet, but she's sent us a summons regardless. One I promptly burned before anyone else spotted it. But she sent another, and another, and *another*, until finally Vlad noticed. I told him there's no way we're responding. A trip to Europe sounds romantic and all, but the reality of this situation isn't as pretty. And why should I be the one to pay out of pocket to die? If the queen wants me dead, then it seems only fair she cough up the airfare.

The optimistic side of me hopes this will deter her. Maybe she hates America or maybe she'll tire of waiting for me and move on.

Or *maybe* I'm just daft.

I mean, vampires are eternal, and from my understanding, they hold grudges for an effin' long time. So, something tells me she won't wait much longer.

Lucky me.

Maybe I should get my affairs in order? Because, damn, my life sure has become dangerous since I died.

CHAPTER ONE

"SHH!" I clapped a hand over my best friend's mouth and giggled. "He'll hear you!"

Lucy—the aforementioned bestie—sniggered against my palm. An evil glint shone in her eyes seconds before she slopped her tongue across my hand like a frigging dog.

"Ew!" I snorted a laugh, then smeared my palm—and her drool—across her face.

Seriously disgusting! Everyone knew the human mouth was a dirty, nasty place. Okay, yes, I was a vampire and therefore impervious to all forms of diseases, viruses, and bacteria. But that didn't mean I appreciated being bathed in her gross cooties. And yes, I understood the irony, considering I rather enjoyed playing tonsil hockey with my vampire beau. Then again, Vlad preferred to lick *other*, more pleasurable parts of me.

"I swear, you're as bad as Sam," I grumbled.

Sam was our local Wolfman—aka werewolf—*and* Lucy's mate. We couldn't leave out that little tidbit of info, even though she desperately wished I would. My dear sweet Lucy was trapped in the denial phase of their relationship. It'd only been three months since vampires had announced their existence to the entire world. I think learning werewolves also existed was the overwhelming icing on the mind-boggling cake for her.

Lucy wasn't the sort who rolled with the punches. That was my role in this relationship. I was the go-with-the-flow sort who made impulsive decisions, which usually landed me in trouble. Hence why I was now a walking, talking creature of the night. Freaky, right? Not.

Lucy was the steadfast one and my austere counterpart. Always there to remind me to smarten up—not that I ever did. Where would the fun be in that?

I suspected my life had become a little too much for her. The same day we'd learned werewolves existed, she'd also learned one of them was her mate.

I absolutely shipped their relationship. Not only

because Sam had saved my life by beheading an evil vampire hellbent on burning me alive, but also because I believed he'd be good for her. Force her to loosen up a little. You couldn't have two serious people in a relationship. And I didn't see Sam loosening his reins at all.

From what I'd managed to drag out of Lucy, she and Sam had only spoken a few times over the past couple months. Instead, most of their conversations were through text. It wasn't ideal, but at least she hadn't written him off entirely. Now, if only I could get her to take the next step with him. She'd admitted to me more than once, in confidence of course, that she was absolutely hot for his bod. I didn't blame her. Much like Vlad, Sam scored a solid twelve out of ten. They were two different men, but both were abso-fucking-lutely mouthwatering. Except her man's body was going to waste, which was an absolute travesty.

Lucy swatted my arm, then pointed at the television and howled with laughter. "I love this part!"

I glanced up in time to watch as Dracula—a fictional one—leaned over a woman—also named Lucy—and bit her. When he started drinking her blood, it sounded like he was slurping it through a straw. I had to admit, there was a definite comedic value to that. One *my* Lucy found downright hilarious. The way she clutched her sides and rolled across the bed had me snickering alongside her. *Dracula Dead and Loving It* was old as balls but so very worth the hour and a half run-time.

"You should include this one in your next vlog," she said between laughter. "Use this scene to show the differences between the movies and reality when it comes to feeding."

Oh, definitely.

Ever since I'd become a vampire, Lucy and I had made it our mission to watch every single vampire flick out there, genre be damned. Then we tallied up all the fiction versus fact points and scored each movie accordingly. Sort of like a report card. Once we finished that, we recorded a video for my vlog and up it went, released into the webosphere. It was a far cry from my previous "the truth is out there" channel, but people were eating this new one up. My online popularity had skyrocketed since I was one of the few vampires pandering to the public. And because of that, not only was I raking in the dough, but I was also considered the first "vampire influencer."

My connection to Vlad certainly increased my

popularity, but I couldn't help that. Even now, I had interview requests rolling in. Podcasts, radio shows, guest starring on other vlogs, you name it. Everyone wanted to meet a real-life vampire, wanted me front and center on their channels, even though I had no reflection. But hey, my bank account was loving it. I was twenty-four years old and made more money than all my friends combined. Mind blowing when I compared even half a year ago to now. A real rags-to-riches story.

When vampires first came out, the queen had issued a gag order to keep any eager vamps out there silent. But she'd lifted the order two and a half months ago. Lucy had insisted I jump on the opportunity ASAP, and I'd taken her advice, knowing she'd never steer me wrong. She was now my social media and content manager and made a beautiful chunk of change herself.

Unfortunately, I hadn't told Vlad yet. Part of me feared he'd disapprove, the other part of me feared this would all blow up in my face. Fame was a fickle beast. One moment, you're walking on air, buying the newest Louis Vuitton pumps, the next buying secondhand shoes from Goodwill. I didn't want him to see any of this until I knew for sure it was more than a passing trend. He adored me, and I wanted to keep it that way.

"Oh, this is just perfect!"

Lucy's voice cut into my thoughts, and I glanced up in time to watch the scene where Van Helsing stuffed their Lucy's room full of garlic in an attempt to repel the villainous Dracula. My Lucy, on the other hand, was laughing so hard, tears spilled from her eyes.

I couldn't help but join her. Garlic truly was a treat for us vamps. And I didn't mean that in a pleasurable way. Even now, I couldn't handle the memory of that scent, and Vlad had only shown me one clove to give me an idea.

The thought of filling someone's room to repel one of us would *absolutely* work. And the image of it was so downright ridiculous, even my stomach had begun to cramp from the hilarity.

"Ohmigosh, Lucy." I dashed blood tears from my eyes. "Keep it down, Vlad's gonna hear you!"

"So?" She threw a handful of popcorn at the screen. "If ole Battikins pisses me off, I'll just chuck some garlic at him and run away."

I burst out laughing at the image, then clapped a hand over my mouth to muffle the sound. Lucy *loved* the new nickname she'd come up with for him. It'd quickly become her favorite after she'd somehow managed to sneak up on Vlad—a feat I still had no idea *how* she'd accomplished. But she'd startled him so badly, he'd spontaneously shifted into bat form. She'd just about laughed herself into an early grave that night.

Vlad didn't approve of our movie selection. Considering he was *the* Dracula, these movies possessed a completely different tone for him. I respected that. I'd gotten my own taste of that when I stumbled across a fanfiction website featuring thousands of stories written about me. I'd tried reading a few but stopped once I'd stumbled across the Anna x Lucy ones. I loved Lucy, of course, but not that way. And it weirded me out to read love stories about us. I had to imagine that was how Vlad felt about the movies based on him, especially considering his deceased wife's name had actually been Mina. Bet that felt like a donkey kick to the nuts.

Halfway through this ridiculously awesome movie, I noticed Lucy's phone lighting up across the room. From the faint flicker in her eyes, she'd noticed it as well, but refused to acknowledge it. Which could only mean one thing.

"Sam?" I asked.

Her jaw tightened, but she didn't answer. Like I said, denial, denial, denial. But I bet she had a journal at home. A diary—because even grown-ass women sometimes needed an inanimate object to bitch at—and I bet it went something like this:

Dear Diary,

Sam is, like, soooo hot. Like fry an egg on his pecs hot. He also has this lumberjack beard that's to die for, and abs worthy of a Norse god. Like Chris Hemsworth. I know he wasn't actually Thor, but he did portray him, and his body is absolutely lickable. The things I would do to him, if I wasn't a little scaredy cat afraid of my own shadow.

I stayed in New Orleans so I could eye hump him every time we saw each other, but I never let it go any further than that. Because I'm a celibate nun at heart, even though I think I love him.

Then she'd probably draw Sam's name with hearts all over the page, and doodle Mrs. Wolfman in the corner. Yeah, that sounded about right. Girl had damn googly eyes for him, like I did for Vlad. But at least I had the ovaries to jump Vlad's rickety old bones. Frequently. Happily.

Lucy's phone lit up again, distracting me from my immature thoughts. I couldn't help but chuckle at the image of Emo Lucy, scribbling in her journal, her hair draped in front of her eyes.

Hmm. If she didn't want to speak to Sam, maybe I would. He and Vlad didn't get along at all. But Sam liked me. He thought I was a breath of fresh air in Vlad's otherwise stuffy life. I didn't find Vlad stuffy at all, but he held grudges. And he disliked Sam because of some... uncouth behavior. Let's just say, while in wolf form, Sam behaved in an unbefitting way. If I remembered correctly—and I did because it was funny as shit—Sam had urinated on Vlad's coffin as a giant *fuck you.* The two definitely didn't get along.

When her screen lit up a third time, I smirked, then dashed across the room and snatched up Lucy's phone.

"Anna Perish!" Lucy shrieked, her face a mask of pure horror.

I grinned, held my fingers to my lips, then answered the call. "Sam! Hi!"

"Anna?"

"Yup!"

Silence crept across the line. Sam wasn't loquacious at the best of times. One-word answers were his repertoire. I often wondered what the hell he and Lucy talked about, or if they just sat there in awkward silence, panting and lusting over each other's bodies.

"I take it you're looking for Lucy?" I dragged out my words, hoping to get him talking.

He grunted.

I almost busted up laughing. *Of course* he grunted. I was really starting to wonder about the man's vocabulary. Did he just prefer not to speak? Or maybe he didn't know many words? So many questions!

Lucy, on the other hand, was shooting daggers my way. Ah well, she'd get over it once she got *under* him. Their relationship needed a little nudge anyway. The guy definitely had to be worth it considering he kept trying even while being strung along. Don't get me wrong, Lucy was incredibly hot for him, but the second the word "mate" or "werewolf" came up, she slammed on the brakes so fast, we all had whiplash.

Maybe I could help. Or interfere, whatever way she wanted to look at it. I needed to get these two somewhere they couldn't avoid each other anymore.

Somewhere small and cozy. Somewhere Lucy would be forced to sit and speak to the poor wolf.

A nefarious plot bloomed in my head like a Venus Flytrap.

If Lucy wouldn't go to him, then I needed to bring Sam to us. And I knew exactly what to do. Lucy would *hate* me, but I could handle a little best friend hate for this.

"So, Samuel..." I rarely used his full name. Even Lucy's eyebrows rose. "Lucy's and my parents have been begging us to come home. They're getting pretty insistent, actually, and I don't see how we can avoid them any longer."

The blood visibly drained from Lucy's face. Look how quickly she caught on. Oh, I was going to be paying for this for the rest of her life.

"Whatd'ya say? Wanna come with? Meet our families? I'm gonna drag Vlad along too, so we can make it a sort of double date type sitch. You in?"

"Where's home?" Sam asked.

"Perish. About an hour and a half from here. We can have you back by the end of the weekend. So you can... do whatever it is you do with your time." I literally knew nothing about him other than he turned into a wolf. "Just think, four days with Lucy. Maybe you two can resolve some matters."

Lucy chucked a pillow at my head. Too bad I saw it coming a million miles away. And too bad my vampire reflexes were far more advanced than her human ones. I snatched it out of the air and whipped it back at her. I choked on a laugh at the sight of a pillow knocking her flat on her back. Maybe I'd used a little too much force.

"Sure," Sam said, drawing my focus back to our conversation.

I grinned mischievously. Lucy didn't possess supernatural hearing like me, but my smile told her everything. She swatted the pillow off the bed, then sat up and mouthed very slowly, "I hate you." I mouthed back, "Love you too."

"Welp! Guess it's settled then. We'll leave on Wednesday night if that works for you." It was currently Sunday. Which left him a couple of days to get his stuff in order for a small road trip. "Be here around nine p.m.?"

"Fine."

When he didn't hang up, I winced. He was waiting for me to hand Lucy the phone. "She isn't available to talk right now."

"I can hear her in the background."

Right. Werewolf. Forgot they could hear as well as us.

"Ah, well. Truth be told, she's too busy having a panic attack to speak. But don't worry! I'll calm her down and make sure she packs something super sexy for you."

"Anna!" she shouted, knowing her cover was blown.

"Okay, see you Wednesday night. Byeeee!" I ended the call before Lucy could snatch her phone back and slid it into my back pocket.

"Give me my phone right this second, Anna!"

"Nah." I backed away from her, then darted for the door, once again using my unmatchable vamp speed. Poor Luce. She really didn't stand a chance.

"That's cheating!" she shouted at me.

I paused at the door and threw a sassy glance back over my shoulder. "Oh, sweetie, it's only cheating if you're caught. And you can't catch me."

"I won't forget this!" Lucy cried out as I vanished through the door and raced down the steps.

Laughter bubbled in my throat.

Sometimes it was good to be a vampire.

CHAPTER TWO

I WAS STILL CHUCKLING to myself as I snuck into Vlad's office. He sat at his desk with his back to me, his rigid posture the absolute definition of him. He drummed his fingers against the veneer top while his other hand held a phone to his ear.

Before I could utter a word, he canted his head in my direction, showing me he'd heard my approach. Because of course he had. So how the hell had Lucy startled him? Every time I insisted she tell me, she just laughed harder and harder. She loved lording this over me. Somehow, she'd snuck up on Count Dracula, the Big Bad himself. What wasn't there to love about that?

"That's right, yes," Vlad murmured into the phone.

I paused and perked an ear. It was rude to listen in on private conversations, but honestly, nothing was private in this house, thanks to our heightened senses. Privacy was a thing of the past, especially considering Camilla, one of Vlad's friends, now lived with us. She seemed utterly convinced Vlad and I would die without her annoyingly persistent presence. I'd never imagined myself living in a communal household, but it'd happened. Vlad's mansion was practically bursting at the seams with its many residents. His staff alone inhabited the lower floor guest suites, while the second floor contained the main bedrooms for me, Vlad, Camilla, and Lucy. Then, of course, there was the attic where we vamps kept our coffins for sleeping.

Usually, this sort of arrangement wouldn't bother me. Except, Camilla had taken it upon herself to tease me whenever she overheard Vlad and I being intimate together. It was like living in a college dorm, for crying out loud. I'd walk downstairs and she'd make kissy faces at me, or she'd provocatively flash her fangs and tongue the instant Vlad turned his back. I was hardly shy, but it did squick me out knowing she could hear everything that went on between me and Vlad in the bedroom.

At least Lucy had human ears. The most she

overheard was a loud giggle now and then. But Camilla overheard the sweet words Vlad whispered to me—among other things. Trust me, it wasn't fun sitting across a room from someone who suddenly started dramatically acting out the sounds you made during sex.

We needed to kick Camilla out, as simple as that. She had her own house and harem, which was on a permanent hiatus while she hunkered down here. But that didn't mean she couldn't leave. In the past few months, she'd grown distressingly obsessed with me. If she wasn't bashing in my skull while teaching me how to fight, or teasing me like some high school bully, then she was updating my wardrobe, introducing me to other random vampires, and texting me stupid historical vampire facts.

I appreciated her efforts, but holy hell, there was only so much a girl could take.

"And your company guarantees complete UV protection?" Vlad asked, drawing my focus back to him.

Ooo, now *this* sounded promising! Back when Vlad first changed me into a vampire, he'd promised to look into new and improved sleeping arrangements for me. I absolutely loathed waking in a stupid coffin with a stupid lid and stupid small walls. It made me feel like a real monster from all the creature features Lucy made me watch. There had to be other options, especially now that vampires were no longer a secret. Everyone and their dog were starting up new business ventures catering to us fangers.

The problem wasn't with the products, it was with my crusty old boyfriend who was set in his traditional ways. Having lived this way for five-hundred years, he didn't see any other possibilities. Because sleeping in a coffin was safer than sleeping out in the open where any human could stumble across him and ram a stake through his chest. I tried telling him the same thing could happen in a coffin, but he'd completely ignored my comment.

So, instead, I'd suggested blackout curtains. His response? *They're not foolproof.* Of course. Anyone could fling them open, thereby frying us in our sleep. Fine. How about blacking out the windows with paint? But that "isn't aesthetically pleasing and will lower the house's resale value."

After that, I'd gone a wee bit overboard and suggested full military security, complete with trained werewolves to guard our rooms so no one could assassinate us in our sleep. I believe his exact answer had been, "Very amusing, Anna."

Ugh. Fine. If he wanted *serious* suggestions... I went and did some research and found there was a new company launching a product called SunGuard. Fancy-dancy windows that would protect us from those dastardly UV rays. In the words of their company, "SunGuard defends and protects you from the sun, allowing you the best sleep money can buy." I would be the judge of that, thank you very much.

From what I'd read on some forums, there were a few vamps around the country who'd experimented with basement suites now that we no longer had to hide. But thanks to our location, Vlad's estate didn't have a basement. And when I asked why we couldn't turn the attic into a suite, his answer had chilled me to the bone. *Because a hurricane could rip through and tear off the roof, leaving us unprotected.* Yikes.

Thanks to Petrik's blood, the sunlight wasn't *as* big a concern for me anymore. I still couldn't withstand direct sunlight—*boo*—but I woke earlier than Vlad, and so long as the sun's beams didn't touch me directly, I was safe. That didn't mean we didn't need to take the right precautions though. And I would do anything to sleep in a bed again. Coffins were morbid and downright ghastly. I would empty my bank account for these SunGuard windows, so long as it meant never crawling into the dank darkness again.

"Has this product received approval from all required channels?"

Vlad's head bobbed as he listened to the other side of the conversation—as did mine. Queen Genevieve and her council had recently approved their windows, as had the new Vampiric Health and Safety Division created by the humans.

My excitement grew.

According to the man on the phone, they'd recently installed a set of windows in a local vampire's house, who hadn't reported any problems. So, either the product worked, or the vamp had been fried crispy in the middle of a bed somewhere and no one had noticed yet.

I couldn't wait to try out these new windows. I wanted nothing more than to go to sleep cuddled up next to Vlad on a California king, surrounded by mountains of pillows and blankets. I'm talking quilted and down-filled duvets on top of a plush pillow top mattress. One upside to vampirism was we didn't overheat, even in southern temperatures. Tell me that didn't sound like heaven.

"Very well. When can we book an installation?"

I nodded eagerly. Yes, yes, when? Tonight? Tomorrow at the latest?

"August sixth will suffice."

My heart dropped. That was two damn weeks from now! *Whhyyy?* I mean, part of me understood. They likely needed to order in parts, then fit us into their installation schedule. But damn it, how many jobs were they doing that we had to wait so long?

I guess it didn't matter. We would be leaving for Perish in a few days anyway. After we returned, it'd be another week of waiting, which sounded agonizing. Impatience was a weakness of mine. When I wanted something, I wanted it now. Waiting was the absolute definition of torture.

Vlad thanked the customer rep, hung up, then finally turned in his chair, giving me the chance to really look at him. I never tired of admiring his beauty. There was something about his darkly hypnotic eyes that always seemed to entrance me. I knew he didn't possess the power of compulsion, so it was definitely just an effect he had on me. His dark, wavy hair fell to his ears in a purposely tousled look that made me want to comb my fingers through it. And then came his chiseled jaw and strong chin. All in all, the man rated "sexy AF" in my book.

Certainly sexier than me, but I didn't mind that one bit, since I was the one doing all the looking.

Clearly enjoying my attention, Vlad's mouth curled into a slow smile. He wasn't big on showing affection, but for me, he always made the effort. We may be vampires, but that didn't mean we couldn't enjoy life. If I was going to spend an eternity with someone, then our romance needed to be epic and all-consuming. None of this simply putting up with each other for the sake of the relationship.

I gestured to the phone on his desk and chuckled. "You remembered."

Just when I thought I couldn't love this man more. Of course, Vlad didn't know I was in love with him yet. That was one part of our relationship I'd been holding back on. The thought of uttering those three little words terrified me. Part of me worried I only *thought* I loved him. I mean, we'd only met three months ago. Was it possible to fall in love with someone that quickly?

Vlad, on the other hand, had always known we were destined to meet, so he saw things differently than me. Thanks to his gift of foresight, he'd dreamed of me for fifty years, knowing that one night, we'd meet. His gift wasn't infallible, and it often withheld more information than it provided—for instance, the fact that I would die the night we met—but he'd never doubted that we were meant to be.

That pretty much told me how he felt about me. But I hadn't been given the same advantage. I hadn't dreamed of him for fifty years, longing and waiting for this mystery man. For me, this was all so new and fresh and exciting. I wasn't ready to say those three little words yet. I wanted to make sure this was real and not some trick being played on us by some unknown deity with powers beyond my comprehension.

I mean, who even controlled our fates anyway? What if the rush of emotion I felt for him was nothing more than me lusting after a sexy, famous vampire who made me all mushy in the knees? What if it was all purely physical? So many people confused good sex with love. Add in Vlad's drop-dead gorgeous looks, and a girl was bound to be a little confused.

Thankfully, Vlad hadn't told me he loved me yet either. Which helped a lot. Took the pressure off. Except I kept fighting the urge to just blurt it out. Especially during sex, thanks to Vlad's mad skills in the art of pleasuring the female body. When he touched me, I melted into a pitiful puddle of goo. Then there was the way he looked at me—

like I was the only thing that mattered in his eternal life.

But that definitely didn't mean love. At least, I didn't think it did.

Gah! I was a mess of emotions and confusion. Lord, someone send help. Seemed my hormones were screwing me up six ways from Sunday.

"Of course I remembered. You might wake earlier than me now, but I'm still aware of your dislike for the coffin."

"It's just so cramped," I complained. "And dark. And stifling. Now picture us snuggling together in a bed full of pillows and soft blankets, holding each other, touching each other...."

"That doesn't sound like sleeping to me," Vlad mused.

"That's the joy of sharing a bed. We can sleep *after*."

Vlad chuckled.

"Trust me. You'll love it. You haven't experienced luxury until you've slept on a pillow top mattress, snuggled in a bunch of soft blankets."

Vlad lifted a brow and gestured to the room surrounding us. I couldn't help but snicker. His entire house was the definition of grand luxury. Chandeliers, marble tubs, velvet couches—which I despised—and top of the line technology, thanks to me and Lucy. Pre-Anna, as I liked to call it, the Count had lived like it was the nineteenth century. No televisions, stereo systems, computers, tablets, nada. Lucy and I had changed all that. We'd taken his house under our wing and modernized it. Now, we had a computerized fridge that informed us when supplies were low, and two family rooms complete with big screen TVs and gaming consoles —one for Vlad's employees and one for us vampires. I'd recently convinced Camilla to play a zombie apocalyptic game called *Last of Us*, and I regretted it. That woman loved murdering her some zombies. So much so that Lucy and I never got to play anymore.

I closed the distance between us, then eased onto Vlad's lap. I looped my arms around his neck and slid my fingers into his thick, wavy hair. "You're gonna love it. After five centuries of sleeping in a coffin, even a twin-sized bed would be an improvement."

"If it makes you happy," he told me, his nose brushing against the hollow of my throat.

It was one of Vlad's favorite places on my body, among a few others farther south. I never complained—I'd quickly learned my throat was incredibly sensitive, and his touch often sent little pleasurable shivers coursing through me.

"This house could be a hovel, and I'd still be happy," I whispered as I leaned my head to the side to grant him more access. When his lips brushed my throat, I shuddered. "All I need is you."

Vlad chuckled, his breath brushing my flesh. "Well, in that case, allow me to call SunGuard back and cancel the installation."

I playfully slapped his hand away from the phone, then lowered my head and eyed him. "Don't even think about it. Or I will feed garlic cloves to your harem for a month."

"Vicious," Vlad mumbled, laughter rumbling deep in his throat. In our time together, I'd noticed he didn't laugh with anyone but me. So, I took a moment to revel in the sound. I loved that he let down his walls and opened himself up to me.

"What were you and Lucy doing up there? Sounded like the two of you were having fun."

I bit my lip to smother a laugh. "Uh, watching a movie."

Vlad's eyes narrowed teasingly. "What *kind* of movie?"

He knew of our recent fascination with vampire movies. Again, no privacy in the house. But he didn't understand *why* we were watching them. I still wasn't ready to tell him about my new vlog, and we'd somehow managed to keep it a secret.

"Lucy wanted to watch another vamp flick. A satirical one."

Vlad grimaced. "Do I want to know more?"

"Well, an aging white-haired man with a penchant for the ucipital mapilary played you," I said, referencing a specific part of the movie.

Vlad's eyes widened. "Penchant for what?"

I pointed to the hollow notch at the base of my throat. "This right here."

"Mm. Well, it is lovely," Vlad said.

"You also had a man-servant who enjoyed eating bugs."

Vlad's mouth thinned. "I think I've heard enough."

"Probably." I leaned over and gently nipped at his bottom lip, hoping to perk it back up. "It's just a silly movie we used to watch while we were in school." I smiled at the memory. "We weren't really popular, so when no one invited us to the cool kids' parties, we spent the night at my place, binging on B-rated movies."

"I don't know what either of those things mean."

I chuckled. "Means indulging in low-budget

films. Thing is, though, most B-rated movies have a warped charm about them that makes them better than the mainstream releases."

"As long as you're enjoying yourself."

"I know another way I could enjoy myself," I suggested, hoping to lure him away from this topic. The last thing I needed was for him to question my purpose behind watching these movies.

He lifted a brow. "Oh?"

I wiggled mine in response.

Vlad's smile grew until his fangs winked at me. And damn, did that make me shiver. His dick wasn't the only thing I liked inside me. I couldn't drink his blood anymore—a decision we'd made after I'd feasted on Petrik like it was no big deal. But that didn't mean Vlad couldn't bite me. Luckily, my blood seemed to have no effect on him, considering he was ancient in his own right. Our sexcapades usually ended with both his fangs and his dick buried so deeply within me that I had no idea where I ended, and he began. I was A-OK with that, and I was quite sure you could guess why.

Mind. Blowing. Orgasms.

Who knew that was all it took to make me happy?

Well, not all. But enough to distract me from the

other issues in my life. And there were so, so many. Queen Genevieve for one with her annoying, holier-than-thou summons. My vlog, which demanded a lot of attention. Then my family, who I really didn't want to think about right now. Not while seated in Vlad's happy little lap with his fingers gripping my happy little ass.

"Is Camilla here tonight?" I whispered, while running my teeth down his throat.

I couldn't bite, but that never stopped me from teasing. It teased me too. Just the thought of sinking my fangs into his throat nearly brought me to the edge of climax. I *loved* biting Vlad. But it was too dangerous. Younger vamps who consumed older vamp blood tended to go a little bit insane. The older the blood, the more powerful, and we youngins weren't able to process it well enough. I'd tasted Vlad before, but after I'd fed off Petrik—a thousand-year-old ancient—Vlad had insisted we cool it on his blood. Much to my dismay.

When my teeth scraped his flesh, Vlad's breath hitched, and his fingers squeezed my butt. I could feel the tension building within him and the hardening of his body in every delicious way possible.

"I sent her on a few errands," he murmured, his fingers almost bruising my ass cheeks.

"Thank Jeebus." I seemed immune to most godly curses, but other vampires weren't, so I took care not to mention the G-word in front of them.

With no time to waste, I ripped off Vlad's shirt, then unzipped his pants and freed him through the open fly. I'd barely glanced at the Count's gloriousness before he pushed me back onto his desk, popped open my pants, and wrenched them around my thighs.

Vlad leaned over me and devoured my mouth seconds before he slid his fingers into me. Usually we took our time, teased one another, lavished in every form of foreplay known to man. But neither of us knew how much time we had before Camilla returned or someone else came knocking at his door. We were literally racing the clock. Vlad knew *exactly* how to work me up, which he proved right now with his talented fingers.

It didn't take long to send me spiraling toward a climax. The second my inner walls clamped around his fingers, he withdrew and filled the emptiness with a different, albeit deliciously harder organ. He wrapped my thighs around his waist, then clutched my hips and began moving within me.

I nearly screamed with delight but managed to bite it back into a moan.

His desk shuddered against the floor, the force of his movements sending his papers and stationary scattering to the floor. Neither of us so much as paused to look at the mess we'd made. Instead, I slid my fingers into his hair and fisted them, tugging gently on his roots. Vlad's eyes shuddered closed, and he groaned. He loved when I did this. He seemed to enjoy a bit of an edge to his lovemaking, which didn't surprise me. He was a vampire, after all. He liked to bite, pull, and push, but he especially loved to withhold orgasms as a form of beautiful torture. Lead me to the edge until I was ready to scream with frustration before finally letting me fall over it.

Tonight was different though. Tonight was rushed and merciless. And yet still so wonderful, I could have died—again. He drove into me with a divine force that had my head thumping against the wall. But I didn't care.

When I finally cried out my release, Vlad wasn't far behind me. His head dropped forward as he groaned, his hands convulsing against my sides.

Quick, dirty, and amazing.

Just the way I liked it.

CHAPTER THREE

A DOOR SLAMMED open seconds before Camilla's not-so-dulcet voice rang through the room. "Oh, good. You're done."

I *screamed* and flew off Vlad's desk. My hands scrambled to fasten my pants, but I couldn't seem to get them to stay done up. The damn button kept popping back out! I nearly tore the stupid thing off in my panicked attempt to redress myself.

Once I finally got my pants buttoned, I whirled around and swept my mussed hair off my face. "For fuck's sake, Camilla! What the hell is your problem?"

"No problem." She stood in the doorframe, inspecting her nails as though she hadn't a care in the world.

I eyed her tall stature, from her golden heels to

her wavy black hair, and snarled. She looked the picture of beauty and grace, while I probably looked like... well, freshly fucked.

"Would it have killed you to knock?"

I shot Vlad a glance to find him standing deathly still, his hands gripping his office chair as though his deceptively calm temperament relied on it.

"No, but where's the fun in that?" She sighed and pushed off the door.

I listened to the sound of her clacking heels as she approached, my eye twitching with every step. I liked Camilla. I truly did. She'd been a key factor in my survival a few months ago. Since my little adventure with Petrik, she'd taken her role as my trainer quite seriously. But this was pushing it too far. We had zero privacy with her around! If she kept goading me, she was going to find herself dumped in a pit right before sunrise.

And from the look on Vlad's face, it seemed our thoughts aligned.

"This is entirely inappropriate, Camilla," Vlad snapped.

His deep voice sent a shiver down my arms.

"I'd apologize, but maybe you two shouldn't engage in freaky sex in the middle of your office."

"This is my house," Vlad stated, his upper lip

curling back to reveal his fangs. “If you’re unhappy with the circumstances, you do have your own home. Perhaps you should consider leaving.”

“Can’t. Too busy,” she said. Her gaze darted to me seconds before her hand clamped down on my wrist and she wrenched me toward the door. “Come on. We have places to go and people to see.”

I backpedaled. We so did not. The only plan I had consisted of a shower. Right this second. Vampire or not, sex was delightfully messy. Fuck, I hadn’t even had a chance to bask in the afterglow. Okay, scrap my earlier comment. I no longer liked Camilla. Rob a girl of her post-orgasm bliss and you rob her of life.

“Quit squirming,” Camilla shot back at me. “We have a date.”

“Excuse me?” I tugged on my arm.

With a dramatic sigh, Camilla whirled around to face me. “Look, while you’ve been content just existing, the rest of us have been busy trying to keep your ass alive. In case you’ve forgotten, the queen sort of has this personal little vendetta against you.”

Man, the sarcasm was thick tonight. Sometimes I wondered if my presence was having an effect on her.

“So, let’s go. You have an appointment with VA.”

"With... what?" I glanced back at Vlad. I could only imagine the unpleasant thoughts running through his head.

"VA. Vampires Anonymous. Hurry up. Go shower and put on something a tad more appropriate."

What was wrong with my current outfit? I glanced down at my clothes. Jeans and a long-sleeved designer shirt. I mean, wasn't this a pretty standard look for most women my age?

Camilla growled. "Let me spell it out for you, sweetie. The queen doesn't like you. Which means other vampires don't like you. Your first week of life consisted of you slaughtering Petrik. And while no one *knows* you're responsible, they *know* you're responsible. Get me?"

Talk about stating the obvious. "So?"

"*So*, we're trying to fix your reputation. One of the requirements for new vampires is that they attend Vampires Anonymous."

"That sounds like something for humans who are addicted to vampire bites."

Camilla rolled her eyes and stared at the ceiling, as though begging it for patience. "I texted you about this earlier tonight."

"You so did not!" Okay, even I winced at that one. I sounded like a whiny teenager.

"I *so* did," Camilla mocked. "Check your damn phone."

Cursing under my breath, I stuck a hand in my back pocket and came up empty. Right. My phone had probably fallen out during—well, just *during*. I eyed Vlad's desk, heat rising to my cheeks at the sight of the mussed papers. I'd never be able to look at his desk the same way again. Sure enough, laying amidst his scattered documents were both mine and Lucy's cells.

I snatched mine up and flicked it on, only to find Camilla's missed text. Along with half a dozen more explaining the vampire hierarchy to me. Well? How the hell was I supposed to know she'd actually texted me something useful among the countless boring texts about the monarchy?

"Alright, *fine*. What the hell is Vampires Anonymous?"

"A nonprofit, self-help program for all newly turned vampires."

"Um, I think I'm a little beyond that now, don't you?"

She shook her head, her waterfall of inky black hair glimmering beneath the office lights. Once upon a time, I'd been jealous of her beauty, but that envy had dimmed once I'd gotten to know her annoying personality. Looks only went so far.

"The queen has been looking into you. We need her to believe you're like all the rest of us."

"But I *am* like all the rest."

"You aren't," Vlad commented. "No newborn vampire can wake before sunset or walk around during the day like you. Such a feat will attract the attention of the queen, considering she would know Petrik possessed the same talent. I understand Camilla's concerns, and while I absolutely do not approve of her methods, I think you might benefit from this program. If anything, it'll show your commitment to the vampire community and allow you the opportunity to network."

To network with whom? And why?

"Hurry up!" Camilla hissed. "It starts in an hour, and you need to make yourself presentable. If the queen is watching, you can't go looking like...this."

Again, I stole a glance at myself. Maybe I was biased, but I thought I looked fine. What'd they expect? For me to show up in a dazzling ballroom gown complete with heels and tiara? It's not like I had a crown or anything.

"Just go shower." Camilla shoved me toward

Vlad's office door. Apparently, I wasn't even allowed a kiss goodbye. "I'll have an outfit waiting for you on your bed by the time you're done."

"Lucy is in my room," I warned Camilla. Not that I needed to. The two didn't like each other—a little best friend animosity, I suspect. But I still felt the need to warn Camilla.

"Fine. She can help, I suppose."

Oh, Lucy would love that.

Not.

CRIPES, this was ridiculous. What the hell was Camilla thinking bringing me here? I suppose on some scale, I was still considered a newborn vampire, regardless of the three months I had under my belt. But I was a happily adjusted fanger, right? I had a werewolf buddy, a human sidekick, a deliciously sexy boyfriend, and well, Camilla. I didn't need *therapy*.

Camilla had practically dragged me kicking and screaming into the room—albeit without the dramatics and just a whole lot of glaring—then forced me into a chair before she beat a hasty retreat. Couldn't be bothered to stick around, I guess.

Now I sat in a large half-circle, surrounded by at least eight other vampires. And boy, did the majority look green, both in experience and appearance.

Hell was a four-letter word, and I was in it.

What did Camilla and Vlad expect from me? To make friends—or network, as Vlad put it? To open up to these *strangers* about my experiences as a vampire? I couldn't do that. If I revealed anything too personal, that information could somehow get back to the queen.

So, here I sat, dressed in a flowy skirt, strappy sandals, and silk blouse. All because Camilla had insisted. The entire ride here, she'd lectured me on the importance of maintaining mystery. *This isn't high school*, she'd said. I wasn't here to make a new bestie or join the undead chess club. I was here to make an impression. To show the queen I was a good little vampire, brushing my little vamp fangs, and making vamp friends.

Ugh. Just stuff me in a box and mail me to Transylvania. I did *not* want to do this.

"Hi," someone murmured at my side.

I glanced over to find two people seated next to me, one a young woman, the other a bedraggled looking man. Both stared at me like I was the most interesting person to have walked through the door.

Damn. They were in for a shocking surprise. I was just as boring as the rest of them. Of course, the little voice in my head chose that moment to laugh at me. Since it was my voice, I was essentially laughing at myself. There really wasn't anything normal about me at all. And I wasn't sure how I felt about that.

I focused first on the woman, biting my inner cheek to keep from sighing. Her outfit absolutely *screamed* college student, and I secretly hated her for it. Jeans, a light sweater, and scuffed sneakers. Was that so much to ask? Well, not the scuffed sneakers bit. Wouldn't catch me *dead* in beat-up, no-name shoes. But skirts? Dresses? Both were emphatic hell no's from me. Why would anyone want to wear anything that limited their movement? If I wanted to run, I sure as shit didn't want to be worried about flashing someone my lady bits. Camilla didn't give two craps about my feelings, though, and had dressed me in exactly that. A stupid skirt that showed far too much thigh for my liking.

"I'm Violet," the woman said.

I bobbed my head. "Nice to meet you."

The disheveled man next to her leaned forward and flashed me a gap-toothed grin. "And I'm Graves."

Holy guacamole. I mean, I'd seen people with

missing teeth before, but never quite like this. Dude had zero teeth *except* for his fangs. What a mildly disturbing sight. And by mildly, I meant immensely. He was all... gums and fangs. Fangs and gums.

"Um, sorry, did you say Grays?" I reached out to take his extended hand.

"Graves," Violet repeated for me, rolling her eyes. "Don't pay any attention to him. He has fake teeth he could wear, but he refuses to."

"Ain't comfortable with these now, are they?" Graves gestured at his sharp fangs. "And we ain't need fake teeth for nuthin' now."

He wasn't wrong. And I couldn't imagine fake teeth felt too comfy with his fangs pressing against them. I wasn't even sure if dentures would work with fangs. I wasn't a dentist. But I did know implants wouldn't. His body would reject anything surgical like that while he slept during the day. We were the undead, which meant unchanging. We would forever look the same as we did the night we transitioned. So, instead, I merely nodded and forced my gaze away from those gaping, pink gummy holes.

"What's your name?" Violet asked.

Right. Introductions. Strange how something as completely simple as missing teeth had befuddled my brain. "Oh, sorry. Anna?"

"You askin' or tellin'?" Graves questioned.

"Um, telling."

"It's nice to meet you." Violet tucked a strand of pastel rainbow-colored hair behind her ear. I had to wonder if she'd dyed it that way before transitioning or if she woke up every single night and colored it. I also wasn't sure which sucked more. I would hate to be stuck with permanently dyed Easter egg hair, but coloring my hair every single night sounded worse. Far too much effort.

It made me stop and think though. My mother used to always tell me to make sure I had clean panties on in case I—wait for it—got hit by a car and died. There were so many things to unpack in that sentence, like one, *of course* I changed my underwear daily, but also, did doctors really care about a dead person's underwear? Seemed to me they had more important things to waste their time on.

I didn't extend Violet the same compliment, because honestly, it wasn't nice to meet her. Or anyone else for that matter. I was here under protest, and I wanted to make sure everyone knew it. Screw the queen and her "spies." I honestly didn't give a fuck about any of that anymore.

"So, haven't seen ya here before, darlin'," Graves mumbled.

Great, another southern boy with a penchant for calling me darling. Had to be something in the water. I was as southern as they came, but I didn't walk around calling people sugar or sweetheart.

"First timer," I said.

"Oh!" Violet clasped my hand and threw me a sickeningly sweet smile. "Welcome to the group!"

I grimaced and slowly extracted my hand from hers. An image of Emperor Kuzco flashed through my mind because I was definitely feeling a *no touchy* moment coming on. Instead, I asked, "You?"

"Two months."

I blinked. I'd been hoping for a one-and-done sorta deal. Definitely wasn't looking to come here the next eight Sundays—or longer! I was all for mental health and healing yourself, but this wasn't for me. I didn't need therapy, and I certainly didn't need to make a good impression for the queen. She'd already formed an opinion of me, and I doubted it was a good one.

"It's Graves's third time here. He's fairly new too," Violet continued.

I shot dear old Graves a passing glance. He ran his hands through his greasy hair, then rammed a finger right up his nose and started picking. Oh wow. Charming.

Violet scoffed and leaned in close to Graves. "You know, just because we don't have reflections doesn't mean other people can't see you."

I almost burst out laughing when he shrugged and dug a little deeper. Someone was mining for green gold, that was for sure. I looked away before he did something disgusting, like wipe a goober the size of his knuckle on his leg.

Violet sighed and straightened in her chair. "I'm so sorry. I'm his sponsor, but I haven't been able to instill any manners in him. The man is like a cockroach."

"Sponsor?"

"Sure. You know, helping those who don't have sires."

My eyes widened. Wait. There were vampires out there without sires? I thought sires were required? I'd read through all the information the queen's people had sent me after transitioning. After transitioning, the newborn vampire had to remain with their sire for three months. Afterward, they were free to go.

But the more I thought about it, the more it made sense. Much like how mothers abandoned their newborn babies, surely vampires did the same thing.

I just couldn't believe it'd taken me this long to clue into that. Man, I really didn't know shit.

On the upside, Violet had been attending these meetings for the past two months, so she likely knew everyone here. Meaning I could now begin networking. Maybe I could needle her for information, find out who else was new here. I still believed Vlad and Camilla were overreacting a wee bit to this whole situation, but it couldn't hurt to investigate a little, right? Make a new friend? Then grill her for all the information I could?

Famous last words and all that.

"So, how do these things usually go down?" I waved a hand toward the other six vampires.

Graves gave a wheezy chuckle that made me wonder if he'd smoked in his previous life, then flashed his gums at me once more. I had to admit, they fascinated me. And I truly didn't understand why.

"The speaker"—which sounded like *theaker*—"will welcome us, chat 'bout himself, then open the floor to us plebs to share anything we might wanna yak about."

"Like?"

"Anythin', darlin'. Becomin' a vamp is hard. Some people ain't got a support network to help, ya'know? So, they come here, spillin' their secrets and spinnin' their yarns for y'all to listen to and offer sympathy."

Made sense. Especially if they didn't have a sire to help them through these trying times. I mean, just because the council dictated that a newborn had to remain with their sire for the first few months didn't mean everyone followed the rules. The council had also made it illegal to change nonconsenting humans into vamps, and see how well that one turned out for me? I was a prime example of how much people loved to break the rules.

Violet shot me a haunted look, as though she understood my thoughts. Hell, maybe she did. Damn vampire tricks. "The point of this group," she said, "is to know that we're all going through the same thing."

"Aw, sweetheart"—which sounded a whole lot like *thweetheart*—"the real point of this group is to meet other fangers and get lucky. Amiright, Miss Anna?"

I shot Graves a startled look. "What?"

"Come on, now. Don't play all shy and innocent with me. I know the look. Seen it in your eyes the second you sat down there. Scopin' us out with a hunger I only seen on them prowlin' ladies."

"Prowling?"

"Ya know, them cougar ladies. Yer a bit young, but you got that look aboutcha."

I snorted on a cough, then started laughing. "I'm most definitely *not* here looking to get lucky."

"Sure ya ain't." Graves winked, then grinned at me. "But don't you worry, I won't tell. A lady's gotta keep her secrets, amiright?"

I gave another chuckle, one I had to swallow when someone at the front of the room cleared their throat.

My head snapped up and I spotted the presumed so-called *theaker*. He stood before a small podium, his fingers rifling through a stack of papers. When he lifted his head, his sharp blue eyes snagged mine before moving through the rest of the room.

"Alright. Welcome everyone." He gathered his papers and knocked them against the podium, straightening them into a flat pile. "Welcome to Vampires Anonymous. My name is Noah Bradshaw, and I'll be leading this meeting. Before we begin, I'd like to remind everyone that this is a safe place for all newly turned vampires. However, no humans are allowed. So, if you haven't been turned yet, please excuse yourself."

"Yeah, no bleeders allowed," Graves teased.

I squished my lips together to keep from chuckling. Graves was a character, for sure.

Movement caught my attention, and I turned in time to watch as two humans slipped out of the room. With them went the subtle sound of their heartbeats. It wasn't until they left that I realized how silent the room had become. Humans moved, squirmed, twitched, breathed, blinked, and fiddled. Vampires... didn't. We sat still as the grave. Unnerving to say the least.

"Okay." Noah tapped his papers once more. "As most of you know, and as I just said, my name is Noah. I've been a vampire for going on ten years and have mentored my share of newborns throughout that time. When Queen Genevieve announced our presence to the world, I saw the opportunity to expand this service and help others on their journey."

Next to me, Violet nodded. When I spared her a glance, I noted the reverence with which she watched him. Graves, on the other hand, looked entirely too bored for his own good. He kept tapping his tongue against his fangs, a sight I definitely hadn't prepared myself for. Who'd ever heard of a toothless vampire before? He must have lost them all before he'd died. Either that or—and it twisted my stomach to think of this—he pulled them out every night after rising.

Oh, I was gonna throw up just thinking about that.

"Usually, this is the part where I allow everyone to introduce themselves. Let's begin, shall we? How about you?"

It took me a few moments to realize Noah meant me. For cripes' sake, why did I have to sit *right next* to the podium.

"Me?"

Noah nodded.

Great. Me.

Graves chuckled, then leaned in and whispered, "*Theaker's* pet."

I nudged him back over into his own chair, then lifted my head and faced the group. Wow. There were... a lot of vampires. And all eyes appeared to be on me. You'd think I'd be used to this now, thanks to my vlog's recent success, but here was the thing. The viewers couldn't actually see me on the channel. All they saw were the heaps of clothing Lucy piled onto me to make me visible on camera. Sweaters, scarves, massive sunglasses, wide-brimmed hats. Everything she could think of to give me some semblance of shape on camera. Knowing my audience could see me without actually seeing me lent me a freedom I adored.

This? This wasn't freedom. And I most certainly did *not* adore the many eyes tracking me, waiting to hear my woeful tale.

"Um. Hi, everyone." I gave a pitiful wave. "My name is Anna Perish—"

A quiet murmur spread through the room. Even Violet appeared shocked by this information. Insulted, even. As though she didn't appreciate me withholding that information earlier.

Graves, however, chuckled and leaned back in his chair with a knowing smirk. "So, you really ain't looking for some vamp-on-vamp action then, huh? Pity. Mighta been interested, ya'know?"

"Graves," Noah warned.

I laughed, hoping it would silence the whispers. "Right. So, like I said, Anna Perish. I've been a vampire for three months thereabouts, and this is my first VA meeting."

I had every intention of leaving it at that, but apparently Noah had other plans for me.

"Care to share a little more?" He leaned his elbows against the podium. "How were you changed?"

If my heart could still beat, it would have

sputtered to a dead stop right this second. I didn't want to discuss this. Even now, months later, I still felt Petrik's breath on my throat, and the heat of the sun on my skin. The bastard had tried to murder me. Twice. Once in a dark alley, the other in a cement crypt. I didn't enjoy thinking about him—he wasn't worth the brain power. And it seemed a safe bet to assume the people here had already seen plenty of images online. Just my luck, a reporter had stumbled across me and Vlad in the middle of him turning me. Since I'd still been human—albeit pretty much dead —I was entirely visible in the images. Too visible. Those photos haunted me to this day, and there wasn't anything I could do about them. On the upside, they were a direct line to my bank account, so that had to count for something.

"Right. I was... uh..." My gaze shot to Noah, who nodded in open understanding.

"This is a safe place, Anna. We don't share other people's secrets or stories."

Well, my story was far from secret. The whole world had seen the pictures. So, I highly doubted Noah's assurances. In my experience, whatever I said here would soon be posted online. Therefore, anonymity really wasn't a thing for me. I couldn't let fear stop me, but I also had to be careful with my secrets. Guard them in case the queen truly was watching.

"Well," I hedged, wondering how much to say. "I'm sure most of you already know my story. It's no secret. A friend and I were partying at Fallen when I was attacked." I lifted my hands, palms up, as though to say *what can you do*. "I got more than I bargained for. I thought we'd be safe, thanks to the treaty, but I was naïve. One thing led to another and a vampire—who shall remain nameless—dragged me outside and drained me before tossing me into the trash."

I think that was the part that stung the most. He'd discarded me like I was nothing more than garbage. A wasted meal he hadn't had room to finish.

Soft whispers swept through the room. I did my best to ignore them *and* the memories sweeping through me. Petrik didn't deserve the real estate in my head.

"Lucky for me," I continued, raising my voice above their murmurs, "another vampire found me and saved me."

"Dracula," someone whispered reverently, confirming my suspicions that I was no stranger here.

I rolled my eyes, a small smile tugging on the corner of my lips. "Yes, *Vlad*. He sired me and has been teaching me the ropes for the past few months."

Noah's nod drew my attention. When our gazes met, I noted the emotion flashing within his eyes. Pity, definitely. But perhaps a hint of something else? Something I couldn't quite put my finger on. Admiration, perhaps?

"And what happens now that your sponsorship is coming to an end?"

My mouth parted. I'd asked Vlad months ago what would happen to us when our time finished. He hadn't explicitly said we'd remain together. But Vlad loved me. And I—*ahem*—loved him. Surely, he wouldn't kick me out, right?

"I, uh..." Truth be told, I didn't know the exact answer to this. Hell, he didn't even know we were visiting my family this week.

Noah's head bobbed before he addressed the rest of the group. "These are questions you all need to ask. Regardless of your relationship with your sire"—he pinned me with a quick but piercing glance—"you need to know specifically what happens to you at the end of your term. Will your sire leave you? Will he or she expect you to branch out on your own? These are all important questions. As new vampires, it's in your best interest to prepare yourselves. To ensure you know how to survive on your own when that day arrives. Know what your future holds, otherwise..."

His gaze lingered on me for a few seconds longer before he studied the group. "Who would like to go next?"

Violet raised her hand and started regaling the group with her story. Honestly, I didn't catch most of what she said. My mind was too busy running in circles. I had no reason to doubt Vlad. He meant far more to me than a sire, and vice versa. He'd waited for me for fifty years, promised to protect me from Petrik. We'd slept together, expressed emotions for one another.

But Noah's words kept circling my head, along with the knowledge that Vlad had never explicitly explained what would happen to us at the three-month mark. I didn't want to be set free from him. New Orleans and Vlad's mansion had become my home. The thought of leaving literally made me ache.

No, I couldn't let a stranger's words upset me. Vlad and I were soulmates. I had to trust in that.

CHAPTER FOUR

Somehow, I found myself wandering City Park after VA wrapped up. Camilla had left me strict instructions to wait for her in the parking lot, but the meeting left me with a great deal of restless energy. I found myself longing to be alone, even if only for a few minutes. I hadn't noticed it until Noah pointed it out to another vampire, but I hadn't had any time alone since I'd been turned. The other vampire had confessed that he was too scared to even go for a walk by himself, afraid he'd lose control and kill someone. Memories of me attacking Harold had flashed through my head, and I'd sympathized. But things were different now. I wasn't fresh out of my grave. And damn it, I wanted a few minutes to myself so I could think.

For three long months, everywhere I went, Vlad or Camilla followed. My only time away from them was when Lucy and I vegged out watching a movie or gave ourselves pedicures. But even then, Lucy was there.

So, after the meeting, I'd bailed. Slipped out the back door and just... started walking. It wasn't until I reached City Park and found myself staring at a gondola that I realized where my feet had led me. This place was special to me. Vlad had brought me here on a quick date to get us out of the house and away from the madness. He'd wanted a few moments for us to enjoy each other's company without someone breathing down our necks. And I'd loved every moment.

I stood on the dock and stared out at the lake. It was incredibly quiet tonight. Hardly any tourists on the water, and the wildlife was calm and subdued. Almost as though the world matched my mood.

I'd always loved New Orleans. Even as a child, before my parent's divorce, my family and I had come here frequently. The city was always so vibrant and full of life. It stank to high heaven, but that was part of the charm.

As a vampire, I still appreciated the beauty, especially when the city lit up the night sky. But I also understood the darkness a bit better now, like the monsters that lurked in the shadows and the businesses that catered to them. The Vampire Lounge, for instance. Located in the French Quarter, it was a vampire blood brothel. As a human, I'd thought it nothing more than a tourist trap. A Gothic "bar" catering to a certain crowd. Their true crowd, however, had sharp fangs and no reflections.

Like every other human out there, I'd lived my life in this safe little bubble, believing us to be the most dangerous creatures in the world. Then we'd learned about vampires and had been forced to adjust our worldly perspective.

Such a change had forced me to grow up and to open my eyes to the truth. It'd taught me to ask the hard questions. And right now, there was one *very* hard question I needed answered. It shouldn't frighten me to ask Vlad about his future intentions, but damn it, the reality had me quaking in my newly purchased Valentino shoes.

What if I didn't like Vlad's answer? What if *his* truth was different from mine? What if this all came crashing to an end? Was I ready for that? Ready to branch out into the world on my own, knowing that eternity literally meant *forever*?

One day, Lucy would die. And my family would

be gone. Without Vlad, I'd be left with nothing but memories that would eventually fade.

I'd thought of these things in passing, but never really *considered* them. Passing thoughts in the night that meant nothing because I still had Vlad and Lucy. But what if I didn't?

Sighing, I took a seat on the nearby grass and stared up at the stars.

Now, *this* was something I loved about being a vampire. The stars were virtually impossible to see here with human eyes, thanks to the light pollution, but my eyes were sharper now.

"Beautiful, right?" a soft voice murmured next to me.

I glanced over, a small frown furrowing my brows at the sight of Noah. Had he followed me here? And what was beautiful? Me? The backdrop? Or the stars? Better not be me... just saying.

"Anna, right?" he asked.

I refrained from rolling my eyes. Like I believed he wasn't sure about my name.

When I didn't immediately respond, he seated himself next to me, then pulled his knees up to his chest and stared up at the sky. He let out a long, albeit unnecessary breath. "It really is beautiful here."

"Did I forget something at the meeting?"

"No, of course not. I just wanted a chance to speak to you privately."

I caught the inside of my cheek with my teeth, my senses now on high alert. I'd already told him and all the others my story. There was literally nothing more to know about me.

Again, when I didn't respond, he lowered his head and caught my gaze. His eyes were a warm honey brown color, his hair sandy blond. No distinguishable features that I could see, but when he smiled, I noticed one of his teeth had a small chip.

"You can tell a lot about people from the things they say," Noah commented. He paused briefly, then finished with, "And the things they don't say."

"Okay..."

"For instance, you never mentioned who attacked you in the alley."

All my inner alarms blared in warning. "Because it's not important."

"Not important to mention the vampire who attacked you?"

"Why do you care?" I retorted.

"That's my job, Anna. I'm here to listen and help new vampires adjust to this world."

"And that involves pestering me about the details?"

"Pester." He chuckled, then picked at a blade of grass next to his knee. "I suppose some would see it that way. You know, before I became a vampire, I was a therapist."

Oh god, a shrink. Yup, he was evil. All that remained was establishing *how* evil.

"As a human, I was pretty tuned in to people's emotions. As a vampire..." He let his sentence hang.

I sighed, taking my time to exhale. "Let me guess, you developed an interesting ability to actually read people's emotions."

Because why wouldn't he? Vampires developed supernatural gifts over time. Vlad had visions of the future. I actually had no idea what Camilla's special ability was. Being annoying? Kicking my ass? Either of those two would fit.

Noah cracked a smile. "An uncanny ability, some might say."

I rolled my eyes. "Great. An empath."

"It's a trait I've come to rely on."

"I'm sure. What does all this have to do with me?"

Noah eased back onto his elbows and stretched out his legs. He looked the picture of ease, as though he hadn't a care in the world. All for show though. I was intimately familiar with vampires and the mind games they played.

"Everything," Noah finally said. "I can feel the disquiet in you."

"Hooray for you. What, you want a cookie or something?"

"I wouldn't turn one down."

He delivered the line so smoothly, I couldn't help but laugh. "You know we can't eat them, right?"

"I'm not here to discuss our peculiar diet." He laid back on the grass and tucked his hands under his head. "You never dealt with what happened to you."

I shot him an unimpressed glare. "Says you."

"Yes, says me. I can feel your emotions, remember? That would make me an unequivocal expert in the field."

"Yeah, well, no one asked you to go rummaging around in my feelings. Especially considering we don't even know each other."

I dusted off my hands, about to push to my feet, when Noah's fingers grazed my knee.

"Just listen, please. What harm can it do?"

I rolled my eyes, then turned to stare at the lake. The fact that I hadn't left yet was permission enough for him to continue. Doubtful I was going to like what he had to say, but once he *said* it, I could move on.

"I know you believe you've adjusted. But I can feel your fear. It's hidden deep within you, buried beneath layers of sarcasm and snippy thoughts. Those feelings need to be addressed and dealt with, otherwise they'll fester like an infected wound."

"Then don't pick at it," I grumbled.

Noah's deep chuckle made my mouth twitch. "Clever, Anna. But cleverness will only get you so far. Until you tackle your unresolved emotions, that wound *will* fester. These things don't heal naturally. If you had a broken limb, you'd see a doctor for it, right?"

I couldn't help but laugh. We were vampires. We didn't need doctors. A fact I'd become intimately familiar with over the last few months. When Camilla trained someone to fight, she didn't hold back.

"Your analogy is dated," I commented. "We're vampires, remember?"

"True. But my point still remains. Have you ever considered speaking with a therapist?"

Hell no. That was the last thing I needed. "No. And thanks for this little chat, but I—"

"Vlad can't protect you from everything," Noah suddenly said.

I froze. "What?"

"You feel safe in his little world. But his world is what killed you in the first place, or don't you remember?"

"No. I remember *me* getting *myself* killed by sticking my nose where it didn't belong."

"Into *his* world," Noah argued. "And what about the queen? Do you think she's just going to let this all go?"

I sucked in a sharp breath and leapt to my feet. "Who are you? What do you know?"

Noah held his hands out peaceably, but there was a fire to his gaze now that wasn't there before. "I mean you no harm."

"Like hell you don't."

"Anna, any vampire with his ear to the ground knows the queen is gunning for you."

Gunning for me? No. She'd summoned me, but there was no evidence she wanted me dead. My frown must have given me away because Noah slowly climbed to his feet. He held my gaze as he plunged his hands into his pockets, as though trying to appear like the friendliest little vampire ever.

"What's the point of all this?" I whispered.

"Why are you here? Why are you digging into my life? What do you want from me?"

"That's the thing. Nothing. I don't want anything from you."

Impossible. Everybody always wanted something. "Try again."

"No, Anna. I'm serious. I just want to help."

"Well, you have a funny way of showing it. Do you work for the queen? Are you spying on me for her?"

Noah chuckled, his fangs flashing in the moonlight. I instinctively took a step back, one he noted with an arched brow. "See, that's what I mean. You don't trust vampires. And why should you? We didn't exactly welcome you into our community with open arms."

"So?"

"So... I think you need to deal with that. Before you can deal with anything else. Before you can happily move on."

"You never answered my questions," I accused.

"True. But then, you really didn't answer any of mine."

I ground my teeth and glared at him. Just like that, I knew I didn't like this guy. Noah was far too pushy for his own good. I may not be an ancient vampire, but I'd survived the last one who'd come after me. I wasn't weak or helpless.

Sighing, Noah shifted his weight, then pulled his hands out of his pockets. Clutched in his right hand was a crisp envelope, somehow in pristine condition. "Here. Take this."

I didn't take it from him. Nope. No way. A sealed letter from an unknown vampire. Nuh-uh. Didn't matter that my curiosity *burned* to see what was inside. I'd grown up *a lot* in the past three months, grown wiser and more worldly—or so I hoped—and accepting this letter smacked of stupidity.

"No thanks." I turned to leave.

"Anna." Noah's voice made me pause. It wasn't rude or mean, but his voice possessed a strength it'd lacked moments ago.

When I glanced over my shoulder, he strode toward me and slipped the envelope into my back pocket, careful not to touch me. Then he threw me a two-fingered salute and vanished.

What the hell had all this been about? Empath or not, this was about more than my unresolved issues. Had he sought me out after class specifically to give me some note? And who was it from?

I slowly pulled the envelope out of my back

pocket and studied it. Absolutely nothing stood out to me. No stamp, no name, nothing but a blank slate. There was certainly something inside though. I could feel the edges of a card.

Nibbling on my lip, I turned it over and let my fingers rest against the sealed flap. I could wait to open it until I was home. Until I stood next to Vlad. I could. Or I could open it now. The nosey side of me won out. Maybe I *hadn't* grown up much then.

Cursing under my breath, I caved to my curiosity, ripped open the envelope, then pulled out what looked like a business card. *Noah Bradshaw, Therapist to the Undead.*

I couldn't help but laugh. Undead therapist? Seriously? Did he actually think I'd call him?

Shaking my head, I slipped his card back into my pocket and headed toward the VA building. It would take a hell of a lot more than this to get me to talk to a shrink—but I had a feeling he already knew that.

CHAPTER FIVE

"There you are!"

I groaned at the sound of Camilla's voice. Busted. I knew she would ride my ass for wandering off, but damn, couldn't a girl get a moment to herself?

Apparently not, considering the way she marched toward me, armed with a fierce glare.

"Whoa," a voice rose next to me.

I glanced over just in time to see a mess of pastel hair bob into sight. Guess Violet had also hung around for a bit after the meeting.

"Is she a friend of yours?" Violet asked, staring at the shitstorm heading my way.

With her nose crinkled and fangs bared like a pissed off kitten, if I didn't know her, the sight might have concerned me. But I was so used to her kicking my ass now that a little temper tantrum really didn't bother me.

"Well, she thinks she is."

Violet chuckled and tucked her hair behind her ears before turning to face me. "I just wanted to tell you how brave I think you are. I know your transition hasn't been an easy one. Oh, and I love your vlog."

I inwardly winced and silently prayed that she didn't start fawning over me. I'd had enough of that recently.

"I don't know why I didn't recognize you when you sat down at the meeting, but—"

"Ixnay on the og-vlay," I said, absolutely mutilating the Pig Latin, then gestured subtly to Camilla.

Violet's eyes widened. "She doesn't...?"

"Camilla," I bellowed. "I've been looking for you."

"Oh, have you now? I've been sitting out there for thirty minutes, waiting for you to show your little ass. Did I not tell you to meet me in the parking lot?"

I mean, close enough, right? We were only about a block away. I didn't argue with her though. I knew better. The woman was a she-bat from the inner realms of hell when pissed.

"Who is this?" she demanded, jabbing a finger

toward Violet. "You know what? I don't care. Let's go."

"Sorry," I muttered to Violet. "See you next week?"

"Oh, um. Yeah. See ya!"

Once she strolled off, I prepared myself for the brunt of Camilla's tantrum. Instead, she huffed and started toward her car. "Let's go. We have a training session tonight."

No, we didn't. She was just pissed that I'd made her look for me, and now she was making shit up as she went. First it was the VA and now training. What was next?

I planted my hands on my hips and faced her. "Camilla, are you ever gonna climb outta my ass?"

She jerked to a stop and unleashed a stare worthy of Medusa. "What did you just say to me?"

Okay, so a wiser person might have retracted their statement, then dropped to their knees and begged for this goddess's forgiveness. But because she wasn't actually a goddess, just a trumped-up vampire with an ego the size of Vlad's dick, I felt no need to prostrate myself before her. Instead, I waved goodbye to Violet, then marched to Camilla's ride.

"Well?" I grabbed the passenger side door handle. "You coming or what?"

"One of these days..." Camilla growled as she circled the front of her car and slipped behind the wheel. "One of these days, Vlad and I won't be around to save your sorry little ass, and that's the day you'll find yourself in deep shit."

"Ooo, I'm shaking in my heels. Just admit it. You don't have a life anymore, and that's why you won't leave us alone."

"Are you kidding me right now?" Her fingers gripped the steering wheel so tightly, I wondered if the leather stitches would pop. "Do you have any idea how much trouble you're in?"

"Oh my god—"

Camilla jerked, her slitted eyes flashing at me.

"—I am so sick and tired of hearing about how much trouble I'm apparently in. You sound like a broken record. I'm starting to wonder if it's all in your head. The queen is pissed, I get that. But where is she, huh? You're all jumping at shadows."

"And I suppose it's all in Vlad's head too?"

I shrugged, then braced my hands against the dashboard the instant Camilla slammed the car into drive and tore out onto the street. I'd learned very early on that she wasn't exactly a safe driver. Some nights I even wondered if she had a license.

"I swear by all things bloody, there is nothing more exasperating than a newborn vampire."

"And yet, you continue to punish yourself by hanging out with me."

I was definitely pushing her buttons tonight. Her flushed cheeks and narrowed eyes told me everything I needed to know. But guess what? The woman had literally burst into Vlad's office postcoital, so if I was needling her, it was because she deserved it. She'd been annoying me for months. A little payback wouldn't hurt.

"I hang out with you to train you. To make sure that when the queen calls for your head, you can defend yourself! And to make sure someone is there to pick up the pieces when she murders your ass."

"She isn't going to murder my ass. Geez. Are all vampires this melodramatic?"

Camilla growled and gripped the steering wheel even tighter. I watched the leather strain beneath her fingers and wondered if the poor thing could handle her strength.

"I want you to listen very closely, Anna. You are in over your head right now. You have absolutely no fucking idea what the queen is capable of. So, when Vlad and I tell you that you're in danger, you need to listen."

"Vlad doesn't seem as concerned as you."

"Vlad is hiding it from you, idiot! He doesn't want to scare you. I've told him he needs to be upfront with you about all this stuff, but he refuses. So you know what, I'll do it for him."

I rolled my eyes and settled back against the seat. This wasn't the first time I'd borne witness to Camilla's theatrics. She had a dramatic flair that rivaled my mother's.

She took a hard right-hand turn, the wheels screeching against the pavement. Distantly, I heard someone shriek, "asshole!" I glanced back but couldn't see anyone. I did spot a stop sign though. One she'd blown right through.

"There was a stop sign back there," I told her, not that she listened.

"Haven't you wondered why no one complains about the queen? Why no one ever fights back against her rules? Why there's never been a revolution against her?"

"Considering Genevieve is actually Marie Antoinette, I always figured it had something to do with her past. Maybe everyone loves her for letting them eat cake?"

Camilla spared me a stunned glance, running through a red light. "You truly are an imbecile."

I shot her a beaming grin. "But you love me."

"I... don't even know what to say to that. Vlad could have chosen anyone, but he chose you."

That didn't sound like a compliment.

"The reason no one argues about the queen's rules is because every time she catches the slightest whisper of rebellion, she slaughters everyone involved."

Well, that got my attention.

"I can think of three times in my lifespan alone where the queen rounded up her inquisitors and unleashed them on the entire vampiric community. Everyone was questioned, and if the inquisitors weren't unequivocally convinced that you were the utmost loyal citizen, they burned you, your house, and everyone you knew to the ground."

"That's murder."

She pinned me with a look that clearly said "duh." "Vampires aren't governed by the same laws as humans. This peace treaty with your president is all for show. The queen doesn't care about peace with humans. She only cares about what humans can do for us. The economy has quadrupled since the treaty. New businesses, new products, new jobs. Where do you think that money goes?"

Was this a trick question?

Camilla sped through a yellow light. "By the blood, you really are stupid. The money goes back to Genevieve and her people. As the principal investor in all these new companies, she's lining her royal coffers while playing nice with the humans. And then you came along and threw a lynch pin into all her plans. Not only that, but you did it publicly. Your photos from the night Vlad changed you are still everywhere. You caused a scene. You gave humans a reason to distrust the treaty, to distrust her. And on top of all that, you killed her sire."

"I didn't kill—"

"He's dead because of you. You're responsible. Sam went tearing in and decapitated the queen's sire to save your life." She shot me another glare. "The queen isn't just summoning you for a quick interview. She wants to make an example of you. To kill you and prove to the rest of us that you're nothing more than a minor nuisance."

My silence seemed to settle Camilla's nerves. Her fingers loosened from the steering wheel, and she stretched them out, all while running yet another stop sign.

"Do you get it now?" she asked.

Oh, I got it, all right.

I was well and truly fucked.

And not in a good way.

"Anna Marie Perish!"

I whirled around at the sound of my name. The first thought that slammed into my head was "Mom?" But that voice definitely didn't belong to my mother. Oh no. It belonged to Lucy. My bestest best friend who was storming down the hallway toward me, anger crackling in her eyes. Damn. Was she seriously still mad at me? So I invited Sam to Perish. So what? It wasn't like she had to sleep with him or anything.

"Where's my cell phone?" she demanded, her long, dark-brown hair swishing behind her back. Ooh baby, she was definitely pissed. "You give me my phone. Right this second!"

I pressed my lips together to keep from laughing. Lucy was hardly a scary person. More like a little mouse. Sure, she had teeth, but they weren't as sharp as mine. She was all bark, no bite. I loved that about her.

"Well?" She came to a stop in front of me, her toe tapping the tiled floor.

"Sorry, girl. I don't know where it is." Which

wasn't true. I knew exactly where it was. It'd fallen out of my jeans' pocket when I was getting my groove on with Vlad. It was probably still sitting on his desk, dinging nonstop. Bet it was driving Vlad insane. He wasn't a fan of technology at the best of times.

"Anna!" she shrieked. "You give me my damn phone—"

"Why?" I asked, interrupting what I was sure would be a fabulous tirade of threats that never frightened me.

"It's my phone! I don't need to tell you why I need it—"

"Nope, but you could tell me why you're so mad about it."

"You took it!"

"And?"

"And I want it back."

"Why?"

Anger tinged her cheeks a wondrous shade of red. Poor Lucy. She'd never been able to hide her emotions. With her fair skin, the slightest thing often set it off.

"Anna..."

"Tell me why you're so desperate for your phone."

"I hate you," she growled.

"You love me. Now tell me what's going on, otherwise you'll never see your precious phone again."

"You wouldn't."

"Please. You know I would. I'm officially holding your phone hostage until you tell me what has your panties in a twist."

Lucy cursed under her breath, then raked her hands through her hair, her nails scraping against her scalp. "I just... want it back, alright?"

"Why?"

"Oh my god, you're a pain in my ass today!"

"Watch it," I warned. The G-word didn't affect me, but I wasn't the only vampire living on these premises.

Lucy sighed, then dropped her arms to her side. "Fine, I'll tell you. But don't laugh at me."

I held up my hand. "Scout's honor."

"Oh, don't you scout's honor me. You were never a scout."

I chuckled, enjoying the exasperation in her voice. Man, I was in a mood today, and it was all thanks to Camilla. It should be against the law to ruin a girl's post-orgasm bliss.

Lucy averted her gaze, then muttered, "I need to text him."

It didn't take a genius to know exactly who she was referring to. And I promised I wouldn't laugh. But that didn't mean I couldn't still tease her. I never promised that.

But the second I saw her face, I bit back my words and instead nodded. She'd masked it with her anger, but I could see now that she was miserable. And I completely understood. Lucy was holding herself back from her mate, denying their relationship. I couldn't even imagine how that felt. Being with Vlad made my world feel complete. If I applied that to Lucy, it seemed pretty safe to assume that her world felt a little broken right now. And since texting was all she allowed herself, it was no wonder she was going a little crazy.

"Come on," I told her.

"Where are we going?"

"Vlad's office."

"Anna, please, I just want my phone."

I offered her a tiny smile, then took her hand and slowly led her toward his office. "I know. It's in there. We'll get it, then you can text Sam."

I sensed the relief in her. Her fingers loosened against mine and her shoulders relaxed. This whole "mate" stuff was serious business. She'd be happier if she stopped fighting it, but Lucy didn't know how to do that. She tended to make everything just a little bit more complicated. But that was part of her personality. Type A individuals didn't know how to easily adapt.

Voices rose to my ears as we neared Vlad's office. At the sound of my name, I gripped Lucy's hand tightly and pulled her to a stop. She glanced up at me, intending to question me, but I held a finger to my lips, then listened. If I could hear them, they could hear us, and I didn't want to give our presence away, not when I wanted to know what they were talking about. Rude, yes, but hey, so was talking about people behind their backs.

"She's being purposely obtuse," Camilla whined. "Either she's deliberately ignoring this or she's so naïve that she literally doesn't understand how much danger she's in."

"She understands," Vlad's voice rumbled. "We must be patient with her. A few months is hardly enough time for someone to adjust to all this. Her entire world has changed."

"That's exactly what I mean!" Camilla's heels clacked against the floor in a sharp pattern. Pacing, I realized. "Yes, her world is completely different, but

I really don't think she understands. She's acting as though she's the same girl who stormed into Fallen."

"I disagree."

"Oh, you disagree?" Camilla's heels fell silent. "Is that why you're sheltering her from the truth? Acting as though everything is perfectly fine?"

"I don't see a reason to cause her undue stress."

"You have to be kidding me." Camilla sighed, then I heard the sound of a creaking chair. She must have sat down. "I swear, you two are utterly perfect for each other. She doesn't want to face reality and you don't want to force her to."

Vlad groaned, and I could picture him pinching the bridge of his nose. "Camilla—"

"You *have* to tell her, Vlad! You can't keep hiding something like this from her. She has every right to know, and maybe it'll smarten her up a little."

My mouth pursed. Tell me what? What exactly was Vlad hiding from me?

"It isn't the right time."

"The right time?" Camilla belted out a frustrated groan. "Listen to me, because I'm going to make this very clear. If you don't tell her about your latest vision, I will."

A chill rippled down my spine. Another vision?

"You've heard the whispers as well as I, Vlad,"

Camilla continued. "The queen wants her head. And if Anna refuses this latest summons, which I expect her to, there's talk of the queen unleashing a few of her inquisitors to track Anna down and drag her before Genevieve. I've heard this from very reliable sources."

"As have I."

"And you haven't told her?" Camilla demanded.

"What would that accomplish? She's terrified, Camilla. I don't think it's that she refuses to believe the truth, but rather that she's too frightened to face it."

Ouch. I definitely didn't like hearing that. Especially from Vlad. Was Camilla right? Was I being purposely obtuse? Closing my eyes to the truth and just hoping for the best?

"Then we have to make her."

I gripped Lucy's hand, squeezing perhaps a little too tight if her sharp intake of breath was evidence of anything. Thankfully, Camilla and Vlad were too busy arguing with each other to hear her.

"Vlad, you have to talk to her about this. She thinks I'm exaggerating because you're downplaying the danger. She trusts you more than me."

"Understandably."

"Yes, because you're her mate! It's your job to—"

"Protect her?" Vlad suddenly snapped. "I know this. What do you think I've been doing? It's my job to help her. Defend her. But it's also my job to love her, Camilla."

Tears sprang to my eyes.

"I will do whatever it takes to keep her safe."

"Including keeping her in the dark?"

Vlad didn't answer.

"You're both fools" was Camilla's parting retort before I heard the door click shut.

Unfortunately, I was starting to agree.

CHAPTER SIX

Lucy dragged me into the kitchen, then wrenched open the refrigerator door and grabbed a bottle of water. I watched longingly as she leaned against the counter, popped the lid, and took a massive swallow. The sight of those wet little water beads gliding down the side of the bottle parched my throat.

Interestingly, it wasn't sweets or even steak I missed the most. It was water. The first cool, refreshing sip. A few months back, I'd attempted to steal a sip, just to see if I could tolerate it. The water had tasted like heaven in my mouth, but it'd scalded like fire on the way down. Lucy suggested just swishing and spitting, but I refused. Why torture myself like that?

Lucy wiped a hand across her mouth, and I

blinked, forcing my thoughts back to the present. She recapped the bottle, then glared at me. "You're being ridiculous. You know that, right?"

Hmm. Much like lipstick, there were varying shades of ridiculousness, from Puckering Asshole Pink to 50 Shades of Perverted Grandma Red. Currently, I ranked somewhere in the middle. Maybe somewhere around the Peachy Orgasm shade.

In all fairness, I didn't feel ridiculous. I actually felt quite justified in my decision to ignore Vlad and Camilla's conversation. Why bring it up? Why even mention what I'd overheard? What would it accomplish?

"Anna, listen. I know you."

Oh here we go. Bring it on. The best friend speech.

"And I know you'll continue to avoid this conversation until it grows into a massive elephant-sized secret. Just *talk* to him. Is it really that hard to do?"

Sarcastic laughter slipped past my lips. "Talk about the pot calling the kettle black."

"Huh?"

I rolled my eyes, then imitated her voice. "*Just talk to him, Anna.*" I shook my head. "Pretty sure I've been telling you to do the exact same thing with Sam for months now."

Her mouth pursed. "That's different."

"Oh, hun. It's so very not."

Lucy grumbled under her breath and slammed back another mouthful of water. Pretty sure she was doing it on purpose just to annoy me. And I seemed incapable of ignoring it. My damn tongue shot out and licked my lips of its own accord.

So I gave her my back and started fiddling with the few dishes left in the sink. "If Vlad doesn't want to talk to me about any of this, why should I force it?"

"I don't know, maybe because it's your *life*? Don't you even want to know what he saw in his vision?"

My fingers paused on a bread knife, and I sighed. "Lucy, stop pushing."

"For crying out loud," she snapped. "You two are like toddlers, I swear. You wax poetic about all this soulmate shit, how you're destined to be together, how nothing will tear you apart when really, the two of you are literally terrified of each other."

I burst out laughing. "I'm *not* scared of Vlad. Please. At least I can be around him without turning into a frightened little schoolgirl."

"Hey!" The scent of blood rose, so I knew she was blushing. "We're not talking about me and Sam."

I glanced over my shoulder and lifted a brow. "How'd you know I was talking about you and Sam? Unless you *know* you're being a little chicken shit."

"I'm sorry, *who's* being the chicken shit here? All you have to do is tell Vlad you overheard his conversation with Camilla and ask him to be honest with you. Tell him you want to know exactly what's going on. Clearly, he's been hiding stuff from you. Doesn't that piss you off?"

On some level, it did. On *all* levels, really. I didn't like being treated like a simpering damsel in distress. And I certainly didn't appreciate that he didn't trust me with the truth. But secretly—or maybe not so secretly—I was terrified. Lucy wasn't the only chicken shit here. This whole queen nonsense was getting way out of hand. If Camilla could be trusted—and I knew she could—the queen hated me. Which was just my luck. But it also raised some questions. Camilla made it sound like those who were disliked by the queen were "handled." As in, killed. So how come no one had attempted to kill me yet? After all, I was a newborn vampire who lacked any real power.

Okay, so I could wake up before the sunset, but that literally meant nothing in the grand scheme. And yes, maybe I was the first human changed into a vampire after Genevieve established the peace treaty, but on a scale of one to ten, that little blip ranked a solid negative five. It didn't matter in the slightest bit.

So why hadn't anyone tried to kill me yet?

I could only think of one answer.

Vlad.

He was well thought of in the vampire community. Famous, rich, powerful, and ancient. The man could shapeshift into two different animals and had visions of the future. He was probably the only thing standing between me and countless vampires hunting for my head.

Of course, I also had Camilla on my side—a three-hundred-year-old vamp with an innate ability to kick anyone's ass. A talent that rivaled what's-his-face in that *Rocky* movie from the '70s or whatever.

Then there was the whole "I murdered Petrik" thing. Not that I actually had. But from my understanding, very few vampires knew about Sam. Werewolves weren't a secret, but the actual werewolves themselves guarded their identities like spies. No one knew *he* killed Petrik. Instead, word spread that I had done it. Lil ole me. That took some *major* skills. Ones I definitely didn't possess, but they didn't know that. I suppose that little tidbit could be giving them pause. If I could kill a millennium-old vampire, imagine what I could do to someone half that age.

Truthfully, the answer was absolutely nothing. But hey, maybe this little white lie could work on my behalf.

"Anna."

I briefly closed my eyes and centered my thoughts. Lucy wouldn't quit pushing this because she *never* quit pushing things. The only way she'd shut up was if I agreed. "Okay, fine. I'll talk to him about all this. Alright?"

"Thank you—"

"But only if you talk to Sam."

Her mouth clicked shut while mine spread into a victorious grin. I had her now. For some reason that she didn't feel obliged to share, the thought of talking to Sam downright terrified her. But both of them were utterly miserable. Someone had to crack.

I hadn't tried it, but I couldn't imagine it was easy to avoid and ignore your soulmate. Even now, I felt the pull to seek out Vlad. He made me happy. He completed me. Why would I want to deprive myself of that?

Lucy lifted her chin and met my stare. I spotted the tightening of her jaw and the steel glint in her eyes. She wouldn't ignore my challenge, which was why I'd issued it. If she could push me into doing something I didn't want, then I could return the favor. She wanted me safe, I wanted her happy. So, I refused to feel guilty about my methods. Sometimes a girl had to fight dirty.

"Fine," Lucy bit out through gritted teeth.

I knew better though. "And I don't just mean a hello and goodbye. I'm talking a full conversation about what the two of you expect from each other. Have you even heard his side yet? Has he told you that he wants you as his mate? That he wants to be with you?"

"Well, no..."

"Have the discussion, Lucy. The full blown 'where's this relationship going' discussion. Learn each other's hopes and desires, wants and needs, likes and dislikes. Everything. Sort out what both of you want from this relationship, whether that means jumping each other's bones or walking away forever. But stop dragging him through your emotional mess and stop leading him on. The man has a right to know."

"You know, I like it better when I'm the one counseling you."

"Sucks when the tables are turned, huh?"

"Oh, shut up."

I grinned, then hopped up onto the kitchen counter, my feet dangling next to the lower row of cupboards. Of all the rooms in a house, the kitchen was the one I missed most. Especially the smell of baking. Not that I could bake. Lucy often quipped that my cooking could kill, and I believed her. Now, my mom... she could cook. Damn woman won the Miss Louisiana Best Pie baking contest every single year, which was totally a point of contention between us. When I was a human, she'd loved to hound me about it, ask me how I planned to provide for a husband if I couldn't create the simplest dishes.

Well, I showed her, didn't I?

Now all I had to do was open a vein—and my legs—to keep Vlad happy. There was more than that to our relationship of course. Depth and substance, and all that razzmatazz. But my mom didn't need to know all the finer details. Just the ones that would piss her off.

Yes, I knew that made me a little bit immature. But I didn't care.

"So, you're gonna talk to Vlad then?" Lucy pressed.

I cocked my head and stared at her. What the

hell had I done in a past life to be gifted with not one but two naggy mothers? Well-meaning or not.

"Guess that depends. Are you going to talk to Sam?"

"I already said I would, didn't I?" she snapped.

"Then yes, I'll talk to Vlad."

"Good. When?"

Oh, sweet merciful baby Zeus. "Lucy."

"No, I'm serious. When? Because I know you. Procrastination is your middle name. You'll keep pushing it off until hell freezes over."

"Hmm. Hell freezing over does sound like fun. I could go ice skating with the devil. My parents would *love* that."

"Anna!" Lucy bit out.

I rolled my eyes. She was sucking the fun right out of this room. "Tonight, alright? Is that soon enough for you?"

"Then I'll speak with Sam this week once we're in Perish, whenever we can find a moment alone."

"Cuz that doesn't sound awkward."

"Well, I can't have that kind of conversation over the phone, now can I?"

Wasn't that the truth. "Guess we both have our assignments then."

She nodded, then stole another sip of water. You

know, I'd never noticed how sensual the throat was. As a human, it hadn't once entered my thoughts. But now? I often found myself staring at the smooth column, watching it bob and dip, staring at the curve, studying the veins—

"Hey!"

Cold water splashed me in the face. I sputtered and mopped at my eyes. "What the hell was that for?"

Lucy stood next to me, her hands wrapped around the bottle she'd just squeezed. "You were doing it again! Gazing all longingly at my throat. It's creepy! Go suck on someone's wrist if you're hungry, but stop staring at my jugular."

"I wasn't gonna bite you!" I yelled.

"I don't care! You don't realize how disturbing it is. Your eyes get hazy, and you flash your fangs. It's just..." She shuddered. "Do it elsewhere."

"Spoilsport," I groused.

Grumbling under my breath, I jumped down from the counter and headed toward the nearby guest rooms where Vlad's harem lived.

Humph, guess I was a little hungry after all.

I PACED the length of the hallway in front of Vlad's bedroom.

After Lucy's and my little chat, I'd snuck a quick nip of blood, then wandered the house and considered my options. Really, there were only two. I could continue to play naïve and pretend like I didn't understand the gravity of the situation, or I could be upfront about it all and tell Vlad I'd overheard his conversation. The first option avoided an unpleasant discussion, the second welcomed a whole lotta trouble into my life. Naivety was starting to look mighty fine right now, but I knew Lucy would kick my ass all the way to the moon if I played that card.

Besides, I didn't run away from things. I'd always been the sort to face them head-on. Fearless and adventurous, 'twas I.

Of course, my last impetuous stint had landed me in a cement room filled with sunlight. But hey, I highly doubted that sort of luck struck twice in a lifetime.

Which left door number two. Being upfront.

Damn. I really wasn't looking forward to this conversation. Yes, we were soulmates. But we'd also only been together for three months. That wasn't a lot of time to build a relationship. And I was already about to test it.

But I'd promised Lucy. And I wasn't a coward.

So I squared my shoulders, pushed my hair off my face, then opened Vlad's bedroom door. This time of day, I often found him in here, undressing and unwinding from the night's events. Tonight, he stood on the attached balcony just outside his window with his back to me.

My eyes widened at the sight of him shirtless, his black slacks hung low on his hips. He gripped the balcony railing and stared out over his land, as though inspecting every last inch of it.

If ever there was a prize for hottest vampire, Vlad would win it hands down. The man was drop dead gorgeous with the hips of an Adonis. I couldn't see that fancy little V-thing right now since his back was to me, but it was always there, directing my gaze *downward* like a bright and shiny arrow. I wasn't a sex-crazed teenager, I swear. It was just my body's reaction to Vlad. He commanded attention, and I seemed completely willing to give it.

"I was beginning to wonder if I would see you again before sunrise," Vlad commented.

My attention dropped to his fingers, and I watched as they tightened around the railing. It surprised me to find him out here. Ever since the fiasco with Petrik, Vlad and I had avoided the balconies. A sort of unspoken rule. We hadn't known it at the time, but according to vamp logic, they didn't consider balconies part of the house, meaning they didn't require an invitation. Petrik had taken advantage of that little loophole and used it to abduct me. Needless to say, I didn't like balconies as much anymore.

I strode into the room. "Missed me, did ya?"

Vlad turned to face me, a soft smile curving his lips. "Always."

Ah, the things he said. Made a girl weak in the knees.

"How did the VA meeting go?"

I shrugged. "As well as expected, I suppose. I met a few vampires, heard a few sob stories that rivaled my own. The speaker was an odd man. An empath apparently, which wasn't fun. He told me I need therapy and handed me his business card."

"I've heard of him," Vlad said, nodding. "He's been around for a while."

"So, not one of the queen's spies then?"

"Unlikely."

Damn. That meant I really had no reason not to take his advice. Oh wait, yes I did. Because I didn't want to. Reason enough in my books.

"So, speaking of the queen..." I hedged, wincing at the horrible segue.

Vlad lifted a brow.

Ugh. I hated these types of conversations. They always set off my nerves and made my body tremble. Deep down, I knew I didn't have anything to fear—I hadn't done anything wrong, after all. But emotions didn't always follow logic. My traitorous hands were already shaking as I considered my words.

Vlad clasped my hands, then slid his upward, caressing my arms. "Whatever's bothering you—"

"I overheard you and Camilla tonight," I blurted. Best to just get it out there.

His fingers paused and his gaze lifted to mine. "Aren't you the one always telling me it's rude to eavesdrop?"

A weak chuckle slipped past my lips. "Yeah. That's me. But it's hard not to listen when you hear your name."

"I imagine so."

I snuck another covert glance, then turned away and braced my elbows against the balcony railing. We were surrounded by lowlands infested with gators, turtles, and a plethora of birds, and I absolutely loved it. Before moving here, I had cared little about Louisiana's wildlife, but living for the night had changed my perspective somehow. I appreciated nature's beauty more now that I was excluded from it.

"Well? Are we going to talk about it?"

"If we must."

"We must," I parroted. "We can't hide things like this from each other. If you had a vision about me, I need to know about it."

He nodded, then turned and pressed his side against mine. Warmth flushed my entire body, but I couldn't let that distract me.

"Am I in danger?" I asked.

He shot me a sorrowful look, then nodded. "Yes, I believe you are."

My nerves kicked into overdrive. I had to fist my hands together to keep them from visibly shaking. "How... How much danger?"

Vlad curled an arm around my waist and pulled me against him. "A great deal, I suspect."

"Tell me."

"It's all flickers right now. Which is how it always begins. It started this way when I first saw you in my dreams. Eventually, the dream becomes clearer. But until then, I'm at as much of a loss as you."

"But you know I'm in danger?"

"Of that, I have no doubt. I saw..."

"What?"

Vlad sighed, and gripped me tighter. "Your death. In my dream, I held you in my arms, and you were gone."

A shiver screamed down my spine. "Anything else?"

"Not as of yet."

"What can we do?"

After a moment's hesitation, he leaned in and kissed the top of my head. "Convince the queen you aren't a threat. We have proof of your innocence. The video you took at Fallen before Petrik attacked you. Allies who bore witness to your abduction from my house. Testimonials detailing what Petrik put you through. Her sire is dead, but it was a welcome, justified death. It may take an audience with her and the vampire council to prove your innocence, but I believe it can be done."

"Then you think the queen is the one responsible for my death?"

"Yes."

"Okay."

Vlad shifted his weight and peered down at me. "Okay? That's all?"

"What else is there to say?"

"I swear, Anna. I will never let anything happen to you. I'd sooner die."

"How about neither of us die? I like that scenario best."

"Me too," Vlad said, hugging me close. "I... apologize for keeping the vision from you. I didn't wish to frighten you. Perhaps we need to work on being open and communicative with each other."

"I haven't had much luck with relationships," I admitted with a nod.

"What's the word you use for that? Twinsies?"

I burst out laughing. "Ditto. It's ditto."

"Ah. Ditto. I like that word."

I snickered quietly. "Speaking of being open and communicative..."

"Mm."

"I told my mother that we'd come home this week."

"You did?"

"And I, uh, may have invited Sam along."

Vlad tensed. "You didn't."

I choked back a third laugh. Vlad and Sam were not the bestest of friends. Not even on the best of days.

"I would love it if you came with us," I said. "I want to introduce you to my mother."

"Anna..." He groaned and dropped his head forward until his brow rested against the railing. "Your mother? Seriously?"

I bit my bottom lip to keep my laughter in check. Our time together had certainly had an effect on Vlad's vocabulary. I wasn't sure he'd noticed the change, but I had. Far more sarcasm now than when we'd first met. And I absolutely loved it.

"We should probably reach out to my father too. Since we'll be in the neighborhood."

Vlad scowled playfully at me, his eyes catching the earliest morning light. We didn't have much time left. "What day did you say we'd leave?"

"Wednesday. Back on Sunday. It won't be a long trip."

"Long enough," he groused.

I stretched up and brushed a light kiss across his cheek. "Don't worry, I'll protect you from my big bad parents."

"You better," he growled.

This time, he lifted his head and captured my mouth in a hungry kiss. One we didn't have time to act upon.

Instead, I pulled back with a pout and glanced back at his bed. "Just think, in a few weeks, we'll hopefully be able to fall asleep together here, instead of locking ourselves in coffins."

With a bemused chuckle, Vlad swept me off my feet and bolted into his bedroom. I squealed and wrapped my arms around his neck. But before I could even blink, he tossed me on his bed and climbed on top.

"Vlad! We don't have enough time," I protested, laughing breathlessly.

"Want to bet?"

His head lowered and my laughter died on a soft gasp.

Best way to end the night.

CHAPTER SEVEN

"UNDERWEAR?"

"Check."

"Socks?"

"Check."

"Ass-kicking Weitzman boots?"

"Double check."

"Garter and bustier?"

"Che—wait, what?" My head snapped up, and I blinked at Lucy. "I don't own a garter and bustier."

Lucy snorted and rose from the bed, notepad in hand. Since it was Tuesday night, and tomorrow we were leaving for Perish, she'd taken it upon herself to help me pack. Organization was next to godliness, or so she claimed. *Snooze alert.* But hey, she always made sure I didn't forget anything, so there was that.

"Girl, just who do you think you're talking to?" she asked, laughing under her breath. "I helped you buy them, remember?"

Ah, yes. That embarrassing moment when she forced me to strut my half-naked self around a lingerie shop, preaching that the right underwear would land me the right man. Cuz apparently, every man must see my underwear to help me decide if he's the right one for me or not. Whatever. She had some strange ideas in that head of hers.

What that underwear had actually landed me was a one-night stand with a man who had more attachment issues than a newborn baby. The experience had scarred me for life, so much so that I'd never worn it in front of Vlad—and never would. In fact, *that* particular underwear was locked in my apartment back in Perish. And when I finally moved out, it would go in the garbage.

"What about you?" I suddenly asked, turning the tables. After all, *she* was the one hopefully getting laid this weekend. I could only imagine what her travel bag looked like. Ziplocked bags full of perfectly folded clothing, separated with flimsy dividers meant to keep her things perfectly organized. Whereas mine, I just shoved everything in, then sat on top, attacked the zipper, and hoped for the best. "Did you pack condoms? Lots and lots of condoms?"

"No, I did not." She stuck her tongue out at me. "The agreement was I'd speak with Sam, not bone him."

"Ha. Bone him." I chuckled before returning to my packing.

"Oh for crying out loud, knock off the dog jokes, will ya?"

"Never," I vowed.

I mean, Sam was a werewolf. That pretty much ensured an eternity of jokes. Unless werewolves weren't immortal. Another question I needed answered. I actually didn't know much about the furrier kind, other than the fact that they knew how to hunt and kill ancient vampires. Sam had taken care of Petrik like it was no big deal. Impaled him with some special kind of stake made of hawthorn and treated in holy water and monksblood. A trade secret, Sam had said. And one I'd gratefully kept to myself. My issues with older vampires seemed to be a reoccurring theme, so that was information I knew to keep to myself. And if I could create such a stake, or maybe convince Sam to hand one over to me, I'd feel a lot better. The queen wasn't as old as Petrik, but she still had a couple hundred more years on me.

I reached for my toiletry kit, about to unceremoniously stuff it into the corner of my bag, when I caught the sound of a sharp, high-pitched sigh, followed by almost indecipherable grumbling. Frowning, I crooked my head and focused all my attention on the sound. It wasn't coming from Lucy. Or even from my bedroom. I strained a little harder, then nodded. The kitchen. Someone was in the kitchen.

"Nasty little vampires. And they call me filthy. Me! I'm a clean girl. Clean. Not them. Not clean. Not clean."

The fuck? Did we piss off one of Vlad's harem members or something?

The grumbling continued. A little quieter now. Yet higher pitched. It didn't match any of the voices I knew. I knew Beauregard's voice like the back of my hand. Dude was always in the way somewhere, tending to *Master Vlad's* needs. And the needs of the harem. Then there was Malinda, the youngest of the harem, and definitely the squirreliest. I still hadn't heard her full story, but for some reason, I imagined it involved a lot—and I mean *a lot*—of candy. The woman was *addicted.* Like, to the point where I never saw her without. It made *my* teeth hurt to drink from her sometimes.

"Filthy vampires!" the shrill voice squeaked again.

Geez, this person reminded me of that Gollum character from *Lord of the Rings*. Hated the movie but loved that little devil. Just the right amount of schizophrenic behavior to keep me invested. Lucy had shaken her head when I told her I was rooting for him. And when he bit off that other hobbit's finger, I was the only one who'd cheered.

Okay, maybe I liked a good underdog, so what?

"No food. No eats. Why? Filthy vampires."

I chuckled under my breath. Someone was definitely having a bad day. We kept the house stocked with plenty of food. Maybe Malinda had run out of candy and was crashing.

"What's so funny?" Lucy asked.

I blinked, the sound of her voice cutting me off from my eavesdropping. "Sorry. Someone's having some trouble finding a snack in the kitchen."

"And that's funny?" Lucy asked.

"You'd understand if you could hear them. They must be hangry. They're bitching about how we don't keep enough food in the house."

Lucy lifted a brow. "Eavesdropping isn't polite, you know."

"Thanks, Mom."

"Hey." She held her hands up peaceably. "You're the one that's always telling Vlad to turn off his vamp ears. You should do the same."

"Do as I say, not as I do?" I retorted with a slight chuckle.

"Sure," she said, shaking her head. "So, have you told Vlad about the vlog yet?"

My smile instantly slipped from my face.

"I take it that's a no," she pressed when I didn't respond.

I eyed Lucy from across my suitcase. She stood next to a window, bathing in the late afternoon light that I couldn't touch, reading off a list she'd put together of everything we needed to bring.

"What's the hold up?" she demanded. "He knows you're a vlogger. I'm not sure he understands it, but he knows that was your profession before turning. Why are you hiding it from him?"

"Lucy..." I sighed. She didn't understand my apprehensions. Hell, I didn't even understand them. "I just haven't found a good time yet."

"Seriously?" She lowered her list and pinned me with an exasperated expression. "The two of you are together pretty much every minute of the night. The only time you aren't with him are the golden hours before he wakes or when you and Camilla are training. You actually expect me to believe that you haven't found a moment to tell him about it?"

I pinched the bridge of my nose and centered my thoughts. Lucy didn't realize this was a sore subject for me. Especially considering Vlad's and my chat last night about how we needed to be more open and honest with each other. That would have been the perfect moment to come clean about it, but no, I'd brought up my family instead. That one had a timeline, or so I'd told myself.

"Look, just tell him. The longer you take, the more upset he'll get. Your vlog is a success, has been for a while now! Have you seen the response to your most recent episode?" She tossed her phone across the gap, and I caught it single-handedly. She'd opened her email for me to look at, and it was riddled with notifications.

"The last episode already has over half a million views, more than a hundred thousand likes, and over five thousand comments. You've made it, baby. That's your tenth successful episode in a row."

"I know," I murmured. "I just..."

"What other proof do you need to see you're a success? Tell him."

"Lucy."

"What's the big deal?" she pressed. "Just walk up

to him, show him the vlog, then tell him you're raking in the dough. He'll be happy for you!"

"Lucy," I growled.

"Stop being such a coward, Anna. The longer you wait to tell him—"

"Lucy! For crying out loud, back off!"

She startled and stared at me with wide eyes, as though shocked I'd raised my voice. Granted, I rarely yelled at her, but for cripes' sake, she was pushing my buttons tonight. Usually, I just ignored her bullheadedness and pushed past it, but tonight seemed to be one of *those* nights. The sort where her scolding and nagging shoved me over the edge.

I wasn't ready to tell Vlad about the vlog yet, and I honestly couldn't explain why. Imposter syndrome maybe? I'd never been this successful as a human. Which made me wonder if my success stemmed from me being a vampire. And if that was the case, how long till the fame faded? Nothing lasted forever.

"What's going on?" Lucy demanded. "I don't understand what the big deal is. You literally just need to shove your phone in his face and show him your channel. Problem solved. You're making this into a bigger deal than it needs to be."

I bit back a curse. Lucy was incapable of leaving anything alone, and I knew that. Just like I knew she'd keep picking at this until I finally caved and told Vlad. But I didn't want to be rushed into it. Nor did I want to listen to her berate me for not being open with Vlad. I *knew* all this already. I didn't need it from her as well.

But this was Lucy. *Peck, peck, peck.*

"You know, I'm getting really tired of you always butting your nose into my business every night," I complained, my words sour. "Don't you have your own life to live? Your own shit to pack? Your own relationship to meddle with?"

The instant the words left my mouth, I froze. I hadn't meant for it to come out so... combative and mean. I loved Lucy. I loved that she loved me enough to involve herself in everything in an attempt to protect me. I certainly didn't want to push her away.

I quietly cursed, but before I could apologize, she propped a hand on her hip and glared at me. "I do have my own life, thank you very much. A very normal, human life. But I can't live that life anymore because *you* went and got yourself killed, dragging me into this mess"—she waved her hands around the room—"you call *your* life. But you know what? Maybe it *is* time I returned to my life. And dealt with my own problems. Have fun packing by yourself."

She stomped across the room and snatched her phone back from me.

"Lucy—"

She lifted a hand, effectively silencing me. "Have a nice night, Anna."

On that note, she turned and marched out of my room, slamming my door shut behind her.

Great. I sighed and plunked myself down on the bed. *Just fucking great.*

I SAT in the kitchen with a steaming mug of blood sitting in front of me, but I couldn't bring myself to take a sip. The rancid smell turned my stomach, and I knew it would taste even worse. But tonight, I had no energy to track down one of the harem members, and even less inclination to sink my teeth into them. Fighting with Lucy always depressed me.

Seeing how our friendship spanned more than a decade, this was hardly our first row. Nor would it be our last. I'd always imagined us as little old ladies with blue and purple hair, sitting on the front porch, clutching glasses of sweet tea, yelling at them there youngsters to get the hell off our lawns. Neither of us had seen ourselves as loving little grandmas who knitted blankets for their kids and grandkids. That wasn't us.

But now that I was immortal, the image of us rocking together on the porch while spraying water at the neighborhood hoodlums and shouting at them to get off our lawns had vanished.

Lucy would grow old and gray, and I would remain exactly the same. It was actually a devastating thought. She was my partner in crime. My sister from another mister. We fought, we argued, we bickered, but we always came back to each other.

For the first time, though, I wondered if maybe I shouldn't apologize. If I should sever the friendship here and now, for her sake.

She'd said it herself: I'd dragged her into my mess of a life. Brought a human into the paranormal world. A world where she could very easily be eaten alive. It'd already happened to me, after all.

When I was first turned, Lucy had made me promise I wouldn't let the same thing happen to her. She believed there was nothing worse than becoming a vampire.

Keeping her in my life made me a selfish friend.

Maybe it was time to let her go. To break all ties and call it a day. Lucy hadn't promised Sam anything yet. She could turn around and walk away. Return home. Get a job at the local grocery store, go to school, find a husband, have a *life*. A human life.

She deserved that, and so much more.

"Well, don't you look like a barrel of sunshine tonight," a voice said, intruding on my thoughts.

I sighed and unleashed a miserable glare on Camilla. She stood in the kitchen doorframe, looking drop dead gorgeous, arms crossed above her chest. I knew that stance. That was her battle stance. The "time to kick your ass" stance.

"Not tonight," I mumbled.

I reached for the mug sitting in front of me and lifted it to my mouth. Heat touched my lips, but it didn't comfort me. My thoughts had taken a dark turn tonight.

"Yes, tonight," Camilla countered. She shoved away from the doorframe and stalked toward me. She hitched her hip against the counter, then leaned down and sniffed at the blood, her upper lip curling in distaste. "I can't believe you drink that shit."

I shrugged. I could count on one hand the number of times I had, and I'd hated it each time. But sometimes, a girl needed to hold a soothing warm mug between her hands. Coffee had been my go-to in my pre-vampire days, but the smell made me retch now.

"Alright." Camilla hooked the nearest chair with her foot and dragged it closer. "What's wrong?"

My lips flattened into a grim line. I so didn't want to talk about this with Camilla. I knew she considered me a friend, and I appreciated her efforts. Over the past three months, she'd molded me into a fighter. Something I hadn't believed possible. I wasn't the best, and I certainly wouldn't be winning any martial arts competitions. But she'd taught me how to attack and defend myself, shaped me into a strong, confident vampire. None of that meant I wanted to open up to her though. At least, not yet. Maybe one day.

When I didn't respond, she sat and braced her elbows against the counter. Then she grabbed my mug and dumped the contents into the sink. I watched as the thick liquid poured down the drain. Ugh. I couldn't blame Lucy for not wanting this. I literally fed off blood. And nothing else. Yes, I'd live forever, but as what? A shell of my human form? This monster that needed the lives of others to survive. We didn't need to kill, but that really didn't change anything.

We were vampires. Nosferatu. Creatures of the

night, if we wanted to go more dramatic. Yes, I woke before sunrise, but I couldn't let the sunbeams touch me. If they did, I burned. I knew the stench of my own seared flesh, thanks to Petrik. And I'd survived with no visible scarring, thanks to my immortality. I woke every night looking exactly the same as the day before. If I cut my hair, it grew back. If I changed my nail polish, it reverted. We literally never changed. There was some sort of magic involved, something that hit the reset button for us every single night. The only thing that had an effect was permanent death. And even that wasn't easy. Decapitation, fire, or magically enchanted werewolf stakes. We never changed.

But Lucy would.

The day would come when she wanted a real life. When she wanted to settle down and have babies. I couldn't keep that from her. That'd make me every bit the monster I already believed I was. I had to be better than that.

Camilla sighed, then pivoted on the chair to face me. "I had a husband before I was turned, did I ever tell you that?"

Surprise widened my eyes. I shook my head, still not ready to speak, but I could listen.

She nodded, her eyes growing sad as she lost

herself to her memories. "James was..." She hummed quietly to herself. "Amazing. James was everything I could have asked for in a husband. Nostalgia has probably made me forget his little annoyances because I only remember the good. He was kind, giving, loving, features that weren't common in husbands back then. Men were raised to be strong, dependable, and women were raised to listen to their husbands. James never expected that of me. He'd always treated me as his equal. And I him."

I wanted to ask what her point was, but for once, I just listened.

She gave a somber chuckle. "The night I became a vampire wasn't anything out of the ordinary. My carriage had broken a wheel. That was it. And while my driver was fixing it, darkness set, and..."

"A vampire found you," I murmured.

She nodded. "Back then, vampires were more akin to monsters than they are now. My maker—and I say maker because he was *never* my sire—slaughtered my driver first. Took his head clean off in his blood frenzy. Horrified, I watched as the creature slurped up the blood, his face bathed in it. Shock had frozen me through and through. Unlike most, I didn't scream, I didn't so much as take a breath. I couldn't move for fear he would see me next."

I forced myself to swallow. I knew the feeling she described oh so well. Petrik had savaged my throat when he'd attacked me.

"It wasn't until he looked up, face smeared in blood, that his teeth caught the moonlight and I screamed. I screamed so loud I thought everyone in the world must have heard me. He was on me before I could even take my next breath. I think he was a freshly made vampire himself, he seemed to have no control whatsoever."

Camilla drew a deep breath and caught my gaze. "He tore out my throat. I remember choking on my own blood. A fear like nothing I'd ever experienced came over me, and while I bled out, I attacked him. I actually managed to tear off his ear and claw up his face."

"He bled into your mouth," I surmised.

"He didn't know that. There was so much blood everywhere, he wouldn't have had any way of knowing whose blood was whose. He left just before I died. Then three nights later, I woke buried in the ground."

I shuddered. I'd woken in a coffin. It wasn't a pleasant experience.

"I did the only thing I could think of. I tunneled out and returned home. At that time, I had no idea what had happened to me. I simply thought there had to have been some mistake. James would never bury me unless he thought I was dead. But maybe there'd been a mistake."

Oh, I didn't like the sound of this.

"I returned home and nearly scared my husband half to death. He'd been drinking, likely for three days straight. He didn't believe his eyes. He thought I was a vision, an angel. The things he'd said to me."

Blood tears shimmered in Camilla's eyes, and she swiped them away before they could fall. "He told me how sorry he was. That he hadn't been there to protect me, that he loved me, that he'd miss me for the rest of his life, that I was perfect. When he finally sobered up, he realized I wasn't dead, he was so relieved, he nearly collapsed at my feet."

"Tell me you didn't hurt him," I pleaded. I couldn't handle that.

A faint smile crossed her face. "No. I was one of the lucky ones who managed to keep from slaughtering their loved ones. I told James what happened, about the monster. He didn't believe me. Thought I'd hallucinated from my injuries. It wasn't until we realized that I *needed* to feed off blood that he fully believed my story. But you know what?" She turned to look at me, her smile a bit fainter now. "He *chose* to stay with me. He told me we would endure. That he'd seen what his life looked like without me, and he never wanted to return to that dark place."

Oh my god. Could my heart melt any faster?

"He helped me find ways to feed. We tried animal blood, to no avail. So, he offered me his. Eventually, we realized we needed more people, so I learned to hunt discriminately. I learned how to sneak a sip here and there without anyone knowing. Lure men into back alleys for a small taste. And James helped. Because he loved me. He wanted me to survive."

"That's an oddly morbid but beautiful story."

"My point is, give Lucy the chance to make her own decision."

I went rigid. "What?"

"Oh, come on. I can see it all over your face. I heard the end of your argument as I woke."

"Did Vlad hear it?" I demanded, shock rippling through my nerves.

She frowned. "Not that I know of. Why?"

"No reason."

Camilla blinked, then shrugged. "I saw you sitting here, moping over your mug, and I figured you were probably considering cutting her loose. Every vampire goes through this thought process at some point. But Lucy is a grown ass woman. And your best friend. Don't make decisions for her. Don't force her to make choices she doesn't want to make. The day will come when she might move on from you, but in the meantime, enjoy your time together. And don't do something you'll regret in a few years. Because living with regret is different for us vamps. It's eternal."

I winced at the thought.

After a moment's pause, Camilla pushed to her feet. "Now, let's go. Time to train since we didn't get to last night."

I groaned and rested my head on the counter.

"No whining. No excuses. Let's go."

With a final sigh, I lifted my head, stared at the empty mug, then dragged my ass after Camilla. At the very least, maybe the training would give me something else to think about—for a few hours anyway.

CHAPTER EIGHT

I WOKE the next night to an unusually quiet household. Generally, I could hear Lucy and the harem members moving around, playing games, talking, laughing, but today was an eerie silence. I laid still and took everything in, but the only sound came from outside the house, considering it would be about three or four hours or so until Vlad woke.

I slowly eased back my coffin lid and sat upright. White noise assaulted my ears, making them ring. The harem members had been given the rest of the week off—thanks to our upcoming trip to Perish—but I hadn't expected them to leave until we did. Seeing as how Vlad's house was quiet as the grave, guess I was wrong.

After a few moments, I climbed out of my coffin

and gazed at Vlad's, right next to mine. Camilla's coffin usually sat near the back of the room. But after our training session last night, she'd moved it back to her house, knowing we were leaving for Perish tonight. I hadn't invited her to meet my mother, and Camilla hadn't insinuated a desire to come. So, for the first time in months, we were without her. It felt almost freeing.

Smiling, I touched Vlad's coffin lid. I couldn't wait until the new windows were installed. No more sleeping alone in a pine box. Soon, my life would return to normal—or as normal as I could get it—and I'd be able to cuddle with Vlad till we fell asleep, and wake in his arms. That sounded pretty heavenly to me, even for damned creatures such as us.

Sound rose to my ears, and I listened. Seemed Lucy was shuffling around downstairs, likely checking her bags for the umpteenth time before we left tonight. She hated forgetting things. And when she did, it would bug her until she remembered exactly what it was she'd left behind.

The thought made me chuckle. Until I remembered last night's fight.

We didn't speak again after it. In fact, I hadn't seen her since. Camilla had kept me absurdly busy with training. For once, I hadn't ended up battered and broken on the floor. Cause for celebration. Even Camilla had commented that I was starting to hold my own. I still hadn't successfully beaten her, but hey, I'd kept her from severely injuring me. A win in my book.

Lucy's and my fight, however... that one I didn't consider a win.

I recalled Camilla's story, and her advice to let Lucy choose for herself. I truly wanted to, but I wasn't convinced that was the right way to go. Camilla had put James's life in great danger. What if they'd been discovered? The authorities would have strung James up and burned Camilla at the stake. Yes, things were different now, seeing as how humans knew all about us, but that didn't make the danger any less real. Especially considering my recent issues with the queen. One day, Genevieve would come a-calling, and I didn't want Lucy caught in the crosshairs when that day came. If I let her choose, and she chose to stay with me, what kind of friend did that make me? I couldn't unlive with myself if something bad happened to Lucy because of me.

Regardless of that, though, I did need to apologize to her. I shouldn't have snapped at her like I did. My business was her business—always had been. And I wanted to bury the hatchet before we began the trip home. I couldn't imagine anything more painful than an hour and a half drive with two feuding friends.

I reached for the attic ladder, about to descend to the main levels, when I heard a strange sound. Soft at first, then a bit louder. Footsteps, maybe? Not Lucy's. She was still in her bedroom, and I could hear her counting something under her breath. No, this came from the front of the house, near the main door.

A visitor, maybe?

If so, that was unusual. First, we never received visitors, because who would willingly visit a house full of vampires? Everyone we knew practically lived with us. And second, it was still daylight out. I didn't have my phone on me, but I tended to wake around four p.m. these days. Which meant no vampires would be awake yet, except me, but we'd kept that little tidbit a secret from everyone. Yes, I woke early, but I'd never announced that to the world, and I was careful to stay off social media until sundown. No need to suggest any further connection to Petrik's death.

I paused with one foot balancing on the first ladder rung and strained my senses. While I could certainly hear someone moving around on the porch, I couldn't smell them. The nearby swamps were a bit overwhelming today in the late afternoon heat, and that was all I could pick up on.

Gripping the sides of the ladder, I quickly descended. I landed soundlessly on the floor, then folded up the ladder. No need to advertise Vlad's resting spot.

"Anna?" Lucy's voice came from her room.

"I'm here," I murmured, hoping not too loud to scare off whoever was mucking around on our porch. I wouldn't be able to answer the door, but that was what Lucy was for.

For as long as we'd lived here, no one had ever just dropped by uninvited. It was an unwritten rule among vampires that you waited for an invitation first.

Lucy padded out into the hallway, arms wrapped around her middle. She looked oddly innocent and vulnerable, and I hated it. It reminded me of her human weaknesses.

But that was a problem for a different time.

First, I needed to focus on this.

Logically, our visitor couldn't be a vamp. Even though some of us could wake early—exhibit A—we still couldn't step out into the sun. Its rays roasted us like a crispy marshmallow. Believe me, I spoke from experience, and that was an incident I hoped never to repeat. So logically, I shouldn't be concerned about our visitor. Maybe it was a delivery person, or someone with the wrong address, or maybe someone's car had broken down and they needed help.

Except, I knew better than to believe that.

"Someone's at the door," I said.

Lucy's mouth pursed, but she didn't say anything.

"I can hear them moving around out there. Can you open the door and see who it is?" I asked as we descended the stairs together. "Peek through the hole first. Let's make sure it's not anything serious."

She gave a single slow nod.

Okay, her silence was disquieting. I shot her a second glance and noted her pale complexion. "You okay?"

She shot me a narrowed glance. "Fine."

Ah. Just great. Nope, she wasn't sick. She was throwing a classic Lucy-esque temper tantrum. Hers never resulted in yelling and screaming, just the effing silent treatment. I knew this Lucy well—and I hated her. Digging any information out of her would be like pulling teeth. Guess I really had stepped in it last night, and now I had some apologies to make.

But again, now wasn't the time. So, instead, I scrubbed my hands down my face in an attempt to wake myself up a bit more, then gestured toward the door. My apology could wait until after we figured this out.

"Are you expecting anyone?" I asked.

She shook her head.

"What time is Sam supposed to be here?"

"Nine."

It took every ounce of willpower not to growl at her. I hated these moods of hers. It always reminded me of my parents prior to their divorce. First came the bickering, then the silence. I never could decide which was worse.

I glanced at the hallway clock. "That's five hours from now."

"I'm aware."

"Lucy." This time I did growl. My upper lip even curled up over my vamp fangs.

She startled at my tone, but immediately gathered herself together. Instead of apologizing for *her* childish behavior, she lifted her chin and held my gaze, almost as though silently challenging me to say something. Oh, I was about to say something all right. The short and terse answers were immature, and she *knew* I hated them. Which, of course, was why she did it.

The sound of scuffling feet on our porch reminded me we had other issues to contend with.

"Just... go look through the peephole." I waved her forward, then pinched the bridge of my nose. Lord love the girl, because some days, I couldn't. "Tell me what you see."

She leaned forward and peered through the glass lens, then shook her head and whispered, "Nothing."

"Can you see the full range of the porch?" I whispered back.

"No. The field of view starts at the stairs. There's no one out there, Anna. Are you sure you aren't mishearing things?"

Well, at least she was talking to me now. An improvement, at least.

I padded closer and snuck a peek. Lucy was right. We couldn't see anything, but I sure could hear something. I closed my eyes and listened. Footsteps padding back and forth on the front porch deck. I followed their movement. They swept from one side to the other, pausing every now and then. Peering through the windows, possibly? Whoever it was, they wouldn't see much. The house was carefully designed so that the common areas were at the back of the house. Not quite so easy to get back there with the brush.

"Someone's definitely out there," I muttered.

"I don't hear anything."

I turned and stared at her, my expression quite droll.

"Oh, right. Vampire."

Glad *she* could forget.

"I can't go out there. The sun is still up."

"Well, I'm not going out there," she whisper-hissed.

"Oh, calm down. It can't be anything too bad. All vampires are a-snoozing right now."

This time, she pinned me with a droll look.

"Okay, fine. But they won't be playing outside in the sun. Just open the door and see who it is. See what they need and send them on their way."

Lucy scoffed under her breath. "Fine." Her hand closed around the doorknob, and she slowly began to turn it. The anticipation was eating me alive here. I almost barked at her to move a little faster, but what would that accomplish?

When she finally pulled open the door, we were greeted with a bright burst of sunlight that sent me skittering back into the shadows.

"Sorry," Lucy mumbled.

I lifted a hand to shield against the rays, then whispered. "Well? Who's out there?"

Lucy shrugged, leaned forward, and peered around the corner. The second her head popped out of the house, she gasped and clutched at her chest. "Jesus, you scared the hell out of me! Who are you and what do you want?"

So someone *was* out there. I knew it! I practically danced a little jig in the foyer.

"Oh, I'm so sorry! I didn't think anyone would be awake," came an unfamiliar voice.

Gah! I was dying to see who it was. But that would require me peeking outside, and hell with that. I'd felt the sun's wrath on my flesh once before. Really didn't need to experience the sequel.

"Then what are you doing here?" Lucy demanded, crossing her arms over her chest.

I could imagine the stare she'd unleashed upon our unwelcome visitor, considering I'd just borne the brunt of it a few minutes ago.

"Oh, um, I was hoping for a few pictures."

I rolled my eyes. A freaking vampire junkie. Awesome.

"Pictures of what? You do know vampires live

here, right?" Lucy shook her head. "They can't be photographed."

"Uh, right. Um." Our unseen visitor sighed. "Look, I'm just going to level with you. Five hundred bucks, and you escort me inside and show me their coffins."

Oh. Sweet. Lord. Was this really happening? Was someone actually attempting to bribe their way into our house?

"A thousand, and you leave, and I don't call the police for trespassing."

I almost burst out laughing, but I was trying my hardest to keep quiet. If this person was some sort of vampire wannabe or whatever, I really didn't feel like exposing myself would help matters.

"I know Anna Perish lives here with Dracula. I'm a reporter for *Fang and Fur Lifestyle*—"

"Great, a gossip columnist," Lucy commented dryly.

Was that the sound of grinding teeth I heard? The woman cleared her throat and tried again. "We're one of the top ten popular magazines—"

"Save it. I don't need to hear your speech. Leave."

"Two thousand," the reporter countered.

"Two thousand bucks. To see a coffin? Are you

serious? All for some stupid article showing how vampires sleep in coffins, which everyone already knows?" Lucy unfolded her arms and leaned against the doorframe. She didn't shoot me a glance, which told me she also didn't want the reporter to know about my presence.

Footsteps echoed on the porch as the reporter neared Lucy. "Two thousand, you take me inside, and show me their coffins. I'll snap a few pictures, then I'm out of your hair. Ten minutes tops. Ever made a cool two G's in ten minutes?"

"Yes," Lucy deadpanned.

This time I did snort. Loudly. In retrospect, that was the moment things went downhill fast. Before Lucy could slam the door in the reporter's face, which honestly should have been the first thing she did, the reporter stepped into sight.

"You," she breathed, her face melting into a look of pure astonishment. "You're Anna!"

Well... shit.

"Close the door, Lucy," I snapped.

"No! Wait! How are you awake right now? Anna! Let me interview you. We can pitch your vlog, get you more followers—"

"Lucy!" I barked, inadvertently flashing fang.

A flash of light blinded us. I cried out and

stumbled backward, my hands lifted to shield my vision. Was she seriously snapping my photo right now? In my own house? And what the hell would that even accomplish?

"Oh my god, you really don't show up in pictures. So, you *are* a vampire. And awake during the day!"

"Lucy! Shut the fucking door!"

"I'm trying!"

I shook my head and blinked back the damn white bulbs glowing in my vision to find the reporter forcing her way inside. She'd braced her shoulder against the door, then lodged her hip against the frame, preventing Lucy from shutting her out. Lucy stood on the other side of the door, her weight pressed against it and getting absolutely nowhere. This damn reporter knew exactly how to keep someone from slamming a door in her face, meaning she pulled this shit far too frequently for my liking.

When she lifted her camera and snapped another photo, I snarled under my breath. I couldn't let her get inside. This was our sanctuary. Not a damn museum.

I stormed forward, violence clouding my mind. Without a second thought, I snatched her camera out of her hand, snapped it in two, then gripped her shoulders. I nearly caved to my hunger right then and there. Seemed the dam had burst, and all my vampire feelings and instincts were rushing to the surface. Enough so that I was incredibly tempted to wrench her to my mouth and bite.

It was the sudden searing pain of heat splashing over my arms and the scent of burning flesh that broke the spell. The sun scalded my hands and arms, and it took every ounce of willpower I possessed not to scream in pain. Instead, I locked eyes with the reporter and wordlessly flashed her my fangs. The woman before me paled, then screamed when I gave her a good hard shove out the door.

Dark memories flashed to the front of my mind, of me trapped in Petrik's cement crypt, the sun burning a path up my legs and blistering my flesh. The familiar scent pervaded my nose, and I had to hold my breath to keep from retching.

"Anna!" Lucy shouted, her voice centering me in the here and now.

Her fingers gripped the back of my shirt and hauled me back inside. I fell back against a wall and slid to the ground, staring at the charred mess that'd once been my arms.

"Holy shit," Lucy sputtered, collapsing to her knees at my side. "What the hell were you thinking?"

"They'll heal," I grunted. Granted, they'd heal faster with blood. But guess what? We were fresh out of harem members tonight, and Lucy would never open a vein for me—I knew better than to ask.

Maybe I should have taken a bite out of the reporter. But I couldn't allow myself to become that sort of monster.

Which meant I would be dining on bagged blood tonight.

My favorite.

At least the situation was handled. Pieces of her camera were scattered throughout our foyer. But there wasn't anything more I could do, other than possibly sue her for an invasion of privacy and trespassing. Reporters like her, though, lived for that sort of drama. They believed that celebrities gave up their rights to secrecy by becoming famous. More than likely, her company would foot the legal fees, knowing all press was good press.

Maybe I should just go back to bed. Forget the whole trip to Perish nonsense. My arms hurt like hell, I was hungry, cranky, and fighting with Lucy. The last thing I needed was to add my mother into the mix.

But we had plans and we'd told Sam to meet us here at nine. My mother was expecting us around eleven. And while most of my mother's lessons never really stuck with me, this one had. You didn't break plans unless you were sick or dying. I was neither. In pain, yes, but blood cured all ails.

"Who the fuck pulls that sort of shit?" I demanded. "Storms into someone's house to take their photo?"

"It's what happens when you're famous. What, in all your years of longing for this, you never gave it much thought?"

"No, I did, but I thought I'd enjoy it more."

Lucy chuckled. "Sorry."

"I mean, we live out in the middle of freaking nowhere. And it's a house full of vampires, for crying out loud. Talk about lack of self-preservation. If we were any other vampires, we would have just dined on her and called it a night."

Lucy shivered. "I really hate when you talk like that. Makes you sound..."

"Inhuman?" I offered.

She had the good grace to look away. "Should we call someone? The police or something?"

"Nah." I waved off her concern. "Her camera is broken, that alone is going to cost a pretty penny to replace. And I saw her eyes at the end. She knows she screwed up. Hopefully, she learned her lesson."

"You sure?"

I nodded. "Help me up, gently."

I extended a crispy arm and caught the flash of panic in Lucy's sharp green eyes. Yeah, I wouldn't want to touch them either. I looked like a deep-fried mummy. Eventually, she cupped my elbows and guided me to my feet.

"Now what?"

"Well, unless you're willing to crack a vein for me—and I'm not saying you should, but just remember I got burned because you couldn't get the reporter out, so a little gratitude wouldn't hurt—I need to get some bagged blood."

"C—Crack a vein?"

"I'm kidding, Lucy." Sort of. Fresh blood definitely would have helped right now. But alas.

"Kitchen?" she asked.

"Kitchen."

If I had to, I'd plug my nose and swallow it in one gulp.

By the time we reached the kitchen, my jaw ached. I had to grit my teeth to keep from crying out in pain. My arms were an ugly rainbow of reds, pinks, and oranges, complete with blisters and scales worthy of a dragon. I must have looked like a hot mess.

Lucy hurried over to the fridge and grabbed a bag of blood. She poured it in the mug, then popped it in the microwave. The scent of quickly warmed blood filled the room and turned my stomach. I definitely wasn't looking forward to this.

"Here," Lucy mumbled as she carried the warmed mug toward me.

"Mm. Yummy."

"Shut up and drink it."

I stared at my crispy palms and winced. This was going to hurt like a mother.

"Let me," Lucy offered before lifting it to my lips.

Our gazes met over the rim, then I held my breath and nodded. I truly did hate this stuff. But right now, there was no other choice. So, I opened my mouth, placed my lips on the ceramic edge, and waited for Lucy to upend the liquid.

She hadn't warmed it enough. Dear god, it was tepid and horrifyingly disgusting. My throat closed off in rebellion, but I squeezed my eyes shut and chugged as fast as the sludgy liquid would allow. Best to just get it over with, but someone definitely needed to give Lucy lessons in preparing blood, because sweet lord, this was like drinking copper flavored mud.

"Better?" Lucy asked once I drained it dry.

My stomach convulsed, and I turned away, pressing a partially healed hand to my gut. No. Not better. Not even remotely. Not only were my arms on fire, but now I had to worry about vomiting up nasty ass blood.

"Anna?" Lucy's hand touched my back.

"Might... wanna... move back," I rasped. Because she was totally standing in the splash zone.

I forced myself to draw a few deep breaths. For some reason, it seemed to help soothe my stomach. Might have been a placebo effect, but I honestly didn't care. It worked.

After a few gut-wrenching moments, the nausea passed. I glanced at my arms and grimaced. I wasn't sure what was worse. Drinking more of that shit hoping it sped up my recovery, or just waiting for them to heal naturally. At the moment, I was leaning toward the latter.

"More?" Lucy asked.

The second she wafted the cup near my face, my stomach lurched. "No."

Maybe my arms didn't hurt that bad after all. In fact, I could barely feel them now. Whatever lie I needed to tell myself so I didn't have to drink that nasty shit again. Imagine swigging absinthe and this was similar. They tasted completely different, but both were abhorrent swill that made you retch.

Except, my arms didn't feel better *at all*. And with about three hours more to go till sundown, I really didn't feel like wallowing in misery for that long.

So, with a brave face, I pointed at the microwave. "Warm it some more."

Lucy did so without a word. Once she returned with a steaming mug, I blew on it to cool off the fetid liquid, then plugged my nose, closed my eyes, and chugged back every last drop. Once finished, I lowered the mug and pressed a hand to my cheeks. Thanks to the blood, they were warm to the touch.

"I think I'm just going to lie down," I mumbled.

"Really? Did the blood not help?"

"It did. But I just... I'm going to lie down." Maybe I'd feel better after a nap.

"Okay." Lucy reached out and touched my shoulder. "Feel better."

I threw her a grim smile, then dragged myself back up to the attic and into my coffin. I laid my arms on my stomach and winced. Hopefully, after a small nap, they'd be healed, and I could get a fresh start on the night.

CHAPTER NINE

For crying out loud, what would it take for a dead girl to get some honest rest around here?

It felt like I'd only just closed my eyes when a heated argument woke me. I released a heavy breath, then forced open my eyes and stared at the attic ceiling. Wooden rafters hung over me, and for the first time, I wondered about my safety. Vlad had once told me we slept in coffins, even in the attic, because if a hurricane rolled through, we needed as much protection as possible. At first, I'd thought he meant from the sun, but staring up at those rickety old rafters, I now had another fear impregnating my poor, innocent brain. Nothing like sleeping beneath wooden beams to understand the fragility of life.

"You expect me to believe you could not handle

one single human? That you are so frail and so utterly incompetent that you failed to push someone outside and lock the door?" Vlad's heated voice penetrated my morose thoughts.

Oh, yikes.

Someone was pissed.

"Of course not—"

"Then explain to me why *she* is burned."

Still, huh? I glanced at my arms. In all fairness, they were much improved, but apparently not enough to appease my boy toy. I didn't blame him for being mad, they actually looked pretty damn gross. Blistered in some places, crusty in others, charred in most. I honestly looked like I'd held my arms over an open flame. Felt like it too. Stiffness had settled in nicely, and I knew if I so much as moved, I would be in utter agony.

A great start to my Wednesday night.

"Vlad," I muttered. The last thing I needed was him developing a hate-on for Lucy. Or vice versa.

Darkness settled over me as Vlad suddenly appeared at the side of my coffin.

I caught his gaze and smiled. "I'm fine. It wasn't Lucy's fault."

"In your immortal words, the hell it isn't."

The absolute sassiness in his voice made my grin grow. His sarcasm was coming along just fine.

"Honestly. It wasn't. It was mine. Lucy said something funny, I laughed, and the reporter heard me. I should have just kept quiet."

"I don't see how that has any relevance to this."

"She was determined to get in once she spotted me. Lucy tried to shut the door, but the damn reporter fought back. She was pretty damn good actually. But I got mad when she started forcing her way in. The last thing we need is someone writing an article about how I'm awake during the day."

Vlad's expression darkened.

"Yeah," I said, nodding. "Figured that'd be a bad thing. That reporter thought we'd be asleep. She was trying to break in to photograph our coffins."

"Bold and utterly stupid." He sighed and pinched the bridge of his nose. "I suppose we'll need to take proper precautions to ensure this doesn't happen again. Security, perhaps."

"Yay, more people in the house."

His lips twitched with amusement. "Yes, well, we can't ignore this."

I agreed. But under protest.

"I'll look into this after we return from Perish. Perhaps others are experiencing similar annoyances."

I grimaced. There were probably some, but I had to imagine my vlog was contributing. Vlad and I were one of the most popular vampire couples right now. Every night, Lucy showed me a new article regarding us. Even the tabloids loved to feature us. They always seemed to claim one of us was having an affair, or we were splitting up, or my personal favorite, I was pregnant with baby bats. Considering we both had a lot of fame surrounding us—him with his Dracula persona, and me and my vlog—I had to imagine things would only get worse from here. The last time we'd ventured out into public, a woman had practically swooned at the sight of him. I didn't blame her—I swooned every night. But at least I had the grace to do it in private.

I opened my mouth to mention the vlog, confess about everything right here and now, when Lucy swept into my peripheral.

"How are you feeling?" she asked.

Vlad curled a lip in response, clearly still angry with her.

"I'm fine," I answered.

But the judgy arch of Vlad's brow told me he didn't believe me. He shot Lucy an accusatory glare. I could practically read his mind and hear the many questions he still had whipping around in that brain of his. Why hadn't she been able to force the reporter outside? Why not stop me from stepping into the sunlight? Why let me get hurt?

I didn't answer his unspoken questions—I didn't want to admit aloud that I'd lost my temper.

When Vlad's lips parted—I assumed to ask the questions I suspected—I subtly shook my head. No point beating her over the head with it when the damage was already done.

Vlad's mouth thinned, but he finally nodded. "Fine." Then he eased one of his hands beneath mine and held them to the dim light. "You need blood."

"I had some bagged before napping. Honestly, they feel much better than they did." *Liar.*

Vlad's sharp stare told me he saw right through me.

He helped me out of the coffin, then studied my full arm. After a moment's consideration, he lifted his wrist and pressed it to my mouth. "Drink."

"What?" The scent of his arm beneath my nose did funny things to my body. Funny, sexy things. I *liked* biting Vlad. If I started now, I wasn't sure I would be able to stop. Which was why he never let me bite him anymore. Too dangerous. Too addicting.

"You need fresh blood. I assume you still wish to go to Perish tonight?"

I nodded.

"Then drink. Your mother would be distraught at the sight of you."

He wasn't wrong. And not the good kind of motherly distraught. More like horrified and disgusted. "Are you sure about this?"

His only response was to brush his wrist against my lips. I stopped thinking and let my instincts take control. My mouth parted and I bit.

The second Vlad's blood washed through my mouth, I moaned and sank into him. My arms began to slowly knit themselves back together and the pain abated.

Vlad's other hand swept my hair back from my neck, and his fingers began caressing. Oh boy, if he kept this up, Lucy would need to leave ASAP. I grabbed his wrist with freshly pink fingers, all healed and blister free. Relief coursed through my body, then sparked into something a tad more dangerous. Desire. Heat. Need.

Vlad's arm slid around my waist and pulled me flush against him, his stuttered sigh telling me everything I needed to know. Warmth bloomed within me, and I leaned against the swell of his chest, struggling to tamp back the emotions rising within. I had to remember Lucy was present.

When we parted, I gazed into his eyes and slowly licked my lips. Lust flashed in his dark depths, promising me a wickedly sinful time. Just not right now.

Instead, his fingers trailed down my healed arms, and he lifted them to the light. "Much better." He brought my fingertips to his lips and pressed a soft kiss against each one.

My dusty ovaries nearly burst right then and there. Some nights, I wondered how the media could see him in one light when I saw him in an entirely different one. To the movie and literature industries, Dracula was an evil, maniacal creature who murdered without conscience. Vlad was the stark opposite of that. He was kind, caring, sweet, and attentive. Moments like these made me fall all the more in love with him. And I wasn't even sure that was possible.

After kissing all ten fingers, he leaned in and pressed a firmer, final kiss to my lips. "Do you still wish to visit Perish? I can cancel our plans and handle the fallout with your mother if you wish us to stay here."

That he even thought to offer... I swear, I

probably had a little bubble heart emoji flying around my head right now.

"I'll be fine," I assured him. "They're healing up nicely, and my mother would probably set me on fire if we didn't show up."

"She sounds like a lovely woman."

I chuckled. My mother wasn't *really* the harbinger of evil, but it was my responsibility to prepare Vlad for the worst, because guaranteed, she was going to bring her A-game tonight. And not in a good way.

"Everyone is all packed and ready to go," I continued. "I don't want to disrupt our plans. The sooner we get there, the sooner we can come home, which means the sooner we get our new windows and can sleep together during the day."

Vlad frowned. "Time will pass at the same speed regardless of when we leave."

I chuckled. The man was so literal. My sarcasm appeared to be rubbing off on him, but I was far from a perfect teacher.

"Anna, I-I'm sorry," Lucy suddenly spoke up.

So swept up with Vlad, I'd almost forgotten she was still here. When I glanced her way, I found her standing next to my coffin, arms wrapped around her waist, and her gaze locked on my pink arms.

"I should have been able to handle that reporter," she muttered. "I could have—"

"Pointless to focus on the what ifs," I told her. "It's done. I'll heal. Don't worry about it."

She nodded, then swiped at her unfallen tears and left, quickly descending the attic ladder.

"I was perhaps a little hard on her," Vlad observed.

"You think?" I teased.

"I'll apologize. I admit I lost my head a little when I woke up and saw you laying here in an open coffin, half-burned." Darkness tinged his eyes, and I knew why.

I reached up and cupped his face. "Are you still having visions about my death?"

He nodded, then turned his face into my palm and kissed me. "I had another tonight. Unfortunately, I've yet to see anything new. Right now, it's little more than me holding you after you've died. And I can't, I *won't*, go through that, Anna. I refuse to lose you."

"Hey..." I rose on my tiptoes and pressed my forehead against his. When his eyes fluttered shut, I allowed mine to do the same. "I promise you, I'm not going anywhere. We'll figure it out and stop whatever it is from happening."

"I failed last time," he whispered so low I almost didn't hear him.

"What do you mean?"

"The night I turned you. I was almost too late. Another minute and I would have been."

"I remember," I said. It was a moment forever burned into my memory. "But let's not focus on what could have happened. We'll use your visions to figure this out. I promised you an eternity, and I plan to deliver on it."

He kissed the tip of my nose, then straightened. "In the meantime, I'll apologize to Lucy for yelling at her. Did you by chance know this reporter? Perhaps I will speak with her boss. Put the fear of Vlad in them."

"No. But she did mention her magazine. *Fang and Fur Lifestyle*. She had shoulder length brown hair and green eyes, a splattering of freckles across her nose. I'm sure that description will help them figure out who she was."

"Very well. Why don't you go gather your things for the weekend, and I'll give this magazine a call they won't soon forget."

I kissed his cheek, then descended to the lower levels. Sam would arrive soon, so I only had an hour to handle all the final arrangements. We couldn't waste any more time playing out this melodrama.

AT NINE O'CLOCK on the dot, the sound of the house's dignified doorbell brought a grin to my face. I legit dropped everything I was holding—makeup (because even a dead girl needed to look like a hot girl), hair products, and my fang brush—and bolted down the stairs. From the corner of my eye, I spotted Vlad strolling casually toward the door, so I put on a little more speed and beat him there.

"I see you're feeling much better," Vlad commented wryly.

Ignoring him, I threw open the door and squealed, "Sam!"

All six-foot-five of him ducked into the house. "Anna." His nose wrinkled. "Your house reeks of burned flesh."

"Thanks for the reminder," I said, laughing. A typical Sam greeting. Right to the point and with little warmth.

I chuckled, then reached up for a hug, one I quickly modified into an awkward shoulder pat the second I heard Vlad growl. Regardless of my attempts, the two men still loathed each other, and would till the end of time, I suspected. Vlad wasn't jealous of me hugging another man, but he certainly didn't want me getting all snuggly with his self-pronounced archnemesis. Their animosity toward each other cracked me up. The whole vampire versus werewolf nonsense. I was proof that it was exactly that. Nonsense. We both had fangs. Sam just happened to be half-furry. I, however, had always loved the canine kind.

"I'm so glad you're here." I stepped back and took Vlad's hand, as though to reassure him that I hadn't switched teams on him.

Sam's gaze flicked to mine. I caught a hint of warmth in those amber eyes of his, one that turned cold the second his attention latched onto Vlad. "Why does your house stink?"

"We had an incident today."

A dark eyebrow arched high on Sam's forehead. His focus leapt to the staircase, as though he expected Lucy to suddenly appear. I knew better though. She would avoid him until the absolute last moment. Or until I shoved her face-first into the car.

"What kind of incident?" Sam demanded, his already growly voice deepening.

Vlad tensed, his fingers tightening around mine.

"It's been handled and there's nothing for you to worry about."

Sam unleashed a fierce glare on Vlad. "Lucy is my mate. And she lives here. I'll decide what warrants my concern."

Phew. Even I could smell the rising testosterone in this entryway. These two rarely spoke to each other, but when they did, tempers tended to spike. Sometimes it made for good drama, but more often than that, their arguments sent me and Lucy for the hills.

"It's fine," I assured Sam, giving Vlad my own reassuring squeeze. "Some reporter tried to bust in on us today. No one was hurt"—except me, and Vlad's sharp glare reminded me of that—"and we're all perfectly fine."

Sam's grunt had me biting my lip to keep from laughing. "Where is she?"

"Upstairs. She's moping."

This time Vlad grunted. "As she should be."

Even I tensed when Sam shot Vlad a scathing scowl.

"Okay. Alright." I pulled my hand from Vlad's and held them up peaceably for all to see. "I'd like to take this moment to remind certain people that we have a long drive tonight as well as an entire weekend together. My family is batshit crazy, so how about we take a breath and remind ourselves who the true enemy is?"

Vlad lifted a questioning brow.

"My parents," I said. "We're vampires about to descend into the seventh circle of hell."

"An interesting concept," Vlad mused.

With a small, encouraging smile, I leaned in and brushed my lips against his cheek. His arm instantly snaked around my waist and pulled me into him seconds before he stole a heated kiss.

I scoffed and playfully slapped his chest. Dead or alive, men were men. And my man apparently felt the need to mark his territory.

"My bags are upstairs," I commented. "I'll go get them and drag Lucy down. Are we taking one car?"

"Absolutely not," Vlad barked at the same moment Sam uttered a resounding, "No."

My gaze flicked between the two men. "We're not?"

"If this weekend will be the epitome of hell, then I want to spend some time alone with you beforehand. Sam and Lucy can take his vehicle." Vlad shot him a droll look. "Assuming the mutt knows how to drive?"

"Vlad!" I hissed.

Sam rolled his eyes. "The mutt can drive better than a corpse."

"Sam!" I shouted. "What is the matter with you two?"

The two stewed in competitive silence, one that had me shaking my head. And people thought *women* were catty.

I started up the stairs. "I'm going to get my bags and Lucy. Try not to kill each other."

"No guarantees," Sam muttered.

"I heard that."

"Meant to."

Still shaking my head, I took the stairs two at a time, afraid to leave them alone together. I'd learned of their little feud when Sam and I had first met, but I'd hoped they'd outgrow it. Especially considering Lucy and I were best friends. Guess my hopes were aiming a little too high. I just hoped I didn't find them at each other's throats when I came back downstairs.

I hurried into Lucy's room and saw her seated on the edge of her bed, staring morosely at the wall. I didn't want to startle her, so I rapped my knuckles against the doorframe and murmured, "Sam's here."

Her head rose, almost of its own volition, but her gaze was distant when it landed on me. "Hmm?"

"Sam? He's here. We're ready to leave if you are."

"Oh. Right." She didn't move.

Frowning, I slipped into her room. "Want to tell me what's going on?"

She blinked and her vision seemed to clear a little, sharpen with clarity. She seemed a bit shocked to find me here, as though she hadn't really realized who I was at first.

"Lucy? What's wrong?"

"Would you say I'm a good person?" she asked, her voice barely a whisper.

"What? Of course. I don't befriend assholes."

That gained me a tiny smile. One that faded as quickly as it came on. She dropped her gaze and picked at the bedspread, her movements almost aimless.

"I knew the sun would hurt you," she finally said. "I knew. And yet, when you dove forward and grabbed her, I did nothing. I could have pulled you back right then and there. Except, I didn't. Vlad's right—I let you get hurt." She lifted sorrowful eyes. "What kind of person does that make me?"

"You didn't know that woman would be so brazen. It doesn't mean anything, Lucy."

"Please." She scoffed under her breath. "I've

seen a hell of a lot worse than a reporter trying to break into the house. I'm friends with you, remember?"

"Um. Sorry?"

She waved a hand. "I was mad at you because of last night. And then when that woman rushed inside, it caught me unaware, sure. But I just stood there and let you handle it... and you... burned."

I wasn't quite sure what the point of this conversation was. "Somehow, I highly doubt you did any of that purposely. Were you standing there thinking 'Muahaha, I'm going to let Anna get hurt? That'll teach her!'"

"What? No, of course not."

"Did you stand back with a grin and watch with a sickening sense of perversion and self-satisfaction?"

"For crying out loud—no, Anna, I didn't."

"Then why make this out to be anything other than a mistake? Okay, so you probably could have done something other than stand there. But you pulled me back in the end."

"Yeah, after you handled the situation."

Sighing, I plopped down on the bed next to Lucy. "Look, I'm all healed." I held out my arms so she could see. Not even a tiny bit of redness remained, thanks to Vlad's blood. The best medicine.

"Why are you dwelling on this? We have places to go and people to see, so let's get moving."

"I'm sorry," she blurted. "I just... wanted you to know that. That I'm sorry."

When she turned to face me, I spotted the tears in her eyes, and my heart dropped. "Lucy. You're not a bad person. You're not even remotely mean. There isn't a cruel bone in your body. I know you better than anyone, and I absolutely do not believe you purposely let me hurt myself. You weren't maniacally laughing or plotting some nefarious scheme to hurt me. Because that's not you. So, let's drop this, okay? There's nothing to forgive you for."

Her bottom lip trembled, but she eventually nodded. "Okay."

"Good. Are we done?"

Another weak nod.

"Great. Because you need to stop beating yourself up. Tonight's gonna be hard enough for you as is."

Fear flashed across her face. "What? Why?"

"Because you and Sam are driving to Perish together, alone, in his car. Vlad and I are taking his car."

The color utterly drained from Lucy's face. Her

hands clutched mine, and she squeezed so tightly, I thought for a moment it might hurt.

"No. No. You can't do that to me. Anna—"

Her panic almost made me laugh, but I didn't want to ruin the moment. "It'll be fine, Lucy. Sam can't make you talk about anything you're not ready to talk about. Just remember that."

"That's not what I'm worried about!"

"Then what—" Understanding dawned, and this time I did burst out laughing. "Ohmigosh, you're worried you might jump his bones!"

"Anna!" she hissed under her breath, her wide eyes darting to the door.

"Oh, please. They've both been listening to this entire conversation, and you know it. Here, I'll make it simple for you." I drew in a deep breath and shouted, "Sam! No hanky panky in the car tonight, no matter how horny Lucy gets!"

"Oh my fucking hell! I hate you, you know that?" Lucy spat out, her face red as a beet. "I can't believe you just did that! Maybe I *should* have pushed you into the sunlight today!"

So glad we could laugh about it already. I snickered, then leaned in and brushed a light kiss across her temple. "Maybe you should have. Now, get your things. We have to leave. You know my mother, she will be pissed if we're even ten minutes late, and we're pushing it already."

"Nope. I'm not going." Lucy sat firmly on the bed, arms crossed over her chest.

"That's okay. I'm sure Sam wouldn't mind staying here with you all weekend, alone in this big ole mansion, with no one here at all to stop things from getting too heated. Just think... four days alone with him."

Her anger bled away. "You're just the worst, you know that?"

"You love me."

"I *hate* you."

"I love you too."

Lucy muttered a string of curses at me, but she finally rose from the bed and started gathering her belongings. Which only meant one thing. It was finally time to go home. To introduce Vlad to my parents. To see my family for the first time since dying.

Hell was starting to look more like a vacation now.

CHAPTER TEN

"Woooo!" I lifted my arms above my head and cheered, all while reveling in the feel of the wind against my face. I'd always had a thing for convertibles, a love affair I shared with Vlad, apparently. The second he'd unveiled his baby—a black 1962 Ferrari Cabriolet—I squealed, screamed "shotgun" even though there was no one else to claim it, and dove into the passenger seat.

"Enjoying yourself?" Vlad asked from the driver's seat, his hands lovingly wrapped around the leather steering wheel.

I leaned back against the seat and sighed contentedly. There was something so freeing about the open road. For a brief window of time, I could leave behind all my worries and concerns and just *exist*. Which was exactly what I planned to do. I refused to think about this weekend's impending disaster or Lucy or the queen or anything.

Instead, I lowered my arms and rested my hand on Vlad's thigh. The hard muscle packed beneath his slacks brought a smile to my lips. One advantage to road trips at night was fewer people to witness any naughtiness. Naughtiness such as, say… stroking his inner thigh.

Vlad's mouth quirked and his gaze briefly flicked to mine before returning to the road.

With an impish grin, I unbuckled myself and scooched closer.

"What are you—"

Vlad's question cut off the instant my mouth found his earlobe. We hadn't had time alone in ages, as Vlad had pointed out earlier, so I wanted to take full advantage. I tongued the edge of his ear while continuing to rub his inner thigh, my fingers achingly close to the mark I knew we both wanted me to land on. The thought of unzipping his pants and having my way with him out here on the open road had me squeezing my own thighs together.

"You're aware of how dangerous this is?" Vlad rasped.

"We're vampires," I murmured, my fingers climbing just that little bit higher.

Vlad twitched in his seat, and I caught the sound of the steering wheel leather straining beneath his grip. I would have laughed if it wasn't so damn hot seeing him this close to losing control. Careful not to prick his flesh with my fangs, I moved south, my lips landing on his throat. Every inch of me fired up the second my mouth found that perfect little bite spot. I wouldn't, of course, but the temptation always turned us on.

"Anna..." Vlad rumbled.

"Yes?"

"You're going to cause an accident."

"Focus on the road then," I told him, grinning.

I marched my fingers up his thigh, then paused at the junction between his legs. For one moment, I hesitated. I could do what I longed to and free him from his pants, or I could sit back and enjoy the ride.

Vlad seemed to hover on that precipice as well, his body rigid in all the right ways.

Nuzzling his neck, I glanced behind us and noted the dark open road. Not a single headlight in sight. I wasn't sure what route Lucy and Sam had taken, but apparently it wasn't the same as ours. And right now, I was A-OK with that.

A smile claimed my lips when I remembered her deer in the headlights look as she climbed into Sam's car. It was a memory I quickly banished. Tonight was about me and Vlad. And just like that, my decision was made. I gave into the temptation.

The second my hand cupped Vlad through his pants, he shot to the side of the road and slammed on the brakes. My laughter carried on the wind as he parked the car, rolled up the windows and roof, then shut off the engine. I barely had a chance to utter a word before he shoved his seat back. Next thing I knew, he had me by the hips and swung me up onto his lap. He buried his fingers in my hair and pulled me down for a searing kiss that no amount of thigh squeezing would cool.

He broke from the kiss and pushed my hair back from my face. "Is this all right?"

My dead heart swooned. Because of course Vlad would think to check before taking action. Nodding, I returned to my favorite pastime. His mouth definitely qualified as the eighth wonder of the world, one I fully intended to take advantage of from now until forever.

"Take off your pants," he mumbled against my lips.

Hot. So fucking hot.

I did as he commanded and stripped bare from the waist down, not even asking if he wanted my panties gone or not. Then I made quick work of his. I couldn't remove them entirely in this position, trapped as we were in the front seat of this ridiculously sexy car, but I was able to shuffle them down past his hips, granting me full access to the gearshift I wanted most of all. The car was nothing compared to him. He had more horsepower than any vehicle ever, with one hell of a piston that I definitely wanted to ride until the end of time. Whatever, I didn't know enough sexual euphemisms for cars. Nor did I care about that right now.

Vlad's fingers got to work, preparing me for the main attraction. If I were an amusement park, he'd be slicking up the slides right about now. I shuddered above him, reveling in the feel of his expert touch. Warmth pooled in my stomach and spread through my limbs, all in anticipation of that perfect moment. So attuned to my body, Vlad knew I was about to climax. But instead of granting me that bliss, he grabbed my hips and seated me on top of him, thrusting upward in one smooth motion.

Ah. So that was what heaven felt like. I'd always wondered.

Bracing my hands on his chest, I closed my eyes

and slowly began to move, riding him like the stallion I believed him to be. Sweet, sweet torture. If I moved even the slightest bit faster, I would be *right there*, about to tumble over the edge into ecstasy. But I wanted to drag this out, make him moan a little. So, what if we were a few hours late. Totally worth it, right?

Tap, tap, tap.

Vlad and I both froze, my eyes now wide open and locked with his. We couldn't have both misheard that, right?

Tap, tap.

A shadow moved outside the vehicle. Thanks to the steamed windows, I couldn't see what it was, but I could *definitely* see the flashing red and blue lights behind our car.

"Oh my god," I whispered, the words slipping past my lips without thought.

Vlad flinched at my quiet curse, but didn't scold me. Likely because he'd realized the same thing as me.

We'd been caught. Having sex. In the middle of nowhere. By the cops.

"Sir?" a voice carried through the closed windows. "Ma'am? Please step out of the vehicle."

"Holy shit!" I cussed, biting back the startled laughter threatening to rush past my lips.

I'd never been caught canoodling in a car before! And from the astonished look on Vlad's face, neither had he. I clapped a hand over my mouth to silence my nervous giggles, then dipped my head forward, my hair brushing Vlad's throat.

"I swear, I never heard him," I whispered.

"Nor I," Vlad admitted.

Which said *a lot*, considering we were vampires. Had we gotten so wrapped up in each other that we hadn't even heard the vehicle approach? That seemed impossible, right? But one glance at Vlad, and I knew it wasn't. He absolutely befuddled my senses on a daily basis.

Even more unfortunate, Vlad didn't possess the stereotypical Dracula hypnotic qualities, meaning we'd have to talk our way out of this.

I lifted my head from Vlad's chest and finally put my ears to use. The officer was pacing the vehicle, likely jotting down the license plate number. Just behind him, I caught wind of a wheezy half-chuckle, half-bark of laughter. His partner, most likely, sitting in the car as he typed in what information they'd gleaned so far.

"Bet they're humping it up in there," a rough voice commented. "Classic."

I groaned. "Yeah, they know what we're doing in here."

"That much is obvious. Would you mind...?" Vlad gestured to the passenger seat.

"Oh, right."

As much as I enjoyed riding Vlad, now *really* wasn't the time. With as much grace as I could muster, I climbed off Vlad and started scrambling back into my pants, which wasn't as easy as it sounded. It was one thing to rip them off in the heat of the moment, and another when you were frantically rushing, without knowing which way was the front or back, or where your underwear had run off too. Worst. Sexual. Experience. Ever.

"This has never happened to me before," I mumbled, unable to bite back a bewildered giggle. "I can't believe this. Who gets caught screwing in the middle of the highway?"

Vlad shot me a strange glance, then fixed his pants and climbed out of the car. He certainly seemed more confident than me. I was practically sweating blood, freaking out about what the hell we were going to say to the officer. The thought of joining him out there horrified me. It was different for men—they congratulated one another on their embarrassing sexcapades. Not women. We took the slack and bore the insults. I had to be a slut if I was willing to screw in a car, right?

Still, I couldn't let Vlad face this alone, and the officer had requested we both step outside. So, I did what any woman would. I straightened my clothes, fluffed my hair, wiped my face, then stepped out of the car.

"I understand, Officer."

"I do remember what it's like to be young and in love," the cop continued.

I nearly choked on my saliva. Vlad was *far* from young. Then again, I'd been the one to initiate the sexy times, not him. Guess his comment still applied then. Just to the wrong person.

"But it's illegal, you know. Indecent exposure, even though there isn't anyone around this time of night. Next time, keep it in the bedroom, 'kay?"

"Of course." Vlad gave a respectful nod.

The officer shot me an appraising glance. I had to wonder about the questions running through his head. Like what sort of girl would willingly hop on a man's joystick out in the middle of the boonies. Thankfully, he didn't ask. Instead, his mouth curled into a sly grin, then he retreated to his car.

My focus shot to the passenger seat, but I didn't see anyone.

Huh. Odd. I'd definitely heard someone earlier. I lifted my chin and scented the air, but could only pick up the scent of the single officer. When the cop's hand grasped the door handle, I finally caught movement in the back seat of the car.

A criminal then?

But finally, two giant pointed ears popped up. And even though it was pitch dark out, I could easily see the furred face and lolling tongue. A German Shepherd.

"You dawg!" came the same growly voice, quite rough around the edges.

A voice that had distinctly come from the dog.

I gasped, then shoved my finger into my ear and wiggled it around. Surely, I'd misheard or had imagined hearing it? I stared at the mutt, waiting for him to speak again, except he did nothing but pant, his eyes latched onto his handler.

"Alright, you two," the officer drawled in a classic southern accent. "Drive safe."

"Thank you," I mumbled, half-assing a wave.

The cop slipped into the car and started pushing buttons on his computer system. The K-9 in the back seat simply rose on all fours and repositioned himself so he could look over his handler's shoulder, absolutely silent. Because *of course* he was silent! He was a freaking dog. And dogs couldn't talk.

I'd officially lost my mind.

"Anna?"

I turned at the sound of a voice and found Vlad standing next to the driver's side door, his hand extended toward me. Right. We had places to be, but at least we'd be on time now.

Hurray?

CHAPTER ELEVEN

WELP, we'd finally arrived.

After what felt like an eon of waiting, we were here in Perish. And absolutely nothing had changed. It was still the same small town I knew and hated. Compared to New Orleans, Perish was more like a blip on a map, a place most people didn't even know existed. I wish I didn't know it existed. That would make my life much happier. Alas, this was my hometown, born and raised, and my entire family still lived here. No escaping that.

Sam and Lucy had beat us here, unsurprisingly. For some reason, I didn't really feel the need to indulge her with the tale of Vlad and Anna versus the police right now. We'd just pretend that we drove a little slower.

After parking, Vlad circled the car and opened my door, offering me his extended hand. I took it happily and climbed out, all while running my thumb across his knuckles. Unfortunately, our little rompus interruptus hadn't quelled my lusty desires. So even just touching his hand sparked that fire within me. From the tiny smirk curving Vlad's lips, he knew it too. One downfall to vampirism, a girl couldn't maintain mystery anymore. Half the time, he knew what I was feeling before I did. Ah well, didn't mean I couldn't play it up and tease him. A concept I very much implemented when I squeezed his ass with my other hand.

Vlad's eyes shot wide, and his gaze dropped, as though startled I would dare do such a thing. Glad I could still keep him on his toes.

Chuckling, I headed toward Lucy and Sam. Now, *their* scent was that of frustration. Guess the car ride hadn't gone as well for them as it had for us. I'd hoped they would talk out their differences, but Lucy was a stubborn ole girl. It would take more than trapping her in an enclosed space with Sam to get her to open up.

I shot Sam an apologetic glance, then glared at Lucy.

"What?" she snapped in an extremely bitchy tone.

Alrighty then. Someone wasn't in the mood to share. I didn't bother responding. I refused to let her foul mood sully mine. Regardless of the cop, our ride had been quite pleasant, once I banished the cop's K-9 partner from my mind. No reason to worry about something I had no clue about.

"Y'all ready for this?" I asked.

My gaze scanned the neighborhood. Everything looked exactly the same here too. Mrs. Bitterly still lived next door, according to her pompous little mailbox, and the family just down the road was still here, if the mountain of toys piling up in the front yard meant anything. Behind us was the local school with the dilapidated monkey bars I'd hung from every day at recess. Everything was the same. Sure, it'd only been three months since we'd left, but my entire world had changed, so for some reason, I thought Perish would have changed too.

"Um, Anna?" Lucy murmured.

I glanced over, only to find her staring at my mom's front yard. I did the same.

And my jaw dropped.

"Holy. Hell."

Honestly, I didn't know what else to say. What

could I say? My mother and I had spoken on the phone a few times since I'd agreed to come home. She *knew* we'd be arriving tonight. I'd explained how we would leave New Orleans the instant the sun set and would arrive in Perish no later than eleven p.m. A quick glance at my phone showed it was quarter to. So, I'd held true to my estimate.

How could she not prepare for my arrival?

Or, holy shit, was *this* her way of welcoming us? I knew my mother inside and out. Knew her habits, her beliefs, her mannerisms. I *knew* she was a narcissistic drama queen with a penchant for gossip. I also knew she was a former Miss Louisiana runner up. Lastly, I knew she'd married my father out of necessity, since she'd been baking a cute little bun in her supposedly virgin oven—aka my brother.

So, when I said I knew my mother, I meant it.

But this? This was beyond the pale. And I had absolutely no fucking idea how to respond.

"Is that...?"

I nodded when Lucy's voice trailed off. Oh, it was indeed.

My vainglorious mother had put the nativity scene on full display. Yup. In the middle of her yard. At the end of July. Complete with baby Jesus and angels. And we couldn't forget the three wise men who weren't particularly wise, oh no.

Was I blaspheming?

Probably.

Did I care?

Not particularly.

And why? Because I was a vampire. And my mother had chosen to welcome me home with baby Jesus. Now, this didn't affect me. Thanks to my atheistic ways, religious artifacts, items, and words didn't bother me. Vlad, on the other hand, very much believed in the Big-G up high.

I swallowed and shot him a wary glance.

I wasn't sure what to expect. Anger? Annoyance? Neither apparently. Instead, he wore a bemused expression I found a little off-putting. As though he found this little display to be the cutest thing he'd ever seen.

Not for the first time, I wish I could take a selfie right now. Because my *mother* had chosen to greet me and my vampire mate with a bunch of religious crap.

My mouth parted, but no words came out. So I closed my trap, swallowed, and tried again. This time I managed to squeak out, "I'm so sorry. My mother... she's..."

"Insane." Lucy's gaze leapt from the scene to my face. "She's freaking insane! You know that, right?"

"Considering I was raised by the woman, yes, I would say I'm well aware of her mental status."

My mother had never been diagnosed as clinically insane, but there were days I wondered about her mental health. Her ability to blatantly ignore the truth while only focusing on the things that mattered to her was impressive. A few years back, I'd found out that she'd known about my father's affair the entire time. Politician he may be, he was still a shitty liar. The only reason she hadn't said anything was because she'd liked being the mayor's wife. It wasn't until Caleb and I found out that she did anything, and even then, it was so she could play the victim. Then came the fake tears and temper tantrums and drama. She'd stomped around town calling my father's mistress a floozy, a grave robber, a bimbo, a desperate doxy, you name it. But prior to it becoming public knowledge, she hadn't cared. That was my mother.

And now this.

"I mean... I knew she was a lot of things, but this..." Lucy released a slow breath. "This takes the cake."

"The very religious cake," I quipped.

"And Caleb allowed her to do this?"

"You and I both know Caleb can't control her, no matter how much they both pretend otherwise. Hell, my father couldn't even control her when they were married, and he's the freaking mayor."

Lucy ran a hand through her hair. "I'm torn. On the one hand, I'm dying to know what else she has in store for you. On the other hand, I have my own family to see. I also need to get Sam settled in the hotel."

I shot her a look. "He's not staying with you?"

Crickets. That was all I could hear. Sam and I shared a glance, but he resorted to his signature half-shrug. Oof, I felt bad for the poor bugger. Perish hotels weren't known for their quality. But I couldn't offer him a room here. Between me and Vlad, my brother, and my mother, there weren't any rooms left. I only hoped Lucy was footing the hotel bill, since she was making him stay at one.

There really wasn't any point in arguing with her either. I could hear Lucy's reasoning in my head without even asking. She and Sam hadn't slept together, but if she asked her parents to put him up, they'd automatically assume they were a couple, and she still wasn't ready to take that leap.

"Go," I told them. Whatever else was waiting for

us beyond those doors, Lucy and Sam couldn't help. "Your parents have been dying to see you. At least your mother is sane."

"I don't know about that," Lucy grumbled.

"Please. The worst thing she did was send you to school with little 'I love you' notes. My mother slept with the football coach, then egged his house when she realized he was married. She knew his wife, for crying out loud! Who does that?"

Lucy choked on a laugh. "I forgot about that!"

"I see where you get your impulsiveness from then," Vlad commented.

"Do not start with me," I growled. "Allow me to impart one life lesson to you. Never compare me to my mother."

A smile teased Vlad's lips.

"Oh, seriously, don't." Lucy shook her head. "Not unless you want to suffer an eternity of itching powder in your pants."

"Hmm. Not good enough. An eternity of garlic shavings in your underwear, holy water in your shampoo, wooden stake shavings mixed in your blood."

Vlad's eyes widened. "Diabolical. And they call Vlad Tepes the most notorious torturer of all time."

"And don't you forget it," I harrumphed.

Still chuckling, Vlad leaned in and pressed a kiss to the top of my head. "And your father? Should I concern myself with him? What sort of antics await me?"

"A shotgun to the chest?" Lucy shrugged. "I swear, when they were handing out responsible, well-meaning parents, you got shafted."

Didn't I know it. "I doubt my father will even notice you. We speak to one another once or twice a year, and all the conversations revolve around him, his life, and his wife, who is only a few years older than me. Did I ever mention that?"

"You didn't."

This time, I sighed. It was like the Fates had conspired to bring together the worst couple ever, just for shits and giggles. When we were younger, Caleb and I begged our parents to get a divorce. Thankfully, they'd listened, but not until after my father's affair, and after their incredibly public separation that to this day was considered the worst town scandal.

Made me wonder if my undead status rivaled it now? We Perishes sure did bring a good name to the town named after us. Guess scandals ran in the family.

"Alright, get lost, you two," I said. "And tell your mother hi for me."

Lucy rolled her eyes, but after a quick wave, she and Sam ducked out of the front yard and climbed back into his car.

"Dare we go inside?" Vlad asked once we were alone.

That was the million-dollar question, wasn't it? A part of me wanted to run back home to New Orleans. I honestly wasn't sure what we'd be facing here. This was my mother, after all. The woman who'd stuffed a hive full of pissed off bees into my father's car, then blamed someone else.

With a wish and a prayer—which was just so ironic at this point that I couldn't help but laugh—we braved the front porch. I studied every nook and cranny, searching for anything out of place. A bucket of holy water teetering atop the door? A cross nailed to the frame? An army of Jesus statues scattered across the entryway?

Who the hell knew?

I squared my shoulders, then opened the screen door and knocked. Technically, I'd lived here my whole life, but thanks to the whole "invitation" rule, I couldn't enter my family home without one. Talk about awkward. At least I wouldn't need another after this. Once a vampire was invited in, the invitation was good for life or until a change of ownership.

The door flew open, and the putrid stench of garlic smacked us in the face. Both Vlad and I choked back a cough and stumbled down the front step. Sweet baby Zeus, the place reeked of it. Had she diluted it in water and cleaned the entire house with it?

I waved a hand in front of my face and blinked back stinging tears. The damn stench assaulted my eyes and nose. What the hell was she even cooking in there?

I intended to ask, but froze when I spotted my mother. She stood before me, hovering on the threshold, clad in—I shit you not—a *Catch Up With Jesus* apron. And draped around her neck were two massive cross necklaces that had to weigh an effin' ton.

"Oh!" My mother's jaw dropped at the sight of me and Vlad cringing on her stoop. "Anna, I didn't realize you were bringing home a guest."

I choked on the poisoned air. "Wh—what the hell are you... cooking?"

"Dinner?" Her perfectly drawn brows rose as though she had absolutely no idea what I could possibly be talking about. "It's just pizza. You like pizza."

"That isn't pizza," I rasped.

"It's chicken and herb."

"And what herbs did you use?"

"Oh, a little bit of everything. You know how I cook. Some paprika, rosemary, basil, and—"

"Garlic?" This time I coughed.

My mother's cheeks pinked. Not a hint of confusion lingered in her eyes. She knew exactly what she'd done. The only thing I didn't understand was why. Was this all some sort of test? Or an insult? Or maybe she found it hilarious?

"Well, are you coming inside or what?" She waved a spatula in the air.

"Or what," I parroted. "First, you need to open some damn windows."

"Anna Marie," she hissed. "I raised you better than that. No cussing in front of guests."

I threw Vlad a look of exasperation. He hardly qualified as a guest, but who was I to argue with my mother?

"Windows, Mother."

Her mouth pursed.

When she didn't move, I drew my lips back and exposed my fangs. "Now!"

I wasn't sure what I expected, but a scowl wasn't it. "Anna Marie!"

"It's just Anna, Mother. Has been my entire life, and that's not about to change now."

"I'm your mother. I think I know your name."

"Do you?" I eyed her sternly. "And are you going to handle this situation or not?"

After a moment's hesitation, she sighed and stomped back inside. From the porch, I could hear her slamming open windows and muttering under her breath about her ungrateful wretch of a child. Lucky for me and Vlad, we could hear every word.

An eternity later, she returned, minus the spatula but still donning that ridiculous apron.

"Well?" She waved at the kitchen. "Is that better?"

Considering we were no longer under assault, yes. Though I still had so many questions about the apparel. I'd lived with this woman for eighteen years before moving out, and never had I laid eyes on this stupid thing. Or the necklaces.

"Hurry up then. Dinner is getting cold."

Dinner. With vampires. I blinked and stared at my mother as though she'd grown two heads. Was she going senile? Surely, she knew vampires didn't eat food, right? I mean, *everyone* knew that. And I highly doubted she was inviting us to snack on her, so…?

I decided to start with the more obvious problem. "You need to invite us in first."

"What? But you lived here."

"Lived, as in past tense. I don't live here anymore, and didn't when I was turned, so we can't enter until you invite us in."

A flicker of emotion flashed in her eyes before vanishing just as quickly. Almost as though she feared the idea of welcoming us inside. Was that what this was all about? Her way of pushing me out the door without having to say the words? She'd been the one nagging me to come home. But maybe now that I'd agreed, the idea of having a vampire under her roof terrified her. As much as it pained me, I didn't blame her for it.

"Mom."

"Fine, fine. C-Come in. Please."

Vlad and I shared a glance, then together stepped over the threshold. To this day, it baffled me how one moment there could be a barrier holding us out, and the next, presto, nothing but air. Magic, obviously.

Once inside, I kicked off my shoes and gently placed them aside.

My mother chuckled when she saw my fancy Weitzman boots. "Some things never change."

I glared at her offensive rubber croc shoes. I'd never understood her fascination with them considering her upbringing. Thankfully, she never wore the atrocities in public. Small favors. "No. They certainly don't."

"Well, introduce me already," my mother commanded.

I grimaced at the sight of her standing in the kitchen doorway, hands planted on her hips, with her Jesus apron just... staring at us.

"Can you take that off, please?" I sounded as exasperated as I felt.

Her brow furrowed. "But Mrs. Bitterly gave me this. It was a gift."

"And let me guess, she gave it to you after she learned I'd been turned into a vampire?"

"Oh, darling, don't be so absurd. Not everything is about you."

I arched a brow. Right. Because it was absurd to believe that our extremely Catholic neighbor hadn't done such a thing. Mrs. Bitterly was the sort of woman who taught abstinence at the local high school. And not as a means of preventing pregnancy. More like as a means of keeping girls and boys apart.

Especially "colored" boys and white girls. She was *that* sort of woman—one who wrapped her bigotry in a blanket of religious piety. Needless to say, she absolutely would give my mother such an inappropriate gift after learning I'd fallen from grace.

"Take it off."

"Anna. There's no need. It doesn't bother me." Vlad's hand brushed mine. I nearly clung to his fingers, using him to steady me. Five minutes in my mother's presence, and I was ready to murder her.

"Well, it bothers me. It's rude." I leveled my mother with a heavy glare.

Her colored eyebrows winged up. If there was one way to get her attention, it was by insulting her manners.

With a dramatic sigh, she removed the apron and tossed it aside.

"What's with the display outside? And the necklaces? What's your goal here?"

"My goodness, Anna. It's like you aren't happy with anything I do."

"Because I'm not. You knew I was coming home tonight, and this is how you chose to welcome me? What could you have possibly hoped to accomplish?"

She shrugged, then turned and vanished into the

kitchen without another word.

Ah, avoidance. Another of my mother's fine traits. So maybe I was ragging on her. But believe me, she deserved it. If I didn't ride her, who knew the other stunts she'd pull. Even now, the thought of entering her house terrified me. I could only imagine what the rest of the place had in store for us.

"Maybe we should go," I offered. "She's in a mood. Sometimes it's best to just ignore this sort of behavior. We can go find a hotel or something, come back tomorrow."

"A hotel is hardly required." Vlad braved a quick glance into the kitchen, but he seemed unconcerned with what he found. "I've arranged proper accommodations for us."

"Proper? What's that mean?"

"Well, your apartment would hardly house us and our coffins."

I nodded. I'd considered that. They built my apartment with bachelors in mind. And the windows were westward facing. Which tended to make things a bit toasty in the afternoon.

"When you first mentioned this trip, I purchased a house for us."

It took a few moments for my brain to comprehend that. "Wait. What?"

"I found us a place to live. Perish is your hometown, so I felt it best to own something we could call our own. We certainly can't depend on your family to shelter us. That responsibility is ours alone."

Well, he wasn't wrong there. But still! He bought us a house? And why hadn't he discussed this with me? What if I'd wanted a say in the location or the person we were buying from? He didn't know the town or the people like I did. I could have helped. I could have—

"I can practically hear your thoughts," Vlad mused.

"Yeah, well, I'm a loud thinker when surprised... or mad."

"Why would you be mad?"

I couldn't get into that right now. I wasn't like hopping with fury type mad, but definitely annoyed he'd taken this step without me. Still, we had more than enough to focus on right now. So much so that I needed to put a pin in this whole house thing and come back to it later. Especially considering my mother was returning from the kitchen with her hands full of garlic pizza.

Oh yeah, *way* more than enough to focus on.

Someone remind me why I came home again?

CHAPTER TWELVE

"WELL?" My mother stood in the kitchen, framed between two wooden crosses I knew hadn't been there when I'd left, and tapped her toe. "Are you going to tell me who your friend is?"

"Mom, this is Vlad. I told you about him, remember? The man who saved me?"

She harrumphed. "You mean the man who killed you?"

I bit back a groan. I knew this game, knew her goal. To create drama. If I fed into it, we'd be here all night listening to her tantrums and antics. Instead, I hit her with a few truth bombs. "No, that would be Petrik. Vlad turned me so you wouldn't have to bury your daughter. Say thank you, Mom."

"Thank you, Mom," she parroted in a saccharine

voice. And people wondered where I got my sarcasm from.

"Vlad, allow me to formally introduce you to my mother, Penelope Perish. Mother, this is Vlad Vasek." I left off the Dracula bit. I honestly didn't see a point in bringing that up. As evident by the Christian artifacts tacked to her walls, my mother was a God-fearing woman. Somehow, I just knew mentioning Dracula in any facet would result in an epic meltdown. Best to keep the information as PG as possible with her.

Her gaze swept over Vlad, but from the downturn of her lips and the slight narrowing of her eyes, I knew she didn't approve. The classic "mom look." The one she broke out every time I brought a boy home. Manners dictated that she behave politely, but the second they left, she'd break out into one of the many lectures she loved to spout at me. Not that they ever worked. I pretty much did what I wanted when I wanted, and I never stopped to think about my mother's preferences, much to her dismay. More than once, she'd told me I should try to be more like her. All proper and polished. Then I'd remind her it wasn't the 1980s anymore, a comment she never appreciated, which of course was why I'd bring it up. Anything to shut her up.

"He's dark," she finally said.

I... honestly didn't know what to make of that comment. Vlad's skin was quite pale, thanks to his ethnicity and the fact that he was the undead. Maybe she meant his clothing? The man didn't own a single piece of colored clothing. Everything was black, right down to his socks. He did have an image to uphold, after all. Or maybe she meant his features? His raven black hair and midnight eyes definitely stood out against his stark pale face.

"And he's tall," she continued, as though his height offended her somehow.

I simply laughed and shook my head. She was looking for something to complain about, and there wasn't anything I could do about that.

"Don't you need to eat?" I asked her. "Before your food goes cold?"

She blinked as though waking herself from some little reverie, then nodded and marched into the kitchen. "Yes. Let's eat."

Vlad and I shared a startled look. I didn't think I'd have to explain this to my mother, but apparently, I'd been wrong.

"Um, Mom?"

She glanced over her shoulder with a raised brow.

"Vampires... don't... I mean, we don't..."

Her other brow rose. "Don't what?"

I sighed. Best to just jump in feet first. "Eat. We don't eat."

"You don't eat," she repeated, her brows furrowing as though this concept baffled her. "Then how do you—" She gasped, her hand leaping to her throat. "Oh dear. Oh my. No, I can't... You... drink... *that*?"

Shame colored my cheeks. I didn't think I'd have to explain this to her. Everyone knew vampires drink blood. It was the one myth that never changed.

"Oh God," she panted, collapsing into the nearest kitchen seat. "Oh dear God."

Vlad stepped back, as though the sound of her curses would be easier to bear with distance. Maybe they would. Pity swelled within me, and I swept into her kitchen and crouched in front of her. I took her hands and held them tightly. Maybe I didn't like my mother, but she was still my mother, and even I could see she was on the brink of an absolute meltdown. I needed to curb it before it devolved into a panic attack.

"It's okay," I told her. "Deep breath."

Her gaze met mine, and she shook her head.

"Yes. You can do this. Deep breath. Come on."

After a moment's hesitation, she finally caved and sucked in a shivering breath that shook her entire body.

"Good," I told her. "Exhale through your nose." Then nodded when she did. "Good. Keep doing that. It's okay. It doesn't matter what we eat. All that matters is I'm alive, and I'm here. Right?"

She gave a jerky nod, her normally perfectly coiffed blond hair slipping free of her bun. When she didn't immediately move to fix it, I realized this was a true panic attack.

I imitated her deep breaths and listened to the slowing of her heartbeat.

"I can't do this, Anna," she warbled, her voice weak. "I hate this. I hate knowing someone hurt you and that you died."

My shoulders rounded and I nodded. "I know. Just focus on the present, okay? Forget the past."

"I can't! Your past is literally staring me in the face. I knew when you left that you were going to get hurt. But I never said anything because you are just like me. Impulsive and careless. If I told you not to go, you'd refuse to listen and would leave just because I told you not to. I thought maybe you'd see the club, see a vampire, and come home. I didn't think *this* would happen."

"No one did, Mom."

"Chris did," she muttered. "Do you know I ran into him at the grocery store the day you left? He told me what happened. How you broke up with him because he forbade you from leaving. He told me you were going to get yourself killed."

Anger erupted within me. Who did that? Who told someone's mother that their daughter was going to get herself killed? If I ever saw that little shit again....

"Chris is an asshole, Mom," I told her, hoping to make her smile.

When her mouth curled upward, I grinned, pleased with the result.

"Someone should run him over with a car," I said.

She burst into a giggle, then clapped her hand over her mouth. "What a horrible thing to say."

"But oh so true. He never should have said that to you. He was probably still angry with me."

"Yes, you do tend to break little boys' hearts." Her gaze rose to Vlad.

"Don't worry, he's not a boy," I said, winking.

I glanced back and shot Vlad a soft smile. He stood in the living room, simply watching with a keen eye. I appreciated his silence right now, as though he knew it was best to just keep out of the way.

"Believe me, next time I see Chris, I'll slap him for you," I said.

"Probably not a good idea, sweetheart. You are a v-vampire after all."

Ah, she said it out loud. My grin widened. "Look at you, using the v-word and everything."

"Yes, well, I guess I better start owning it. There's no chance of you turning back?"

I shook my head. That she'd asked that question told me how desperate she was for it to happen. "That's not possible, Mom. Vampirism is permanent."

"You just had to go to New Orleans, didn't you?" she scolded gently. "But that's who you are. Always at the front of the line when something new and exciting happens. Nose deep in everyone else's business. I always thought you'd make a good reporter."

Well, those dreams had died alongside me. But that was okay, I had new dreams now. Ones I'd never known existed.

"I guess if you can't eat, then this whole pizza thing was pointless."

"But we appreciate the effort," I said, lying

through my fangs. The house still reeked of garlic, and even if I'd been human, I never would have touched a slice. My poor gut would have rebelled just on principle.

"Do you have plans to see your father while you're in town?"

I sighed. My saint of a father hadn't once called me since I'd transitioned. Guess my father had skipped *How to Be a Good Father 101*, cuz the dude sucked. Miserably. "I texted him a few nights ago and told him when we would be in town. He didn't respond. I was considering dropping by tomorrow night, but I haven't decided yet."

"As much as I would love to say screw the bastard, I really do think you should make the effort. He is your father, after all."

A father who had proven time and time again that he didn't give a shit about us. Why should I make the effort when he so clearly refused to do the same for us? This was the man who'd cheated on my mother, then left her with absolutely nothing before settling with his mistress. Classy, right? I could count on one hand the number of times he and I had spoken in the last five years.

"Anna, listen to me."

I locked eyes with my mom.

"Talk to your father and fix your relationship with him. If this whole lesson has taught me anything, it's that family matters. If you'd died without burying the hatchet, your father would have had to live with that the rest of his life."

"And? How's that my problem?"

She sighed and gripped my hands tightly. "Your father isn't the sort to admit he's wrong. You have to be the one to take that first step."

"Well, that won't be happening."

"Anna..."

"Leave it alone, Mom. I came home so you could see me and meet Vlad. I'll make an effort to see Dad, but I never said I'd forgive him."

She released my hands and cupped my cheeks. "So much of me in you."

Oh, ouch. I definitely didn't like hearing that.

"Now, let me meet this handsome young man of yours."

I snorted a laugh. "Mom, Vlad is five hundred years old."

Her eyes shot comically wide. "Oh my."

I snickered and waved Vlad over. Hopefully, I'd diffused the situation enough that she'd be polite to him.

Sure. And pigs could fly.

THE INSTANT we left my mother's house, I drew in a deep breath in an attempt to clear the garlic from my nasal passages. Man, that shit really stung. And lingered. It felt like it pervaded every single one of my pores and orifices. I couldn't even imagine trying to ingest any. It'd probably rip my stomach to shreds.

"Well. That was... interesting," Vlad commented.

I nodded but kept my gaze locked on his car—our escape vehicle. My mother had calmed down a bit after our little chat, but she'd been incredibly curious about Vlad. More like intrusive, honestly. She'd asked questions I never would have thought to ask. Like what'd it been like living in the Middle Ages. I reminded her that he'd been born slightly afterward, but that hadn't swayed her. She'd also asked him about his parents and his life as a human. Vlad had responded graciously, but holy crap, I couldn't take another minute in there.

"Oh, Anna!" my mother called from the kitchen window.

I grimaced. "Yes?"

"Caleb is coming over Friday night. Do drop by."

Oh yay, another round of *this*. Except this time

with my egotistical yet oddly stupid brother. "Sounds fun."

My mother waved at us through the window, then pulled the curtains shut, likely to keep her nosy neighbors from peeking in on her. Neighbors who had their faces plastered against their windows, openly gawking at me and Vlad.

"Lovely," I muttered with a curl of my lip.

Vlad tracked my gaze and nodded. Every single house surrounding us had people crowding their doorways and porches. I knew we were the most exciting thing to happen to Perish this year, but I honestly hadn't expected this level of prying. They even had their phones out, the distinctive camera flashes giving them away. I clicked my tongue against my teeth and started toward the car. Guess they didn't realize that 1) we couldn't be photographed, and 2) it was the dead of night. What the hell kind of results did they expect? They'd be lucky if the photos showed the trees in their yards.

"Sorry about all this," I said. "Guess you're not used to this level of attention."

Vlad clasped my hand and lifted my palm to his mouth, pressing a light kiss on my wrist. Shivers lifted the little hairs on my arms, and it took every ounce of sanity I had left to remind myself that I couldn't jump him right here and now.

"You have no need to apologize to me," he said. "While I'm not accustomed to meeting someone's parents, I'll survive."

I chuckled. Of that, I had no doubt.

"Come." He gestured to the passenger seat, then opened the door.

I slipped inside and belted myself in, even though I really didn't need to. Still, we didn't need to tempt fate a second time and land ourselves a ticket for not obeying traffic laws. We'd seen enough of the police tonight.

Once Vlad climbed in next to me, I turned down the radio and faced him. "You bought a house."

His gaze briefly flicked to me, then back to the road. He turned the ignition and the car roared to life. "No, we bought a house."

See, that irritated me. "*We* didn't do anything. *You* did it all. You chose the place, you paid for it. All you."

A slight frown marred his perfect features. "Yes. For us."

Yeah, he definitely didn't understand my point here. The old Anna would have jumped down his throat and insisted he treat me fairly and equally.

But the new and improved Anna knew she needed to look at this from both sides. Vlad wasn't a modern man. To him, buying a place for *us* was exactly that. It didn't mean he didn't value me, more like he felt it was his responsibility to provide housing for us.

Keeping that in mind, I centered my thoughts. What could I say to help him understand my concerns? "While I appreciate that you handled this problem for us, I would have liked to have been included. Not only because Perish is my hometown but also because if we buy a place, I want to have a say in it. I want to choose a home with you, as partners."

Vlad fell silent and considered my words, his expression pinched. What I would have given to hear his thoughts right now. After a few moments, he nodded. "Next time I'll consult with you before making such a decision."

I almost laughed. What a typical Vlad response. But I appreciated it. He could have been a typical man from the middle ages and assured me that he could handle it all himself and didn't need the "little woman's" opinion, but he was so much better than that. It was one of the things I loved about him.

Huh.

Just like that, I realized how clear things were. I

did love him. It wasn't physical or all lustiness. I loved *him*. I loved the way he listened to me, and the way he adapted and grew. I loved his generosity and compassion. The way he only shared that side of himself with me. The way he let his guard down to show me the real man behind the Dracula façade.

I loved him.

And he deserved to know. Especially with all that was going on in our lives. I would regret it if I never told him, then died tomorrow.

With a smile, I reached up and gently stroked his cheek. "Did you know that I love you?"

Vlad froze.

I burst out laughing at the sight of him startled into complete stillness as he stared out the window. But my laughter soon died as doubt set in. Oh shit, should I not have said it? Did he not feel the same way? Fear twisted my insides, and when he didn't immediately respond, I drew away from him.

I hadn't made it far before his hand snatched mine back.

Tears pricked at my eyes as dread nested deep in my chest. What if I'd just ruined everything? Could I handle that? Could I walk away?

Noah's words came back to me from the VA meeting, how every young vampire needed to know where they stood with their sire. If Vlad didn't echo my sentiment, at least then I would know. It'd hurt like a motherfucker and would probably take decades to heal my broken heart, but it *would* heal.

Vlad's fingers tightened around mine, and he lifted my hand to his mouth. When he pressed a tiny kiss against my palm, I metaphorically flatlined.

"I love you too," he replied, his voice gruff with emotion.

Relief loosened my muscles, and my whole body seemed to deflate like a popped balloon. "You do?"

He pressed my palm against his cheek and held it there. I reveled in the feel of his light stubble. He must not have shaved before his transition, but I didn't mind. I loved a man with stubble.

"I loved you the second I saw you. You were everything I'd been missing. You're my sun, my light, my heart. All things stolen from me. When I say I love you, know that I mean it, that I've never spoken those words to another."

Shock rendered me silent. Not even to Mina?

"You are everything I've lost and everything I've gained. Know that I'll never let anything happen to you. You're mine, in every sense of the word. And I very much intend to love you until the end of time."

Phew. That gave me all the feels.

I needed a moment to collect myself. The man certainly knew how to give a speech. One that had me tearing up. Startled by the tears pricking my eyes, I half-sobbed, half-chuckled, then wiped them away. Vampire tears weren't a pretty sight, and I really didn't feel like walking around with blood-streaked cheeks.

"Um." I released a shaky breath. "Ditto?"

A knowing smile curved Vlad's lips. "Ah."

My mouth moved soundlessly as I contemplated what to say. I wasn't as loquacious as Vlad. I didn't speak fancy words and make undying proclamations that could spin a guy's head. But I definitely needed to give him more than a *ditto*.

Determined to try, I climbed over the car's console and slowly slid into Vlad's lap. My head was pushing against the roof, but I didn't care. This sort of moment demanded closeness.

"I've never told someone I loved them either. I mean, other than Lucy," I admitted. "I can't even remember the last time I said it to my parents. Before you, I didn't really believe in it. I believed in lust and friendship, but not love. You changed my mind. I've never had that *one* person I thought about more than any other. The one person I wanted to spend every day with. But here you are. You're always on my mind, always invading my thoughts and emotions. We're going to live forever, and I couldn't imagine spending eternity with anyone else."

A small smile spread across his face, one that transformed him into a prince of darkness.

I cupped his cheeks, leaned down, and kissed him, reveling in the feel of his lips against mine. Once I had my fill, I sat back and stroked my fingers through his hair. "So, now that we have that out of the way, how about you take me to our new home? I would very much like to strip you naked right now."

Vlad's grin turned naughty. "That can be accommodated."

I fell back into my seat, but Vlad kept hold of my hand, our digits intertwined. He lowered them to the gear shift and put the car in drive. I wasn't one for symbolism, but I liked to think it represented our willingness to navigate our lives together.

With luck, we'd get our happily ever after, even if we had to fight tooth and nail for it.

CHAPTER THIRTEEN

Ohmigod. He bought the Barker house.

The *Barker* house.

Because *of course* he had. He couldn't have bought a normal house. No. He had to go for the *one* house in Perish that was unequivocally haunted. There wasn't a person in Perish who didn't believe this place was haunted. Usually, parents tried to convince their children that there was no such thing as ghosts, but not with this house. Growing up, our parents had actively told us to stay away from it. They never admitted it was haunted but venturing near this place often landed a child with a blistered backside and chores for months. That's how terrified people were of this place.

I didn't realize I'd taken a step back until Vlad's

hand found mine and he tugged me closer. "Shall we go inside?"

Oh hell no. *Hell. To. The. No.* I wasn't stepping foot anywhere near this place.

Memories of my childhood came flashing back. Some kids like to dare others to go inside and spend the night, but no one *ever* did. And oddly, no one ever held it against them either. Because we *knew*. We knew there was something wrong with this place. The closest I'd ever come was the sidewalk leading up to the house. The second I'd touched the grass, goosebumps had pebbled my flesh and my stomach twisted. You can bet your ass I tucked tail and ran. Who wouldn't?

"Anna?" Vlad's hand touched my waist. "Is something wrong?"

I gave a jerky nod. "That's the Barker house."

"Yes. I bought it from the lawyer managing the estate. The house has been sitting on the market for decades without any interested buyers."

"Because it's the *Barker* house!" I hissed.

"Yes. It is."

"It's haunted, Vlad. Like, deathly haunted." I startled at the sound of his chuckle and whirled around to face him. "This isn't funny! The reason this place has never been purchased is that it's haunted."

"Anna, I assure you, it's not haunted."

"Oh, like you would know!"

"I do know, in fact."

I tried not to sulk, but I had a feeling I was failing at it. "*How* could you possibly know?"

"Come. Let me show you."

I slammed on the brakes and dug my heels into the pavement. Nuh-uh. No way. No how.

"Anna." Vlad bit back a full laugh. "You're being silly."

"*I'm* being silly? You're the one who bought a haunted house. Ohmigosh, we have to sell it. ASAP."

Vlad's hand fell away from my side, and he sighed. "Do you trust me?"

I waved his question off. Of course I trusted him. But he didn't know the area like I did. And clearly, he didn't understand the housing here. One did not just *buy* the Barker house. One kept a hundred feet *away* from the house and never looked at it, lest they upset the spirits trapped within.

The thing even looked creepy. While the foundation seemed to be in decent condition, the roof certainly needed some love. And the yard. Definitely the yard. It was overrun with weeds and dead dandelions that dared grow that close to the house.

Vlad thought I'd want to live *here*? Was he insane?

"It's a fixer-upper," he admitted. "But the price was decent, and the bones are good. I rather liked the thought of renovating it into a place we could call home."

I shuddered at the word bones. I bet the place was littered with them. Like an ancient burial ground or something.

"Okay. No." I faced Vlad and summoned my best *don't mess with me* look. "The Barker house hasn't been occupied since before I was born! And you want to know why?"

"Because it's believed to be haunted?"

"Yes!" I threw my hands up into the air. "Because Beaty Barker's ghost has been haunting this place since before any of us can remember. Supposedly, she lost her mind one night and took a chainsaw to her family, Vlad. A chainsaw! Then she did herself in after."

"Is any of that true?" he asked.

"What? Of course it's true. Why wouldn't it be?"

"Because myths and legends have a way of flourishing. Take me for example."

My mouth twisted. "You're different."

"How so? People believe I am the same person as Vlad Tepes. They believe that I beheaded and piked thousands of men."

"No, just one," I said wryly, reminding us of Eli.

Vlad cleared his throat. "My point is, has anyone actually looked into the story of Beaty Barker?"

"I honestly don't know."

Vlad nodded, his hand finding its way to the small of my back once more. "Well, I did."

"You did?"

"Yes. You think I would buy a home without knowing its history?"

Maybe? I mean, he'd turned me into a vampire without knowing my history. Though I suppose the two things weren't quite the same.

"Beaty Barker lived here until she was eighty-three," Vlad said. "Her husband, Robert Barker, died of natural causes three years prior. Their children, who all grew up in this house, eventually moved on, as children do. All have passed. Only the grandchildren remain, one of which sold us the house. He assured me the legends were simply that. Stories concocted by the townspeople because his grandmother never left the house. She didn't enjoy socializing and in her old age, she'd preferred to remain indoors knitting, until the day she passed. She died with her knitting needles in hand."

Skepticism had me crossing my arms over my chest. "How do you know that story is true?"

"Because, my sweet Anna"—Vlad leaned down and brushed a kiss against my heated cheeks—"vampires can see ghosts. If this was a true haunting, I would know. As would you."

"Wait. What? We can see ghosts?"

"Of course. We're the undead. As are ghosts. They're just a bit more dead than we are."

Okay, that was a bit too mindboggling for me. Because first, "You're saying ghosts actually exist?" And second, "You're also saying we can speak to them?"

Vlad chuckled. "I don't see why that would surprise you. Vampires are real, after all. As are werewolves. Why not ghosts?"

Why not indeed.

"And you're saying the Barker house isn't haunted?"

"Not that I saw. Unless the ghost is a quiet one, which in my experience, they never are."

Well, okay then. I would need some time to wrap my head around this one. I'd been told this house was haunted my entire life. And while I actually hadn't believed in ghosts, I had believed in the haunting. Odd, how people's brains worked. And now Vlad was telling me the opposite. That ghosts truly *did* exist, but the house wasn't haunted.

My life had really become topsy-turvy in the past few months. Almost as though the Fates were trying to teach me that I well and truly knew nothing. Life was a dichotomy, that was for sure.

"Are you ready to go inside now?"

I honestly had no idea. But the one thing I did know was Vlad would never purposely endanger me. So, with a forced smile, I took his hand and let him lead me into the house. From the outside, the place gave off an *Amityville Horror* vibe, but the interior of the Creole cottage told a whole different story. Surprisingly, the interior seemed to be in good shape. Vlad led me through the gallery and into the parlor, stopping to point out the well-kept pine floors and pristinely painted walls. Someone had clearly been handling the upkeep. Or they'd tackled some renovations hoping to sell the place.

Pleased by the house's condition, I dropped Vlad's hand and strolled through the entire place, taking in the different bedrooms and bathrooms. Everything seemed pretty standard. Honestly, with a little love, the exterior could easily match the interior's quality. A new roof, some new shutters for the windows, and voilà.

"Who's there!" a squeaky voice chirped above me.

I jumped in my skin, clapped a hand to my chest, then spun in a tight circle, studying my surroundings. I stood alone in the master bedroom, not a soul in sight.

Before I could call for Vlad, the voice came again. Followed by another.

"Who... Who's there?"

"Someone's here?"

"You don't smell it? It smells off. Like old blood."

"Can you see it?"

"I can't see anything, ya dolt, I'm blind, remember? You go see!"

"I'm not going out there!"

"Chicken!"

"Don't you call me a chicken, ya old bat!"

Holy shit. Holy shit. *Holy shit!* Vlad had promised this house wasn't haunted, but I was very clearly hearing voices, almost as though they were in the next room! And from the smell of it, there wasn't anyone here but me and Vlad and some animals. I'd caught the musty scent of opossum when we'd stepped inside, but that'd seemed normal, considering this house was virtually abandoned.

"Is... someone there?" I asked, my voice pitiful and weak.

"Shh! Did you hear that? I know I heard something. There's someone here!"

"Oh, calm down. They won't find us. We're safe up here. We blend in, like monsters in the night."

My eyes rose to the ceiling. Up here? As in... the attic? Oh god, we had ghosts in the attic! Nope, that was enough. I didn't need to know anything else. I *refused* to stay here if there were ghosts. "Vlad!"

The panic must have carried through my voice.

Vlad appeared at my side seconds later, his hands grasping mine. "What's wrong?"

"Ghosts," I hissed, pointing up to the ceiling. "I can hear them up there, chattering away."

His concerned expression slowly morphed into one of amusement. "Anna, there's no one up there. I would know if someone was in the house."

"They're up there, Vlad! Bickering like an old married couple."

"Shh. There's another one now," the squeaky voice added.

"See!" I jabbed a finger in the air, practically

jumping into Vlad's arms. "I told you! I told you! There's a ghost up there."

"Anna..." Vlad stepped close to me and peered into my face, his brows deepening as he studied me. "There aren't any voices."

I dropped my arm and sighed. "This isn't funny. I'm serious! I can't share a home with a ghost."

"All right." He took my hand and tugged me toward the door. "Let's go upstairs. I'll show you there's nothing to fear."

"Nope." I dug my heels into the floor. "I am *not* going up there."

A hint of frustration chased across Vlad's face. "Fine. Then I'll go look. Will that suffice? I assure you, there aren't any ghosts here."

"Sure, go look. But when you find a pair of ghosts up there, I'll be down here, waiting for an apology."

Vlad threw me a wry glance, then started climbing up the steep staircase.

Fear had me wringing my hands together and straining my ears to listen for any movement or commotion.

"Quiet, quiet!" one of the voices hissed. "He's coming."

"Who is?"

"The person, you nitwit!"

"Don't nitwit me, you wanker!"

I trailed between the rooms, listening to the sound of Vlad's footsteps. "Do you hear them?" I shouted up at the ceiling.

"Anna, there's no one here."

"That's not funny, Vlad!" I shouted.

"Ah, there he is! Go, go, go!" the one with the squeaky voice complained.

"Go where?" the second voice demanded.

"Just go!" Squeaky yelled.

"Vlad..." I bolted to the staircase, ready to climb like his life depended on it. "They saw you. Can you hear them yet?"

No response.

"Vlad!" I shouted.

Oh shit, had something happened to him? Had the ghosts attacked him or something? I couldn't hear any sort of commotion up there, and even the voices had stopped. Everything was blissfully silent again.

"Vlad, answer me!"

His head popped into sight at the top of the stairs. "Everything is fine. There's nothing up here. Would you like to come see for yourself?"

"Are you insane?"

"Generally, yes," he said with a playful wink.

"Come, Anna. The attic will house our coffins for now, so you may as well look."

I cursed and tightened my hands around the railings. I *really* didn't want to go up there.

"Anna."

My gaze leapt to Vlad's. I could see the reassurance in his eyes. Regardless of my fears, he wouldn't let anything hurt me. And for all I knew, ghosts could be benign. Just because I'd watched every poltergeist movie out there didn't mean ghosts were evil. Maybe they were like us, just trying to get by and survive their new existence as some earthly ephemeral being.

"Okay, okay, I'm coming," I said. It helped that I hadn't heard the ghosts speak since they'd supposedly left the room. Maybe Vlad had scared them off? Could ghosts even be scared off? Wasn't it their job to scare us off as the new owners?

I slowly climbed the staircase, then took Vlad's hand as I entered the attic. Dusty, yes, but haunted, no. In fact, the place looked pretty standard. Dusty and unused, but standard. A typical belfry.

"You're sure this is the house you want?" I asked.

"If you don't like it, I can put it up for sale and find another that meets your liking. I would never force you to live somewhere you were truly uncomfortable with."

"What about New Orleans?"

We joined hands and Vlad led me through the attic, taking the time to test the flooring. Once he declared it to be safe—since we *really* didn't want to be falling through wooden floors—he faced me. "New Orleans will always be our home. I merely wanted a place we could use when visiting Perish. Clearly, we can't entrust your mother with our safety. And I haven't high hopes for your father either. Our safety is paramount during the day."

I nodded.

"But I don't intend for us to be here often. I know you prefer New Orleans. As do I."

Relief eased my muscles. "Good. I love New Orleans. Not only because my family isn't there, but it's easy for us to grab a meal. It wouldn't be quite so simple here."

"A few of the harem members have agreed to accompany us whenever we come here."

"Well, isn't that gracious of them," I teased.

"Gracious of *me* to up their salary as recompense."

I chuckled. Now *that* sounded more like it.

"Do you hear any more voices?" Vlad inquired.

Shaking my head, I released his hand and strode across the attic. It was nice, as far as attics went. Nothing spectacular. Just a closed-off room lacking any and all light and fresh air. I understood the need for such a room, but this just made me realize how eager I was for the new SunGuard windows. This place didn't feel like home to me, not like the house in New Orleans. But he was right. We would need a sanctuary here.

"I did hear them though," I told Vlad. "They were bickering, calling each other names, and then ran away when you entered the attic."

Vlad's expression darkened. "I heard no such thing."

I threw my hands up in frustration. "I don't know what else to say. I very clearly heard their voices. I didn't imagine them." My thoughts suddenly screamed to a stop, and I lifted my hand to my mouth, touching my fingertips to my lips. "Wait, I heard another voice."

"What? Just now?"

"No. Earlier tonight. In the cop car."

Vlad crossed the room and grasped my forearms. His hands slid down until they cupped mine. "What do you mean?"

"When you and the cop were speaking, I heard a

third voice. It sounded like it'd come from the patrol car. I'd immediately assumed the cop had a partner in there, but when I peered closer, I saw a German Shepherd." I craned my head and gazed up at Vlad. "He called you a dawg."

"A dog called me a dog?"

"No, he called you a *dawg*, like a player, because of how they caught us... canoodling."

Vlad shook his head. "I often find myself frustrated when you speak. I never understand anything you say."

I would have chuckled if his comment hadn't hit so close to home. My thoughts continued racing back to the strange Gollum voice I'd heard in our house back in New Orleans. It'd been squeaky too, similar to the ones heard here tonight. It called us "filthy vampires," so I'd assumed it was one of the harem members. But now that I was thinking about it, I hadn't recognized the voice. And I knew all the harem members.

I lifted my head and sniffed the air. Smell wasn't my strongest sense, but it wasn't weak either. The air was stale and musty, but beneath that came a note of something subtle. A strange odor I'd never sampled before.

With the scent lingering in my nose, I tracked it.

It didn't take long until I found something in the corner of the belfry, a small pile of dark pellets.

"Hmm. I'll need to hire cleaners. I'll want them here tonight before we settle in for the day," Vlad commented. "I don't recall there being any mention of animal feces when I spoke with the inspector, and this looks fairly fresh. Within the last few days. Bat, I'd assume."

My head snapped up. "What did you just say?"

"I said I needed to hire a cleaner—"

"No. After that. What sort of feces?"

"Bat. That's guano," Vlad said.

What had one of the voices said? Something about being an old bat? "Holy shit," I whispered.

"What? What's wrong?"

No, this couldn't be possible. I mean, if my suspicions were true, then obviously it *was* possible, but it still didn't seem possible, ya'know? But what other explanation could there be? Everything lined up. All the recent strange occurrences, the odd voices... I thought they were in my head, and maybe they were, but not in an imaginary way.

"Anna, talk to me."

"Vampire powers, tell me about them again."

Vlad lifted a brow. "What?"

"Just... I'll explain after. Tell me about vampire powers."

"You already know everything there is to know. As vampires age, we gain power. And as our powers grow, we develop gifts."

"But at what age do they normally present themselves?"

"Often around the hundred-year mark."

"What about for a vampire who's been known to drink ancient blood quite frequently?"

Understanding dawned on Vlad's face. "Are you suggesting what I think you are?"

"I don't know," I whispered. "Maybe?"

I honestly couldn't think of any other explanation, other than maybe I was losing my mind. Could it be true? Could I possibly have the ability to speak to animals?

Because all vampires wanted *that* power, right?

CHAPTER FOURTEEN

I RETREATED into the unfurnished living room, my thoughts spinning in senseless circles. This couldn't be possible. I was far too young to have gained my first superpower. And even if it was possible, why animals? Why their thoughts? That had to be the least helpful power ever. Vlad gained foresight and the ability to shift. Me? I got to hear Lassie's thoughts.

Just my luck, huh?

"Anna, you haven't been undead for half a year. You couldn't have developed your first gift yet."

"Then you try explaining it," I said, tossing my hands in the air. "I've been hearing odd voices over the past few nights, but I kept finding a way to explain them away. A begrudged harem member, for instance. But tonight, that dog. I swear that dog spoke. Not out loud, but in my head."

A shadow flickered across Vlad's face. "Anna."

"Yes, yes, I know. It's not possible. I'm not old enough. Blah, blah, blah. Vlad, I drank the blood of a thousand-year-old vampire. And I've had yours more than once. You're not exactly a young whippersnapper yourself. I've also had Camilla's. She's not as old as you, but compared to me, she's ancient. You told me ancient blood was dangerous to younger vampires because they couldn't handle the power boost. Power boost, Vlad! As in, developing my first vamp gift at a younger age."

He held a hand up to end my tirade. "Be that as it may, I've never heard of anyone being able to hear animal thoughts."

I scoffed under my breath and spun toward the window. I peered out into the night, then squinted at the sight of a moving truck pulling up in our driveway.

"Ah," Vlad said. "Our coffins and such have arrived."

Right. Because we needed those tonight. The red taillights shone in the darkness, signaling their approach. I didn't want to discuss this in front of human movers, but I certainly wasn't ready to move on from the conversation either. This explanation was the only one that made sense to me. My thoughts kept centering on the K-9 dog in the patrol car. I knew without a doubt I'd heard that silly beast's thoughts. I'd heard it so clearly that I'd wondered if it was the cop's partner.

I was right about this. I knew it. It all lined up, regardless of my age.

Turning away from the window, I stared at Vlad. I needed to prove it to both of us. The way I saw it, we had a few options. Either we could randomly stalk the sidewalks in search of someone's pet Fluffy to see if I heard anything, or....

"Shift," I said.

Vlad's brows winged upward. "Excuse me?"

"I need to confirm this. Need to know without a doubt that I'm hearing animal thoughts. I've never been able to converse with you when in your animal form. But I'll bet dollars to donuts I can now."

"Anna, I may be able to shift, but I'm not a true animal."

"Maybe that won't matter. We won't know until we test this theory."

Vlad sighed, but eventually nodded. "If this will make you happy."

"So happy," I groused.

"You know, I may be old, but I'm not ignorant to sarcasm."

I rose on my tiptoes and kissed him. "I know. Now shift."

"When did you become so bossy?"

I chuckled, then dipped my fingers under his shirt and pushed it up. "I can be sweeter if you'd like. Oh so sweeter."

"Well, you did promise to rip my clothes off tonight."

"Once the movers are gone. Can't scandalize the poor humans, now can we?"

Vlad leaned down and brushed the tip of his nose against mine. "I could take care of them right now, if you wish."

"Hmm, tempting. But right now, I want you to shift. As soon as we confirm this, we can do whatever you like for the rest of the night."

Vlad's brows waggled at me. "The rest of the night?"

"Mm-hmm. Hours and hours of mindless pleasure." So long as the movers had a couch or bed in their truck.

"That sounds..."

"Heavenly," I teased. "Now, strip and shift, baby."

Vlad chuckled, then grabbed the bottom of his shirt and tugged it over his head. I took a moment to admire his beauty before I slipped my fingers into the waist of his slacks. Just because he had a task didn't mean I couldn't assist.

"What happened to me shifting," he murmured, nuzzling his nose against my throat.

"You're still gonna shift. I'm just admiring the view."

He hummed under his breath, then hooked his pants on his thumbs and shoved them down. The movers hadn't yet left their truck, but I bent an ear in their direction, determined not to let yet another person surprise us tonight.

Once nekkid, Vlad called upon whatever magic let him shift. The air popped a second before his glorious male form vanished and a cute little bat hovered before me.

I chuckled and *booped* his teeny black nose. I'd always loved bats as a child. I had memories of chasing them around the attic in my parent's house, and Lucy and I watching them from our treehouse at night. We'd always left a single light on to watch as they streaked through the air. They looked like winged puppies, and who didn't love puppies?

"Anna?"

Vlad's voice resounded through my head.

I gasped and cupped my mouth. Holy shit. I was right! "I—I can hear you..."

Vlad's beady eyes blinked at me. *"You can hear my thoughts?"*

I nodded. "Cripes, Vlad. I was right! I was fucking right!"

Vlad's wings beat against the air, pushing my hair back from my face. He stared at me, wonder filling those dark eyes. Seconds later, the air popped once more, and a wolf stood before me, his silvery coat catching what little moonlight streamed through the windows.

"And now?"

I laughed and nodded again. "Oh, wow. This is insane. Vlad, I can hear animal thoughts!" This was astounding, in a boring kind of way. I mean, if I'd had a choice, I would want the ability to fly or move things telekinetically. What good could come of hearing animal thoughts? Honestly, it just sounded like a perpetual headache. But at the same time, I had my first gift! At less than half a year old.

"We need to keep this a secret," Vlad ordered, his grim tone popping my small bubble.

"Why?"

"If the queen learns that you've already developed

your first gift, it'll just give her another reason to hate you. You're threatening enough without suggesting you might be more powerful than most other vampires."

"Pfft. Power has nothing to do with it. It's just because of Petrik. I'm guessing the mixed cocktail of his blood and yours probably did it. Accelerated the process."

He crooked his silky soft head and studied me with ice-blue eyes. Vlad's wolf form was my absolute favorite of the two. Beautiful didn't begin to describe him like this.

"Exactly. It makes you a threat. How do you feel otherwise?" He pressed his nose against my stomach and snuffled. It made me giggle. *"No yearnings for ancient blood?"*

"Only yours," I teased, brushing his nose away from my navel. My desire for Vlad went far deeper than a simple feeding.

"That's a relief," he said, his voice resounding in my head. *"But we must keep this between ourselves. Word would spread and I can only imagine the fallout."*

"What about Lucy?"

His lips curled up over his long fangs, but he nodded his assent. *"Fine."*

"And Sam?"

Vlad snarled, his lips curling up over fangs longer than my fingers. *"Absolutely not. The man is a werewolf, our natural enemy, and you want to hand him this information? That you might be able to hear his thoughts, and the thoughts of his brethren, when they're in wolf form? Think what they might do when they learn that information. Their secrets won't be secret anymore."*

Only when they were in animal form. But I understood his point. "Geez, okay. No Sam, then."

Vlad huffed. *"Thank you."*

Movement pricked at my ears, and I glanced out the window to see the movers unloading the back of the truck. They unloaded my coffin first and set it down on the grass. I swear, every kitchen light in the neighborhood suddenly flicked on at the same time. Nosy busybodies watching as the new local vampires had their coffins delivered. I knew this had to be unusual for them, but my god, they had their noses practically flush against their windows in an attempt to catch sight of us.

Shaking my head, I placed my hand on the top of Vlad's head and stroked his fur. I was the only person he let do this. Lucy had tried once a few months ago, and she'd nearly lost a hand to his massive teeth. *All the better to eat you with, my dear*.

"Might wanna shift back and get dressed. The movers are about to start carrying stuff inside."

Vlad side-eyed the door, then with a quiet huff, he trotted over to the front door and sat. I bit back my laughter and watched as he waited for them to enter. The instant they approached the porch, Vlad stood and yawned, showing off his big ole teeth.

The instant the movers opened the door, they shrieked and fell back on their asses, scrambling to escape the porch. I doubled over with laughter, my hand cupping my stomach. Vlad might be ancient, but his sense of humor seemed more attuned to my age. Or maybe I was just rubbing off on him. Yeah, that seemed more likely.

Vlad vanished before the movers could pick themselves up.

I strolled into the foyer and stared down at them. "The coffins need to go in the attic. Everything else you can put wherever you'd like."

"But... the wolf?" one asked.

My lips twitched with amusement. "What wolf?"

"That... wolf." They fell into a stunned silence. "I... I could have sworn there was a wolf right there."

"Last I heard, there weren't any wolves left in Louisiana."

"But..." The closest of the two movers leaned around the corner of the foyer and peered into the kitchen. Vlad was nowhere to be seen. Apparently, I'd turned the stuffy old bat into a prankster.

"Um. I... We'll get right to work then."

"Thank you."

The movers shuffled out of the house, both rubbing the back of their necks. "I could have sworn I saw a wolf."

"You and me both, brother."

"I told you this place was cursed!"

I snickered under my breath, then gathered Vlad's clothing and retreated upstairs, where I could hear him moving. With luck, he wouldn't have a need for the clothes any time soon. And yes, I paired that statement with a sly wink.

"ANIMALS? LIKE... ANIMALS?" Lucy asked.

It was the next night, and we'd agreed to meet at the coffee shop once the sun set. Lucy sat across from me, her arms crossed, and her coffee forgotten as we caught each other up. I could smell the heavenly beans and the sweet vanilla creamer, and my mouth watered. I used to love a steaming hot cup of coffee. Stupid blood diet. It robbed food of all excitement. All I could do was sit here slavering over Lucy's coffee, wishing I could steal a sip. It didn't help that I hadn't had a sip of blood since Vlad's last night, and my belly was *hungry*, nearly reaching the hangry stages. If I didn't feed soon, god help the first person to cross my path.

"Yup, animals. Threw me for a loop, let me tell you. Damn dog was sitting in the cop car, cheering Vlad on, and I couldn't figure out what the hell was happening."

Lucy snorted back a laugh, then cupped her hand over her mouth to silence the offensive sound. "I still can't believe you got caught snorking in Vlad's car."

"Oh god, call it something else, would you?"

"Like what? Making lurrrve?"

"Egads, Lucy. Even humping sounds better than that."

She snorted again, then finally took a sip of her coffee. I watched longingly, watching the motion of her throat, then quickly averted my gaze, remembering how she felt the last time I stared at her throat.

"It was nighttime," I said, shrugging. "I doubt the cop even saw anything."

Lucy choked on her coffee. "This truly would only happen to you, Anna."

"Please. Like you've never been caught by the police?"

"Having sex? Never! I would die of mortification."

She probably would too. "You're telling me nothing fantastic happened between you and Sam on your way here? The sexual tension is so thick, I'd need a sword to cut it."

"Ugh, crass." She grimaced, then sucked back at least half of her coffee, procrastinating her answer.

I merely sat back and crossed my own arms, watching her with wide open eyes. I knew this game. Lucy would keep avoiding my question until she was blue in the face. You have to make severe eye contact with her and hold that damn gaze until she cracked. Almost like a police interrogation.

"Nothing happened! I swear. We just sat there in awkward silence."

"Bullshit."

Heat colored her cheeks, proving me right. Girl was lying through her damn teeth.

"You really are the worst. Okay, fine. It wasn't

entirely silent. Mostly he talked and I sat there like a nervous wreck, too frightened to say anything. And it's your fault!"

Taken aback, I frowned. "My fault?"

"I was expecting you to be there as a buffer, to crack jokes and break the awkwardness."

I sighed. "Lucy, I can't always be there to help you overcome uncomfortable situations. And it really isn't my place to be that buffer between you and Sam. If you don't want to be with him, then you need to be open and honest with him."

"That's the thing," she said, gripping her coffee cup so tightly, I thought it might collapse inward. "I want to be with him so badly, Anna. Desperately. Like, my thighs vibrate when I'm around him."

A grin spread across my face. *Now* we were getting somewhere. And hallelujah too. I wasn't sure how much more of Saint Lucy I could take.

"Did you tell him that?"

"Oh, he knows." She scowled at the table. "Apparently, he can smell emotions just like you guys can."

I gritted my teeth to keep from laughing aloud. Lucy wouldn't appreciate that. I'd already known that, considering the man had tracked me clear across the city after Petrik had abducted me. Based on that, I think it was easy to assume they had pretty sensitive noses.

"So I can't lie to him," she groused. "He knows I'm hot for him. He knows I'm interested. How do I tell him to back off then?"

"Exactly like that," I said. "You tell him you need some space to think and come to grips with your emotions."

Something flickered behind Lucy's eyes, an emotion I couldn't quite put my finger on. Her lashes fluttered as she glanced down at her hands, a clear sign she was hiding something.

I sat straight in my chair and braced my elbows against the table. "What is it?"

"What?" she asked, playing the part of the sweet little doe.

"You're hiding something."

"Am not!"

The sudden rise of octave told me otherwise, and I didn't need to point that out to her. She'd clearly heard it.

Exasperated, she draped her torso over the table and dropped her forehead down. "Okay, so I need to tell you something. I just learned this last night."

"Okay."

She peered up at me from under her lashes. "You can't freak out."

I held my left hand up. "Scout's honor."

"Wrong hand, doofus."

"Ah, you get the point anyway."

"I ended up bringing Sam home to meet my parents."

Excitement burst in my chest. "You did not!"

"I don't know what I was thinking! I just felt so bad. I didn't wanna force him to stay in the hotel last night. I mean, you know Perish hotels, they're all roaches and mildew!"

She wasn't wrong.

"So I told him he could come with, have a home-cooked meal. I swore he'd love my mother and my mother would love him. I mean my mother loves *everyone*."

"Even me, and that's saying something," I teased.

My joke earned me a slight huff. "Well, he walked in and my mother *lost it*, Anna. She sputtered, turned red in the face, and kicked him out."

I blinked at Lucy, not sure I heard her correctly. "Your mother kicked Sam out? *Your* mother? Sweet little Elly? Your mother wouldn't know how to kick someone out if her life depended on it. She takes in strays of all kinds."

"Yes, I know my mother, thank you."

When Lucy didn't immediately continue, I rocked forward in my chair. "And? What happened?"

"Well, I asked Sam to go check into his hotel and told him I'd call him later. Then I demanded to know what was wrong. Why my mother was so upset about Sam."

"Okay. What'd she say?" Damn, the anticipation was killing me here.

"Um." Lucy's bottom lip trembled.

Oh, this was bad. This had to be really, really bad if she was about to cry. "Hey, whatever it is, it'll be alright. I can talk to your mom, or we can force her to get to know Sam. She'll come to love him like she does everyone else, I swear."

"That's the problem. My mom loves everyone," Lucy whispered. "And apparently, she loved someone else before my dad."

I frowned. I mean, that wasn't surprising, everyone had a past. But I was more confused about how this related to Sam.

"I guess the man she loved before my father was..." Lucy leaned forward and uttered in a conspiratorial whisper, "the werewolf alpha of the Mississippi pack."

Shock rendered me still. Surely, I'd misheard Lucy. Maybe the coffeehouse chatter had affected my nearly perfect hearing? Or maybe I'd picked up on someone else's conversation? It was hard to tune everyone out sometimes. "I'm sorry, but I thought I heard you say—"

"A werewolf, Anna. *And* he's my real father."

A metaphorical bomb exploded in my head. *Kaboom*. "Wait. Your father isn't your father?"

"Not biologically, but he's definitely my father. I don't care who donated the sperm."

Well, that was a very healthy way of looking at this. Kudos to her for that. "But biologically, you're..."

"Half-werewolf," she hissed. "The human half anyway, I guess. My mother says that when a human and werewolf have a baby, the child can swing either way. And I swung human. So this alpha guy discarded us like we were nothing."

Shit. That was harsh. What kind of egotistical, misogynistic asshole did something like that? Oh wait, my father did the same thing. Poor Elly. And poor Lucy.

"And she just knew Sam was a werewolf? Like that?"

Lucy nodded. "I guess it's just an instinct you develop."

"This is a lot to take in," I whispered, understanding her need for a bit of privacy right now. "So, you're the daughter of an alpha werewolf. Oh my god, please don't tell me Sam is his son or something."

"What, ew! No! Two different packs, ya goof."

"Thank goodness."

"Yeah." This time Lucy chuckled. "That would be gross. But my mom thinks Sam is playing me because he knows who my biological father is."

Wow. This was *a lot* to take in. Like a minefield worth of information to navigate. One wrong step and kablooey. "Do you believe that?"

"No. I don't know. Maybe? He swept into my life with all these claims that we were mates and destined to be together and blah, blah, blah. What kind of fool falls for that?"

"Um, me?" I said.

Lucy's eyes widened. "Oh, Anna, I didn't mean..."

"It's fine." I waved a dismissive hand. Her mind

was running at a hundred miles a minute right now. I could forgive her for this small slight.

"The thing is, I don't even think Sam knows that my dad isn't my real dad. He just knows me as Lucy Williams. I don't even know my biological father's name, so how could he? Unless the werewolves keep, like, family records or something? A history?"

"They may. We'd have to ask to know for sure."

"I don't like having these thoughts, Anna. I don't like thinking that Sam might be playing me."

My mouth twisted to the side as I contemplated her situation. First, I couldn't believe her dad wasn't her biological father. That blew my mind. And to know that her mother *knew* about the paranormal and never told us. The secrets she must have kept! The things she must know. I needed to hit her up for some learning.

"Can I offer my opinion?" I asked.

Lucy nodded eagerly.

"I don't think Sam is that kind of guy. I don't think he's the sort to use another. And I certainly don't think he'd care that you're the abandoned daughter of some Mississippi alpha. I mean, what would that knowledge even gain him? It isn't like you're a favored daughter or something. You aren't even a werewolf."

Lucy considered my words, her head slowly bobbing. "I think you're right."

"Look. The only way you're ever gonna know is if you talk to him. And if you want, Vlad and I can be there when you do. I think Vlad can tell when someone is lying. Something about the heartbeat and pulse."

"You would do that for me?"

"Girl, please. What wouldn't I do for you?"

She beamed a smile at me, one that made me feel all heroic inside.

Sadly, it was a feeling that quickly joined me in the grave when a familiar—and *very* unwelcome—voice said, "Ladies. Heard you were back in Perish."

CHAPTER FIFTEEN

THE SIGHT of Chris's leering face made me want to vomit. Not that I could, but I *wanted* to. I knew returning to Perish meant I might run into him, but I'd hoped with every last fiber of my being that I didn't. We'd hardly had the worst break up, but apparently, he'd seen things differently than me. We'd broken up right before Lucy and I left for New Orleans because he had the audacity to forbid me from going. That'd been the nail in the coffin for me. Didn't matter that he was my boyfriend, he had zero rights to forbid me from anything. So I'd shown him the door. A result he hadn't taken kindly to, according to social media.

After I became a vampire, some reporter came sniffing around Perish, trying to dig up dirt on me, and Chris had practically handed it to them all wrapped in a shiny bow. His version of revenge, I suppose.

So when I said he was the last person in the world I wanted to see, I meant it. The bastard was lucky I had a "no biting unless given consent" rule, otherwise I might have taken a big ole chomp out of him right this second in front of all these prying eyes.

"Christopher," I drawled, purposely using his full name. "To what do we owe the honor?"

"Dragged your ass home, I see." His smarmy gaze appraised me. "Like a dog with its tail tucked between its legs."

I let loose a sarcastic laugh. "Is that the best you could come up with? And how long did it take you to muster the courage to come over here? You've been here as long as we have."

"Noticed me, did'ya?"

"Don't let it go to your head." I tapped my nose. "I could smell your foul odor the second I stepped through the door." Which wasn't true, of course. The bitter coffee bean stench had sorta fried my sense of smell at the moment.

"I heard you were back. Heard you and your new vamp beau moved in last night. Everyone's talking about your coffin... Is that what you really sleep in?"

I rolled my eyes. "Man, you really need to work on your insults. If that's seriously the best you got—"

He leaned close, his hands braced on the top of the table. The man knew how to invade someone's personal space, that was for sure. Sadly, he didn't realize that he'd woken the beast within. The one hungry for blood.

"No, an insult would be to call you necrophiliac coffin bait. You're literally nothing more than the walking dead now. A piece of trash that doesn't know how to stay dead. I said you were going to get yourself killed by going to New Orleans, and you laughed in my face. Lo and behold, hey? How the mighty have fallen. So, who's laughing now, Anna? You're nothing more than a filthy leech, sucking the life out of everyone around you."

Anger uncoiled within me, burning my synapses until nothing remained but an irate vampire staring into the eyes of an ex she now hated. I felt the monster within come to life, felt it stretch its limbs out as though waking from a deep slumber. The snack in front of me had dangled himself too close for comfort.

"You might want to back the fuck up," I snarled.

Chris's mouth spread into a victorious grin, then froze the instant his flight or fight instincts kicked in. I saw it in his eyes, the moment he realized he'd become prey. His throat was in pure striking distance, and I was hungry. Oh, I wanted nothing more than to strike like a viper and bury my fangs jugular deep.

With Vlad giving his harem the weekend off, I had no one to feed from tonight. Which meant my stomach was rumbling and my inner vampire was displeased. Then here came this prince, offering the juiciest vein I'd ever seen.

"Chris," Lucy said, her voice soft and low so as not to set me off. "I highly suggest you back down. Slowly. No sudden movements. I don't think she's fed yet tonight."

The idiot made the mistake of glancing away. And the second he averted his gaze, I lunged. My hand gripped his throat, and before I could even consider my actions, I whirled him around and slammed his back down onto the table. Chris whimpered and struggled against me, his fingernails clawing at my arms. But I barely felt it, a touch lost to my blood lust. He was weak, defenseless, and had pissed off a hungry vampire. Why shouldn't I take a bite?

"Anna," Lucy whispered. "People are watching."

"Let them," I growled.

My eyes zeroed in on that blue throbbing vein, my parched mouth suddenly salivating at the sight of it like one of Pavlov's dogs. One taste was all I needed. It wouldn't take long at all.

"Anna!" Lucy gripped my wrist. "You only drink from the consenting, remember?"

"He hasn't said no yet."

Chris's wide, terrified eyes bounced between the two of us. His lips parted as he panted for breath. He tried to speak, but my hand squeezed his throat just a little harder. He couldn't say no if he couldn't talk.

"Maybe he wants this," I murmured, caressing his pale cheek with my fingernails. "Maybe he intended to anger me. Maybe he wants my teeth buried in him. *Maybe* I'm not the only coffin bait here."

I loosened my grip, and Chris immediately sputtered for air. "I—I didn't mean it." He choked on a cough. "I'm sorry, I—Ohhhh..."

An acrid stench perfumed the air. It rose above all the coffee beans and slapped me in the face. I blinked, then stared down at the junction of his legs, where a stain began to slowly spread through his khakis.

"Jesus," Lucy laughed, then clapped a hand over her mouth. "You literally made the guy piss his pants from fear. Can you let him go now, please? People are recording this."

"I can't be seen on videos," I said, shrugging, wondering how much further to take this.

"Well, I can! And I really don't want to be the focus on all the stupid vamp sites now."

I didn't tell her it was too late. Guaranteed the videos would be online within ten minutes. The internet loved anything vampire related right now. Instant fame.

With a slow sigh, I released Chris's throat and straightened. Sure enough, everyone around had whipped their phones out and recorded everything. Not a single soul had thought to assist Chris. No, instead they'd opted for their five minutes of fame by recording this little transgression.

Typical humans.

"Let's go." Lucy tugged on my arm. "We definitely need to find you a willing meal before you do something to Chris that you'll regret."

With what I hoped was an evil grin, I braced my hands on either side of Chris's head and leaned in, hoping I'd successfully mirrored his power pose from earlier. "Next time you want to run your mouth, think about who you're talking to. Running your mouth about me will just get you dead, get it?"

His eyes widened before he started nodding frantically.

On that note, I followed Lucy out of the coffee shop. The second the door closed behind us, we both burst into nervous laughter. I had a feeling the coffee shop would permanently ban us, but it was completely worth it just to see Chris's face.

"He totally pissed himself!" Lucy said, her shoulders shaking uncontrollably. "Like, that's on video. He peed his pants!"

"What can I say?" I brushed imaginary lint off my shoulders. "I'm terrifying."

"Oh, undeniably. I actually thought you were going to bite him at first. Your eyes got this unnatural glint, like you suddenly saw him as prey. Freaky!"

I didn't admit aloud that I'd considered feeding off Chris, even if it'd only been a fleeting thought. Lucy didn't need to know that my control had slipped, all because he'd angered me. I wanted to think I had better control of my temper, but truth be told, even as a human, I'd been a bit hotheaded. I couldn't imagine that changing just because I had fangs now.

"Speaking of, where are you and Vlad intending on eating while here?"

My mouth pursed. "I'm not sure. There's nothing quite like The Vampire Lounge here. I wish he hadn't given the harem the weekend off. Even one of them would have been a big help. The movers were unloading furniture all day today. Thankfully, they didn't disturb our sleep, but it would have been nice to have someone there to direct them."

Lucy nodded. "I still can't believe he bought the Barker house."

"Me too," I chuckled. "But he was right. It absolutely isn't haunted. Unless you consider the bats."

"Did they come back?"

I shook my head and started walking down the street. "The place was empty when we woke. I don't know if they sensed us and decided not to return or what."

"Next time you see an animal, you should try talking to it, see if they understand you as well."

"Because that's what I need, people catching me having an imaginary conversation with a random stray cat in the middle of the street."

Lucy laughed. "I'd definitely pay to see that. What are your plans for the rest of the night?"

"We have to meet with my dad," I said, wincing. "Wanna come? You can be our buffer. You know how my dad and his little tramp are."

"You couldn't pay me enough to tag along. I know exactly how you and your dad are, and I know it isn't going to be a pretty visit. Besides, I have my own daddy issues to sort out."

Fair enough. I slowed and placed a hand on her arm. "You know that this alpha werewolf isn't your father, right? Doesn't matter that you came from his sperm, he's nothing to you. Your father raised you, loved you, kissed your skinned knees, held you when you cried—"

"I know, Anna," Lucy said, laughing. "Surprisingly, I don't even care that he isn't my biological father. He's still my daddy. This information changes nothing for me."

"Good," I said.

"Don't get me wrong. I'm pissed my mom and dad lied, but I'm not going to let this information ruin our relationship."

"Are you gonna go looking for this werewolf?"

Her face knotted. "I haven't decided yet."

"Well, let's start with asking Sam if he knew anything about this and then we can go from there."

Lucy nodded. "Tomorrow. You have enough on

your plate tonight. Tonight, I just want to talk to my mom again and get all the information I can."

I was just about to agree when I remembered my mother had asked me to come back again tomorrow night. "Has to be late tomorrow night. I have to go see Caleb. Ugh."

Lucy grimaced. "That's fine. Caleb, really?"

I nodded. "Mom didn't give me much of a choice."

"Joy. What are you going to do for blood tonight?"

I considered her question. I didn't relish the idea of walking down the street, hollering at anyone who passed to feed me, but next to that, I had no idea how to go about finding a meal. It was so much easier in New Orleans, thanks to the inherent mystical atmosphere.

"I'll figure something out," I told her. "Maybe Vlad has a plan already. But I definitely need to be fed before arriving at my dad's, otherwise, I can't promise I won't bite his wife."

Lucy looped an arm around my waist and rested her head on my shoulder. "You know I'd offer, but..."

"I know, and don't feel guilty about not wanting to feed me. That's definitely not a path I want us to go down."

She sighed and straightened. "All right. Well, text me once you leave your dad's. I want to know all about it. I'll swing by your place tomorrow before sunset with Sam."

I gave her a half-hug, then turned toward the Barker house—er, Vlad's and my place. That was going to take some time to get used to. "Night, Luce."

"Night!"

Now... time to find a quick nip of blood. Otherwise, I couldn't be held responsible for what happened tonight.

THE INSTANT I neared our house, I knew something was wrong. I couldn't explain it. Just this shiver that ran down my spine and the feeling that someone was watching me. I stopped on the porch, then bent down to fiddle with my shoes. They hardly needed the adjustment, but it gave me a chance to inspect my surroundings.

Sound wise, I only heard the wind and aimless chatter in our many neighbor's houses. Talk of bedtime and tomorrow's plans. All normal considering the time—half past ten. Next, I gave the air a sniff, drawing the myriad of scents deep into my nose, yet nothing stood out to me. Moss, leaves, swamp, nothing out of the ordinary.

Fingers still pretending to adjust my straps, I pivoted slightly on the porch. Doing so gave me a clearer view of the street. But even from this angle, everything looked right. A few neighbors stood on their porches, their silhouettes illuminated by dim cigarette light. Others sat on their porch swings, swirling their brandy and wineglasses. A third sat on a rickety bench, reading a book beneath the light.

All living their normal lives.

Yet, still, something felt off. Somehow, I *knew* without a doubt someone was watching me. My brows furrowed as an uncomfortable thought wriggled through my head. Maybe *everyone* was watching me. Which wouldn't surprise me, given the current climate. The last vlog Lucy and I posted had now reached two million viewers. And I would have bet any money there were a ton of videos going up right this second of me and Chris at the coffee house. The neighbors currently peering at their smartphones were probably watching it right now, then me, waiting to see what I did next. All this had to be super exciting for the sleepy town of Perish.

So, maybe that was all this was. The unnerving realization that all eyes were on me. Fame comes at a price, right? I'd learned that lesson at the beginning of all this. And seeing how Perish didn't receive many "VIP" visitors, I needed to expect this.

I dusted off the tips of my shoes and rose with a sigh. When nothing out of the ordinary happened, I opened the door and slipped inside. The second I closed the door, that slimy feeling of being watched vanished, and I stretched out a kink in my neck.

At least it was quiet in here. Safe.

"Anna?" Vlad called out.

I toed off my shoes, then followed the sound of his voice into the kitchen, my bare feet silent on the tiled floor. I found him seated at our spiffy new dining room table with a glass of red in front of him—and no, I didn't mean wine.

When I'd woken this afternoon, I'd found the entire house all furnished, thanks to the moving guys. Vlad must have tipped them well to set it all up for us. That or he'd hired an interior decorator. Huh. Never thought to ask. I'd merely been grateful to have a furnished house complete with books to read to pass the time while waiting for sunset. I'd given Vlad a grateful kiss as he brushed his fangs and hair before I'd taken off to go meet Lucy.

"Mmm," I hummed as I lifted his glass to my nose. "Where'd you get this from?"

"Bottled," he said. "They sell some in town. I had it delivered an hour or so ago."

My gaze drifted to the half-emptied bottle on the table, and I nodded, now understanding how we'd feed while in Perish. Vlad had purchased these bottles before. They belonged to a new company that had sprouted up almost immediately after vampires joined society. Much like donating blood to hospitals, the company farmed fresh blood from volunteers, then bottled it up for the night and sold it to us vamp-folk. Far better than bagged, and only slightly less delicious than fresh from the tap.

Throughout history, humans had always excelled at innovation, and it seemed they'd taken the concept and run with it these past few months. Every time I turned around, there seemed to be a new company idea catering to my kind.

"O positive," I murmured before resting my lips against the cool glass and draining it dry. The feel of fresh blood coating my throat soothed the inner beast within, *and* my murderous intentions. Interestingly, I felt a bit ashamed now for lashing out at Chris. Not that he hadn't deserved it. But the poor guy had literally pissed his pants on video, which guaranteed it was already online. His friends would never let it down.

"By all means," Vlad teased with a wry smile. "Help yourself."

I grabbed the bottle, topped up his glass, then held it to his mouth. His lips twitched, but he played along, allowing me to offer him a sip.

Once finished, he looped an arm around my waist and guided me into his lap, my favorite place ever. "How did your visit with Lucy go?"

I snuggled into his chest and gave him a quick rundown of everything Lucy had told me. Vlad made noises where appropriate, appeared shocked when I mentioned her bloodline, then stiffened when I started to talk about Chris.

When we reached the part about necrophiliac coffin bait and how he called me a leech, Vlad grew deathly still. For a moment, I wondered if I'd just signed Chris's death sentence.

Eventually, Vlad's tension bled away, and his body relaxed. "Be glad I wasn't there."

His statement brought a rousing smile to my lips as I pictured that scenario. Vlad wouldn't have publicly lashed out at Chris like I had, but that didn't mean he wouldn't have handled the situation. I just suspected he would have handled it privately. Somewhere Chris would never again see the light of day. Not that Vlad would murder him... I didn't think. Sometimes, I couldn't tell. The man had beheaded one of his oldest friend's for harming me, after all.

"And how are you tonight?" I asked. "Any more visions last night?"

His expression shuttered. "Unfortunately."

I splayed a hand against his chest and offered him a few soothing caresses. "Any new information?"

"Yes, but nothing helpful. Two shadows, working in tandem. They attack you, kill you, and walk away. And I'm not there. I don't understand. I'm *not* there."

"Maybe it's just a dream."

"It's a vision," he said sharply. "I know the difference."

I nodded. Of that, I had no doubt. I'd only hoped to comfort him. So, I decided to change the topic. "You haven't noticed anything strange tonight, have you?"

"Strange how?"

I tucked into his chest and rested my head in the crook of his shoulder. "I'm not quite sure. But before I came inside, I swear, I could feel someone watching me."

Vlad leaned to the side and studied me. After discussing his vision, I had to imagine this conversation was going to put him on edge. "Where?"

"I couldn't place it. I didn't smell or hear anything odd, but I definitely had this feeling. Like eyes on the back of my neck. You know that feeling? Like you've been marked as prey?"

All emotion vanished from Vlad's face. "No."

I almost laughed. Of course he hadn't experienced that before. He was never prey.

"Did you feel like you were in danger?"

"Hmm. No, I don't think so." I sighed and snuggled back into him. "It's probably just all in my head. Everyone is watching us right now. That's probably all I'm feeling."

He pulled me tight against him. "Let me know if you feel it again."

I agreed with a small smile. I loved that he took me at my word and didn't suggest it was all in my imagination. Vlad was the sort who knew not to discount things simply because they didn't make sense. He trusted my instincts. As I did his.

A quick glance at the clock told me we had places to go and people to see. "Think we can blow off my father?" I asked. Our night had just begun, and honestly, the last thing I wanted to do was spend it with my estranged father and his two-bit whore—

oh, excuse me, wife. "Just think. We could stay here, wrapped up in each other, touching, kissing—"

"Careful what you wish for," Vlad jested. "Keep heading in that direction, and we might not make it out of the house tonight."

"What a shame." I chuckled.

"While I would love nothing more than for us to be alone tonight, I do think we should make an appearance, even if only for a few minutes. Your father would be insulted if we didn't show, don't you think?"

"Relieved is probably more accurate," I muttered. "All he cares about are his wife's new boobs and how much he can play with them."

"I sincerely hope your father isn't that immature." Vlad tilted his head. "Or that crass."

"He's both. The man cheated on my mother for three years before she confronted him. When she did, he simply shrugged and said he was relieved she finally knew, so he could stop hiding. No remorse for breaking his wife's heart or destroying his family. Just relief. Then he kicked us out of our family home and took all his money with him. Caleb and I were already adults, so there was no need for child support, and thanks to my mother's inheritance from her parents, she was denied alimony. So off my father went, spending all his money on his mistress-turned-wife's new boobs, face, teeth, you name it."

"Charming."

"Next came a pool installation in his backyard. After that, a fancy new sports car. The man destroyed our lives and got off scot-free."

"It's a wonder you turned out so perfect," Vlad murmured.

Inwardly, I melted. But outwardly, I chuckled and kissed his cheek. "Now who's the charmer?"

"I aim to please." After a gentle kiss atop my head, he scooted me off his lap and rose. "Shall we get this over with?"

"If we must," I said with a sigh.

"We must. But if it improves your mood, just imagine all the depraved things I intend to do to you once we return home. Such thoughts should help get me through the night."

I sputtered out a laugh and swatted at Vlad's arm. "You're incorrigible!"

"I learned from the best." He offered me another kiss, then gestured to my shoes.

As I slipped my feet in, I watched Vlad step out onto the porch and scan our surroundings, likely searching for some unknown threat. His devotion continuously stirred up emotions within me. And I couldn't help but compare him to my father. Of the three of us, Vlad and I were vampires, but my father was the true monster. At least with Vlad at my side, I felt like I could handle anything.

Ah, the silly lies we tell ourselves.

CHAPTER SIXTEEN

WE'D MADE it a whole whopping ten minutes into the supposed "get-together" before I wanted to rip out some throats. Excuse me, no. I misspoke. Not *some* throats. Just one very particular throat smeared in some fancy Hermès perfume and wrapped like a Christmas tree in the gaudiest diamond choker I'd ever seen.

Christina had certainly dressed for the occasion, even a vamp baby like me could see that. She'd dolled her neck up in every way she could think of. The only thing lacking was a literal "come bite me" sign pinned to her throat.

And all that attractive window dressing seemed intended for one person in particular.

Vlad.

Now, I was hardly a possessive or jealous woman—I prided myself on that—but Christina seemed incapable of keeping her mitts to herself. As though her blatant scent and jewelry hadn't been invitation enough, she'd found a reason to touch Vlad not once, not twice, but eight times. And every single time, she'd waited until my father's attention was diverted.

Not mine though. Oh no. I was blessed enough to witness every arm stroke and finger brush, along with the subtle lean-ins and smiles. If she wasn't flashing her throat, she was brandishing her breasts or displaying those pearly whites. Both of which my father had paid for.

Classy, right?

If she kept this up, I was gonna have to show her *my* teeth. The ones I tended to sink into people's jugulars. Just sayin'.

Fortunately, Vlad was all too aware of Christina's attentions. My father seemed the only blind one in the room. When the ninth touch came, I gave her a slow, dangerous blink, and flashed my fangs in a wide smile.

"Christina," I purred. "How long have you and my father been together now?"

"Oh..." Heat flushed her cheeks as she shot Vlad

a surreptitious glance. "How long has it been, sweetheart? About ten years now?"

"Nine, darling," he mumbled.

Nine. Confirming that they'd definitely begun their whirlwind affair when I was the tender age of fifteen. Explained why he'd missed all my extracurricular activities.

I shot my father a glare, but his back was still to me as he washed their dinner dishes in the sink. He'd barely paid me any attention tonight. And I'd yet to figure out the exact reason why. Either he wasn't comfortable with my new vampire existence, or he honestly didn't give enough shit about me to even look at me. Considering my father and I barely ever spoke—even before my transition—I would bet all my money on the latter.

Such a sweet, caring man. *Cue snorting laugh.*

"Oh, right. Nine," she said with a smile so sweet, it gave me a toothache. "But you don't want to hear about us!" She stroked the back of Vlad's hand with the tip of her index finger.

I ground my teeth, about to say something, when Vlad simply sighed and brushed her advances away like she was an annoying gnat. The sight of her wide, unblinking eyes almost made me laugh. She shot him a stunned look, as though confused someone would dare reject her. My father might have turned her into his little doll, but her intolerable personality rotted through her exterior.

Vlad, on the other hand, barely spared her glance. Instead, he looped his arm around the back of my chair and idly stroked my shoulder.

Now, I was the one smiling oh so sweetly.

Of course, his dismissal didn't sway her. Nerp. What Christina wanted, Christina got. That'd always been her way. When I'd first learned of their affair, I'd asked her how she could sleep with a married man. Her answer had been, "He's cheating on your mother, not me." Such a charmer.

And she wondered why we absolutely loathed her.

"So, tell us about yourself, Vlad." She reached toward him once more, almost as though she couldn't help herself.

That was the last straw.

"Woman, do you want to lose that hand?" I snapped.

She startled, her heavily lined eyes snapping to mine. "Excuse me?"

My father finally turned away from the sink and shot us a quick, but hazy glance. One that told me he was already half-in-the-bag. The man seemed completely oblivious to his wife's actions right now. Which had me wondering how often this happened. Had the tables turned on him? Was his former mistress sleeping around? Le gasp, right?

This woman had destroyed my family. She'd ripped through it like Hurricane Katrina and left nothing in her wake. I absolutely despised her. Tonight was about playing nice and seeing my father, but I didn't give a shit about his wife. Not that he understood or cared about our feelings though. So, her flirtatious advances were risking her life, and I had absolutely zero qualms about telling her that.

"Ever heard the saying 'eyes bigger than the stomach'?" I asked.

"Anna..." Vlad murmured.

Christina glanced between us, but nodded.

"Take that concept and apply it here," I warned her. My lips curled into what I hoped was a psychotic smile. One that said "fuck with me and I'll eat your face off."

Seemed my warning worked because she wrenched her hand back from Vlad and tucked it under her rear.

"Um." She straightened her posture and cleared her throat. "So, Vlad, you were telling us about yourself?"

"I wasn't actually." His fingers continued to doodle on my bare shoulder. "Perhaps you'd rather hear about Anna."

Christina scowled at us both. Guaranteed, the last thing she wanted was to hear about me. I was the fly in her ointment, and the one who made her relationship with my father just that bit harder. I took pride in that small accomplishment. They'd made our lives difficult. Why couldn't I return the favor? Maybe it was petty, but sometimes, being petty felt really damn good.

"Personally, I'd rather hear about you, Dad," I said. The bastard hadn't even bothered calling me after I'd turned into a vampire. Such love. "We've only spoken like once this year. I assume you've been busy?"

"No more so than normal," he mumbled, his back still facing me as he continued to wash their dishes.

"Okay. What have you been up to, then?"

He half-shrugged, then pushed his cuffed sleeves further up past his elbows. "Same as always. Work and whatnot."

I shot Vlad an exasperated glance, one he acknowledged with an encouraging nod.

"Dad, I'm only here for the weekend. Could you maybe... try? I know that's asking a lot—"

He sighed and dropped the plate back into the water. "Don't start, Anna. I'm not in the mood tonight."

"To what, exactly? Converse with me? Or even just look at me?"

"I can't," he confessed, his voice barely above a whisper.

"Can't what?"

He blew out a heavy breath, one that perfumed the air with alcohol. Yup, he'd definitely had a few before our arrival tonight. Calming himself after a busy workday? Or preparing himself for this visit? I had a feeling I wouldn't like the answer if I asked.

"Can't *what*, Dad?" I demanded.

"Can't look at you!" he shouted, slamming his palms down on the counter. He dropped his head, and his shoulders rounded inward while he panted for breath.

Yeah, I knew I wouldn't like the answer. But shame on me for asking, right?

Vlad's hand gripped my arm to keep me from rising to my feet. Instead, I nodded and blew out a completely unnecessary breath. It was no secret that my father and I weren't particularly close. Even as a child, I hadn't wanted much to do with him. His busy work schedule had created the divide between us, but his cavalier attitude had widened it. But if I had to guess, I'd say me becoming a vampire didn't jibe with him.

All that remained was deciding whether we left. One half of me wanted to stay. And no, not to repair our relationship, but rather just as punishment. To annoy him. To force him to spend time with the daughter he'd ignored her whole life, the one he couldn't bear to look at right now. The other half of me wanted to bail. Why put myself through this? Why bother?

The man hadn't even bothered to call to check up on me after Vlad turned me. Even before that, he'd chosen his new life and family, and hadn't been shy about his choice. Some families survive divorce. The parents make the effort to separate amicably, and everyone maintains a polite demeanor. I didn't know of any personally, but I'd heard of them. On the news or some shit.

My family had gone full kamikaze. Imagine World War II. And thanks to my father's position in the political arena, the rest of the town had been dragged along for the ride. Sides were chosen and bonds were broken. Such as mine and my father's.

He and Caleb had tried for a bit. But after a while, they'd called it. DOA. Neither had enough interest in the other to keep on trying. So why continue torturing ourselves, right? Just shout out the time of death and abandon ship. Save everyone the hassle.

Well, this was the result of that.

A tumultuous relationship where a father couldn't even bear to look at his daughter. Not exactly the loving daddy-daughter relationship most people hope for.

"We couldn't even give you a funeral," he whispered.

Anger erupted within me. I took Vlad's hand and pushed to my feet. "Bye, Dad."

"What?" He whirled around and finally made eye contact with me. "You're leaving?"

"Yes. I'm not going to stand around here and listen to you while you mourn me or some morbid shit like that."

"Language!" Christina snapped.

"Bite. Me."

Her face paled. I guess the sight of my fangs had stuck with her because she simply swallowed and pouted in her chair like a petulant child.

"I refuse to stand here and cry with you, not when I'm not actually dead. I'm standing right fucking here"—I shot Christina a warning glance before she could utter a word—"and even if I weren't, you don't give two shits about me. So, I'm not going to listen to you bemoan and complain about how you lost your daughter. You lost me a hell of a long time ago, you're just too fucking stupid to see it."

My hand shot to my mouth as the room fell into stark silence.

"Perhaps we should leave," Vlad suggested.

I slowly nodded, my eyes clashing with my father's. He seemed too stunned to speak, a sentiment I definitely shared. I'd never spoken to him like that before, and I wasn't quite sure how I felt about it. At least it was honest. And that had to count for something, right?

My mouth opened, but nothing came out. And since my father seemed less inclined to speak, I took Vlad's hand and let him lead me out the front door.

And this time, I didn't look back.

I SANK into our new luxurious Chesterfield sofa and just sighed. We'd been gone two hours, tops. Honestly, we should have stayed home, could have enjoyed two hours of mindlessly pleasuring each other. Didn't that sound better than arguing with my dad and watching his wife try to feel up Vlad? Sounds a hell of a lot better to me.

"I must say..." Vlad kneeled before me and eased off my shoes. Knowing their worth and how much my shoe wear meant to me, he gently placed them aside before he started kneading my calves. The instant his fingers dug in, I moaned and practically melted into a puddle of goo on our ridiculously expensive couch. "Your father's quite the—"

"Asshole," I mumbled. "Don't say I didn't warn you."

"You very much did."

"He's always been like that. Everything is always about him, all the time. If he was worth even a grain of salt, he would have at least texted an apology or called or something after we left."

"And did he?"

I plundered my phone from my purse and held it up so Vlad could see the missed notifications screen. A few texts from Lucy, a missed email, and a phone call from my mother. Nada from dear old dad. As always.

"You know what? Let's just forget about him," I said, pushing up from the couch. "The man literally means nothing to me. So why let him ruin our night, right? Let's have a dance party, instead. A naked dance party, of course."

Vlad blinked. "I have absolutely no idea what that is."

"It's exactly what it sounds like. I slap on some music—from my generation—and we strip and dance."

"No."

Vlad's resounding response made me laugh. I could tell from his stern expression there would be no negotiating this either. If negotiation wouldn't get me what I wanted—which was Vlad in his birthday suit—then maybe I needed to lead by example.

With a wink, I turned to our new sound system and quickly found the song I wanted. The dulcet tones of Harry Style's "Watermelon Sugar" swept through the house, and I spun back to Vlad, grinning. It wasn't my favorite song, but even I had to admit, it had a great beat. Something you could wiggle your hips and ass too. Vlad immediately noticed the instant I started grooving. I danced my way up to him, then hooked my thumbs in my pants and slowly started pushing them down.

"Anna, what in the world are you doing?"

I grinned, then stepped out of my pants and spun around, grinding my bottom against him.

"Anna..."

I cast a sly glance over my shoulder. "Yes, Vlad?"

His faint growl was music to my ears. My shirt went next, casually tossed aside. I danced before him in nothing but a bra and panties, shimmying and shaking to the energetic beat.

"Well?" I asked, scootching my booty up against his groin. "You gonna join me or what?"

I needed this. Needed to blow off some pent-up steam. I didn't realize how much my relationship with my father upset me. But being upset about it wouldn't accomplish anything. Honestly, neither one of us had any interest in repairing what was broken. So fretting about it wouldn't help either. What I needed was to dance. To burn off all that excess energy. To have fun. To smile. To laugh.

"This isn't dancing," Vlad said.

But before I could argue, his hands shot out and snatched me by the waist. He pulled me flush against him, then kissed me. The passion was intense, burning through us like a wildfire. Everywhere he touched, heat followed, sparking a familiar desire. It didn't matter that we'd sated ourselves last night for hours on end. Our hunger for one another seemed endless. And I was completely okay with that. I didn't want a relationship that went stale. That became a chore. We were only three months in, so I couldn't speak for the future, but something within me told me this was forever.

Vlad grabbed my thighs and lifted, then locked my legs around his waist. He walked us back toward the couch, then slowly sat, his fingers gripping my flesh so hard, I had a feeling there'd be marks afterward. But I didn't care.

Instead, I succumbed to the kiss and the inevitable pleasure heading my way. We hadn't had a chance to break in the couch last night, but it seemed he had every intention of remedying that right now.

I moaned against his mouth as my fingers found his pants zipper. I'd just opened it when a sudden knock echoed through the door.

Gasping, I pulled back from Vlad and glanced backward.

"Are you kidding me?" I hissed. "Who the hell is knocking on our door at half-past midnight?"

Another firm knock, almost insistent. As though this person had every right to be here.

"The scent isn't familiar," Vlad said, his brows deepening.

Which meant no one from my family. I had friends here, or at least I had before New Orleans. I honestly didn't consider any of them friends anymore. Not after they'd handed over every facet of my life to the reporters. But even I could tell from a quick sniff that it wasn't anyone I knew.

"I don't know them either," I said.

A worrisome concept. Who would come knocking on our door in Perish?

"Get dressed," Vlad said, helping me to my feet.

I threw on my clothes, then followed him to the door. Vlad shot me a quick glance, then yanked it open.

There, on the other side, stood an unfamiliar man. I studied him with a frown, wondering if I should know him. Maybe he was a neighbor? He wasn't as tall as Vlad, and he was thinner. Almost anemic looking. Except he was a vampire. And one thing we vampires weren't was anemic.

"Ah, you must be Anna," the man said, his beady dark gaze appraising me as I had him.

I didn't respond. No point confirming something he apparently already knew.

"And you are?" Vlad asked.

The man barely glanced Vlad's way. Instead, his dark eyes held mine and his thin lips pressed into a thin line, as though he wasn't impressed with what he saw. Likewise, little man. Likewise.

"Well?" he demanded. "Are you going to invite me in?"

"Oh, that would be a no," I said. "Sorry, let me rephrase. That would be a hell no. My mommy taught me not to invite strangers into my house."

His upper lip curled in annoyance. "Cute."

"I try."

"I must insist."

"Insist all you want." I crossed my arms over my chest, hoping I looked every bit as intimidating as Vlad. "Until we know who you are—"

"My name is Michel," he said. "Michel Aubert."

I had every intention of commenting on his very French name when I caught the stiffening of Vlad's shoulders. Before I could ask, his arm shot out and he pushed me behind him, shielding me from sight with his body.

The last time he'd done that, we'd found ourselves squaring off against Petrik in the middle of The Vampire Lounge.

My blood ran cold.

Something was wrong then. This Michel must not be a nice guy if Vlad was that frightened.

"Michel Aubert," Vlad repeated. "How nice to finally meet you."

"And you, I suppose," he responded, his thick

French accent creeping into his words. "The queen sends her warmest regards."

Holy shit. Did he just say the queen?

"Now. Will you invite me in?" Michel asked. "Or do I need to return to England with a report of your reluctance to acquiesce?"

Oh, this sounded bad. So very, *very* bad.

I felt Vlad's muscles coiling, but instead of attacking, which he clearly wanted, he stepped back and gripped my hand, almost painfully.

"Please, come in," he said, his tone cold and unwelcome. "Inquisitor."

CHAPTER SEVENTEEN

THIS MUST BE what a panic attack felt like for a vampire. My body couldn't react physically thanks to my lack of pulse and heartbeat, but my stomach was tighter than a puckered asshole and my vision had gone all fuzzy.

Inquisitor? Had Vlad said inquisitor? As in one of the queen's most trusted warriors?

Hell. This was bad. Extremely bad. Apocalyptic bad.

I struggled to remember everything Camilla had taught me about the vampire hierarchy. I'd only skimmed the messages, thinking I could always come back to them when I needed them. Except I highly doubted this Michel would appreciate me whipping out my phone right now to see where he sat on the vampire hierarchy.

If I remembered correctly, the order consisted of the queen, her consort, their heirs, the council, then the inquisitors. She and the consort were mates, and their heirs had been hand-chosen before being turned into vampires. The council consisted of her most trusted allies, those she could rely on when she needed advice. Then came the inquisitors. Men and women she depended on to eliminate heresy and other issues contrary to her laws. They meted out justice as deemed necessary with the power of the queen backing them. Her own little Gestapo, apparently.

Suddenly, Vlad's vision came to mind. We didn't have much to go off, but he'd mentioned two shadows. Could Michel be one of them? And the queen the other?

I honestly couldn't think of a single soul in this world who wanted me dead—well, maybe Christina —except for the queen. Had she sent her inquisitor here to finish me off? To take care of her little problem? Wasn't that an inquisitor's job, after all?

Michel stepped into the house with a cocky little smile while my entire body kicked into flight mode. Vlad's hands were the only thing keeping me still when every bone in my body urged me to run. No good could come of this. I highly doubted the queen sent an inquisitor to simply investigate. This made me think of the Church in the medieval days. Their inquisitors hadn't been friendly people then either.

"Thank you for that generous welcome," Michel stated, his wry voice grating on my nerves. "I see you two have settled in rather nicely."

"How did you know where to find us?" Vlad demanded.

"We've been keeping an eye on you two for a while now."

I shook my head and scolded myself for not trusting my instincts last night. I'd felt the bastard's eyes on me, and we'd both brushed it aside like it was nothing.

"Must be nice to have such services available to you now, yes?" Michel pointed at our furniture. "Before Queen Genevieve brought us into the twenty-first century, such things like buying and furnishing a house were far more difficult to organize. We'd needed proxies to negotiate on our behalf. Men and women we employed but who remained unaware of our secret—"

"What do you want, Inquisitor?" Vlad

demanded, interrupting the man's annoying tirade. I really didn't care about the days of old.

"I assumed that would be obvious." Michel strode into our living room and studied the furnishings with what appeared to be an approving eye.

I kept my comments to myself. I might be impulsive, but I wasn't suicidal, and I had a feeling anything I said would be used against me in the vampiric court of law, if such a thing existed. Camilla had mentioned something to me earlier, about how the queen was organizing a tribunal of sorts for naughty vampires. A means of showing humans we were more than murderous bastards. But I hadn't heard much else on that front.

"Queen Genevieve insisted I come meet the elusive Miss Anna Perish on her behalf, since all the queen's invitations have gone unanswered."

"What invitations?" Vlad asked, his hand squeezing mine to keep me from speaking.

We both knew exactly which invitations Michel spoke of. The first had arrived shortly after Petrik's death, and it'd soon met a fiery ending. I hadn't let anyone else see it. Then came the second and the third. Eventually, Vlad caught on, but that didn't mean we needed to admit anything to Michel.

"Come now, Vlad. Let's not play that game." Michel turned and tsked quietly at him. "You know as well as I that the queen's council has issued multiple invitations. We're all quite curious about the result of certain recent matters. Such as the condition of one Petrik Kamen. He hasn't been seen or heard from in some months now, which is rather unusual for him considering his close relationship with the queen. Last we heard, your local reeve had issued paperwork requesting Petrik be punished for attacking a human. One Anna Perish. The same woman now standing before me. This raised many questions, ones the queen herself would like answered, had either of you responded to her summons."

"Summons or invitation?" Vlad asked. "Invitation suggests we have the right to decline."

"So, you admit you received the summons then?" Michel asked.

Vlad didn't utter another word.

But my stomach sure leaped into my throat. The queen had sent someone to investigate this whole situation. Did that mean Vlad was in danger of being punished as well? Not only for ignoring her summons, but for getting involved in this entire matter? He'd only ignored the invitation because I'd begged him to. I'd been too afraid to deal with the queen myself, so I'd opted to just ignore it all. And in doing so, I'd dragged him, and possibly Camilla, into this mess.

I couldn't let either of them pay for my stupidity. I refused to. Vlad was my sire, but we loved each other. I refused to let him take the fall for any of this. And knowing him, that was exactly what he planned to do. The man was the "throw yourself on the sword" type. No. No way would I let that happen. I loved him too much to let him sacrifice himself like that for me.

"I did it," I murmured, dragging my hand out from Vlad's. Our fingertips briefly touched before I tucked my hands into my back pockets and walked out from behind him. "I saw the invitations but got rid of them before anyone else did. Vlad had no idea."

"Anna—"

"In fact, I burned them all," I admitted, cutting Vlad off before he said or did something stupid.

Throughout all this, there was one thing I knew without a doubt: Petrik had tried to kill me. Surely, I couldn't be punished for defending myself. No court in the world would prosecute someone for that. Twice he'd tried to murder me. Was it my fault that he'd been killed in the process? That hardly made me guilty of murder. Especially considering I hadn't dealt the death blow.

"You burned the invitations?" Michel repeated.

I nodded, then met his gaze. Maybe it was time for a little honesty. Maybe they would appreciate my candor and return to England. I could hope, right?

"I'm a new vampire. Not even four months old. I had no idea the queen's invitation was a requirement instead of a request. So I burned them. That might seem stupid to you, but I was frightened. I honestly didn't know how else to respond."

"You could have written a letter, an email, made a phone call—all of which were made accessible to you when you were first turned."

Like the queen would have listened to my "no thanks" response card. This wasn't like some wedding where I could decline to show, apparently.

"Let's be real. If you're here now, that means the queen never would have accepted an email or phone call from me. So how about we stop beating around the bush and you tell us exactly what you want."

"Anna," Vlad growled.

"No. Please." Michel held up a hand, his lips curling upward. "I appreciate a little candor. Sometimes picking and choosing my words is exhausting. If Anna wishes to speak openly, I very much would like that."

My eyes narrowed for a fraction of a second. I didn't trust this new direction of Michel's. Camilla hadn't been able to teach me much about the hierarchy, but I could lean on my own education regarding the current English monarchy. It seemed safe to assume that every single thing I said would be used against me. I also suspected the queen would hear all about our little meeting right down to every last detail.

I needed to approach this carefully. Wisely. I only hoped I had it in me.

"Please," I said, gesturing to the kitchen table.

Michel marched past us to take his seat, shrugging his jacket off as he went.

I locked eyes with Vlad and gave him a small nod. We couldn't read each other's minds—at least not while in human form—but I could reassure him the only way I knew how by offering him a small kiss. It was quick and passionless, unlike anything we'd shared earlier tonight, but I felt his hand relax in mine in response. Seemed he'd needed it as much as me.

I followed Michel into the kitchen and took the

seat across from him. No way in hell he'd catch me sitting next to him.

Vlad took the seat next to me and tucked his hands under the table, where he rested one against my thigh. I reveled in the small touch, taking comfort from him. Regardless of what happened here tonight, I knew without a doubt that Vlad wouldn't let Michel hurt me. But I also needed to remember to control my temper. This wasn't just my life on the line anymore.

"Very well then." Michel folded his hands on the table. "Anna asked what I want. The answer is quite simple. I want to find out what happened to Petrik."

Cold fear struck my nerves.

Neither Vlad nor I spoke.

"I shall be perfectly frank with you, Anna. My instructions are quite clear. I'm not to leave until I learn what happened to Petrik and establish whether disciplinary action is required."

"Disciplinary action," Vlad repeated. "Such as?"

"You've been a vampire for over five hundred years," Michel said. "I believe you already know what's meant by that."

"Yes, but Anna doesn't. If you truly mean to be frank, then do so."

Michel bowed his head in concession. "If I deem

Anna's actions to be malicious in any way, it will be within my rights to arrest her."

"Arrest me?" I whispered. "And what? Send me to prison?"

"Vampires have no need for prison," Vlad commented. "Do they, Michel?"

"The queen is trying very hard to prove to the humans that we are more than soulless monsters. I admit, ever since our reveal, she's struggled in this aspect. Humans have centuries of folklore and myths, none of which paint us in a very appealing light. Quite a few politicians have expressed concern regarding our judicial system. They've stated that our process is rather brutal. Humans never understood that we need such extreme measures to maintain control of the population."

"I don't understand—"

"Vampires who are found to be too dangerous are eliminated," Vlad said, filling me in. "It's a quick, merciful death. We don't imprison criminals like humans do because there are too many risky elements at play. Our aversion to the sun, to start. Not to mention how we grow more powerful as we age. How can you lock away creatures who cannot be contained?"

"So someone who is found guilty of a crime is

punished with death," I said, stating it as clearly as possible in the hopes that they'd stop dancing around their words.

"Correct." Michel rapped his knuckles against the table, as though congratulating me. "However, the humans see our methods as barbaric. She wishes to prove them wrong. So she's attempting to implement our first court system. Vampires with legal experience have been brought into the process. Should I deem your situation requires legal action, I'm to detain you until such a hearing can be arranged."

On the one hand, at least it wasn't immediate death. That was something, right?

"Furthermore, I've also been tasked with assessing *you*, Anna."

My gaze bounced between Vlad and Michel. Vlad's hand tightened on my thigh, so I knew this couldn't be a good thing.

"How?" I asked after my hand came down on Vlad's.

"The queen asked that I determine whether you're a danger to yourself or other vampires."

I blinked. A danger? Like psychotic? I could easily prove I wasn't. "Um. Okay?"

"She has placed you in my charge for the time

being. To test your abilities as a vampire, to question you about your intentions, and to investigate your little... what's the word, vlog?"

Vlad's head cocked. "Her vlog?"

Ah. Shit. Holding back on telling Vlad was about to bite me in the ass.

"Yes. That little online channel of hers where she explores fact versus fiction and hands over all our secrets to the humans."

A forced breath rushed past my lips. "What? No, I don't—"

"Don't what?" Michel pressed. "Don't betray our kind to the humans? The last episode I watched, you very clearly explained how to kill a vampire, in great detail might I add. You compared it to the movies, explained how they were wrong, and described the correct method."

I stammered out an illogical response. He made it sound so much worse than it actually was! "It's just a vlog," I whispered. "I just talk about what it's like to be a vampire."

"And our weaknesses and strengths," Michel continued. "To..." He dug his phone out of his pocket and stared at the screen. "Three point seven million followers. Does that sound correct?"

“What? No.” I turned to stare at Vlad. “He’s making it sound so much worse than it is.”

“You’ve been working on your vlog?” he asked, his brows furrowed.

“Well, yes, but—”

“And you didn’t think to mention that to me?”

“Vlad. I meant to tell you. But with everything that’s been going on, I just... I didn’t... Lucy suggested—”

“So Lucy is involved then,” Vlad stated, his eyes turning cold.

I squeezed my eyes shut and took a moment to think about my next words. I could actually smell Vlad’s anger. It perfumed the air like a sharp spice, and I didn’t like the way it pricked at my nose.

“Lucy suggested I strike while the iron was hot. After everything we went through three months ago, it would have been stupid not to capitalize on our fame—”

Vlad laughed under his breath. “Three months ago.”

Oh my god, I was making this so much worse than it needed to be.

“During the last three months, you expect me to believe you couldn’t find a single moment to tell me you'd been working on your vlog again. And successfully, might I add."

"It's not that successful," I murmured.

"You recently had a deposit for one hundred and sixty-two thousand dollars into your bank account," Michel said.

"Christ," I cursed, not caring when both flinched. "Would you shut up for a moment? I'm trying to explain something. And what the hell right do you have to access my bank account? That's illegal!"

Vlad shook his head, then with a tight jaw, stared at Michel. "What does her job have to do with anything?"

"If I deem her vlog to be too dangerous, the queen has permitted me to issue punishment, whether monetary or otherwise."

"Otherwise? What's otherwise mean?" I asked, panic rising in my voice.

Vlad turned and finally met my gaze. I cringed at the sight of his expression. I'd never seen Vlad angry with me before, and I hoped after tonight I'd never see it again. He watched me with such disappointment in his eyes, but even worse was the hint of betrayal hiding beneath. That one stung the most.

"Meaning Michel may decide to arrest you based on your vlog alone," he finally said. "Or worse."

Or worse.

Considering our previous conversation, I immediately understood Vlad's implication. Worse could really only mean one other thing.

Guess my vlog really would be the death of me.

CHAPTER EIGHTEEN

Ugh. This night well and truly sucked. I guess visiting my father hadn't been torturous enough. Now Vlad was angry at me, and I had a French inquisitor hovering over us like an annoying little gnat I wanted to swat across the room. At least Vlad had rejected Michel's request to sleep here. We truly didn't need him seeing how early I woke. But in the meantime, I was hiding, slipping in and out of rooms whenever I heard Michel approach. He kept demanding to talk about Petrik, and I wasn't ready to have that discussion. Not after the whole vlog fiasco downstairs.

Thankfully, after the third failed attempt to corner me, he'd left to sort out his sleeping arrangements with a promise to return tomorrow night. It seriously felt like a giant sword was hanging over my head, threatening to make the cut any second now.

Once Michel left, Vlad vanished soon after, claiming he needed some space to think. About what, I had no idea, but I didn't like the sound of it.

My phone rang, distracting me from those dark thoughts. I glanced at the screen and almost smiled at the sight of Camilla's name.

"Pissed off your old man, hmm?" she said the instant I took the call.

"What? How do you know about that?"

"Vlad phoned me an hour ago," she admitted. "Updated me on the night's events. Asked me to check into your vlog to see what I could find. The man wouldn't know how to google something if his life depended on it. And oh, look, it does."

I sighed. "He could have just asked me."

"Yes, well, that's what happens when you keep secrets. You anger those you care about. How about you tell me about it instead."

My eyes fluttered shut. I was starting to wish I'd never revamped it. I'd even gone so far as to blame Lucy for forcing me into it. Almost texted her that same accusation, but thankfully smartened up before pissing off my best friend the same night I pissed off my boyfriend.

The only person to blame here was me. So, I needed to suck it up, own my mistake, and apologize. I just needed to get Vlad to speak to me. But he was too busy avoiding me, like I was Michel.

"This whole thing is a mess," I mumbled.

"Planning on cleaning it up?" she asked.

My fingers tightened around my phone. When all this began, I'd hated Camilla. She was so beautiful, like an Egyptian goddess come to life. Her sun-kissed skin and long, dark hair had probably been the envy of most women when she was alive. But her attitude sucked. She was sarcastic and sometimes purposely malicious. But I'd come to expect that from her now, and almost idolized her viciousness. I never thought she'd become a friend, but here we were, gabbing on the phone together in the middle of the night, like some slumber party.

"He won't talk to me," I said, resting one hand under my head.

"Oh, sweetie. He doesn't need to talk. He needs to listen."

I chuckled and shook my head. "Tell him that."

"Not in my job description. So, rumor has it you've been giving away vampire secrets?"

"No!" I grunted loudly and shook my head. "I swear, I didn't! *Everyone* knows how to kill a vampire, Camilla! Seriously. Everyone knows about stakes and decapitation and fire. So why is it so bad that I simply confirmed it? How is it any different from someone walking down the street, thinking to themselves, I bet a stake could kill a vampire?"

"I don't think it's the information so much as you not telling him," she said. "He feels betrayed."

"Yeah, I get that. But it's not like I gave up any state secrets or something. I don't tell my viewers where they can find us, or mention anything that might endanger us. All I do is take a specific movie and discuss its accuracy. I mean, come on, how is that dangerous?"

"My sweet summer child," Camilla said, which told me I was in for a verbal smackdown. "It's dangerous because of *who* you are. The humans consider you some sort of ambassador because you were the first one to be changed after we became public knowledge. They relate to you. They follow you in every way they can. Which means every single thing that leaves your mouth is taken as gospel. Maybe the information isn't dangerous, but what they can do with it is. And that's how the queen and every other vampire is going to look at it. Right now, they're wondering if you're more loyal to the humans than your own kind."

"My own kind," I repeated harshly. "What the hell is that supposed to even mean? I was a human for twenty-four years, Camilla. I've been a vampire for three months. And I'm supposed to what? Forget I was ever human?"

"Yes. That's exactly what it means. Especially to the queen. By revealing our secrets, or whatever you want to call it, she sees you as a traitor."

"Oh for crying out loud. Has anyone ever told you that vampires are dramatic?"

Camilla burst out laughing. "Many, many times, my dear. As for Vlad, I think he's just angry that you didn't share this part of your life with him. I don't believe he thinks the vlog is dangerous. More that you kept something from him, withheld a part of yourself. Is it true you earned nearly a couple hundred thousand dollars this week?"

"Okay, yes—"

"How much have you made in total since you started your vlog up again?"

"I... actually don't know the full value," I admitted. "Lucy has been handling it for me."

"So, more than enough, since you don't know how much."

"I suppose that's one way to look at it."

"Do you see why Vlad is upset then? This is a massive change for you. From rags to riches, and you didn't share it with him, didn't tell him about your success. He loves you, Anna—"

"I know."

"You do?"

I nodded, then scrubbed my hands down my face. "And I love him, Camilla."

"Have you told him that?"

"Yeah, last night. After we visited with my mother."

Camilla gave another laugh. "It must have been a horrible visit if it got you to confess your love to him."

I snickered and nodded. "Yeah, it was pretty damn terrible. Did Vlad tell you about it?"

"No, he didn't."

I placed my phone on speakerphone, then sat cross-legged on the bed and started idly braiding my hair, all while regaling Camilla with "The Tale of My Mother." Camilla's responses went from amused to horrified pretty damn fast.

"She wants us to go back tomorrow night to meet with Caleb, but no way in hell that's happening now. I may not like my family, but I refuse to put them in any danger. And Michel is like a freaking viper. He's coiled to strike. I won't put my family in harm's way."

"I agree. What's your game plan then?" Camilla asked after I finished telling her about the wretched visit with my father.

"I can't say I have one at the moment. I just need to prove to Michel that I'm not a danger to anyone or anything and hope for the best."

I could practically hear the wheels turning in her head through the phone. "Maybe you should go to England."

My jaw dropped. "Are you kidding me?"

Camilla sighed. "The queen clearly wants to meet you, Anna. So much so that she's sent an inquisitor. Now, I know you didn't pay much attention to my texts, but inquisitors are about as bad as it gets. Do you remember what I told you back in New Orleans about them?"

I racked my brain in search of her words. "Something about how the queen used them to squash any and all uprisings."

"Correct. But it's more than that. Inquisitors are steadfast in their beliefs. In the case of vampires, their beliefs always align with the queen's. Because she doesn't accept anything else. It isn't the inquisitor you need to convince, it's the queen. Only she can fix this."

I rubbed my temples and considered Camilla's advice, but I couldn't see the logic here. Yes, changing the queen's mind was important. But I didn't see any wisdom in placing myself directly in the line of fire. The queen might be interested in me, but maybe that interest would wane the less fascinating I became. If that meant shutting down my vlog and playing the role of a docile little vampire, so be it. Yes, fame was my dream. But not at the expense of my life. I'd already experienced death once, I really wasn't keen to experience it again.

"No," I finally said. "England is out of the question. There has to be another way."

"Sometimes, it's best to face a problem head on."

"Yeah, when that problem doesn't want you dead."

Camilla chuckled. "Okay, true."

"I need to convince Michel that I'm not a threat. Then he can report back to the queen that I'm just a naïve young vampire who means absolutely nothing in the grand scheme."

"I think you're forgetting one important part."

Except I wasn't. I knew exactly what Camilla was going to say. "Petrik."

“Petrik,” she repeated. “The moment the queen learns that he’s dead, she’s going to come looking for blood again.”

I sighed and closed my eyes. When had my life become this? And why? It always came back to Petrik, didn’t it? The bastard had attacked *me*. Not the other way around. He’d killed thirty-four women before me. In my eyes, Sam was a hero for killing the bastard. Seemed the queen didn’t agree. All because Petrik had sired her. Well, la-di-fucking-da. If Vlad had killed thirty-four girls, I would never forgive him, because it was vile, reprehensible, *evil*. Sam had done us a favor by putting the mad vamp down. The world was a better place without him. But apparently, we were the only ones who saw it that way.

“Michel isn’t going to leave until he learns what happened to Petrik. He’s likely under orders to remain until he has any information he can bring back. From there, the queen will render her verdict.”

I shook my head. “No, apparently he can arrest me. I guess the queen is trying to create a court system for us vamps, to prove to humans we’re more than bloodthirsty monsters.”

“Oh.” Camilla quietly tsked. “Because that’s going to go over so well.”

I nodded. It sounded like a clusterfuck to me as well.

"So, she's trying to make an example of you then," Camilla murmured.

"What?"

"She's trying to show the world, both humans and vampires, that we can obey, and if we don't, here's how the situation's handled. But she needs a scapegoat. Someone she can show off as the first criminalized vampire."

Oh, just freaking fantastic. "I absolutely hate this."

"Me too."

"What are our options then?"

"We don't really have any," she said. "Either we let this play out or we take action. It always boils down to those two choices, doesn't it?"

Seemed that way. Seemed like these were the same options I'd been given with Petrik as well. And he'd opted to take action on our behalf, which had nearly left me deep-fried and crispy in that creepy crypt of his. I really didn't relish the idea of going through that again.

"So, Vlad mentioned you can talk to animals," Camilla said, changing the subject. I could have kissed her.

"It seems that way. I had Vlad shift into his bat and wolf form, and I could hear him in both. There were also a couple bats in the attic when we moved in, but I guess we scared them off because they haven't come back yet."

Camilla chuckled. "Trust *you* to develop some weird inane power like that. I've never heard of a single vampire who could speak to animals. How is that even helpful?"

"Oh, thanks," I half-teased. "Talk about kicking a girl when she's down. I'm supposed to be celebrating my first gift, not listening to you tease me about it."

"Sweetie, I developed my first power at a hundred and twenty years old."

"What?" I demanded. "I didn't know you even had one!"

"Well, it's nothing flashy like Vlad's, but it's useful. Far more useful than communing with animals."

"Yeah, yeah, yeah," I muttered. "What is it?"

"They call it 'battle-sense.' It's the ability to read my opponents in a fight. I'm able to see how they're going to attack and see the fight play out in my head."

"What?" I screeched, practically falling off the bed. "Are you kidding me? Is that why Vlad put you in charge of teaching me how to fight? And why you *always* kick my ass?"

Camilla started laughing. "Yes to both. It's not the same as reading minds. It's more like this innate ability to be able to read the fight and my opponent's movements. Sometimes I get it wrong, like that night you jumped on my back and bit me. But it's almost impossible to defeat me in a fight."

"Well, isn't that just handy to have around," I sniped.

"Why do you think Vlad keeps me so close? I'm like the perfect strategist."

"So you can see when someone is about to attack you? See all the moves they're going to take?"

She hummed an agreement. "It's like a movie in my head. Once that adrenaline kicks in, I can see the entire fight play out. Then it's just a matter of taking them down."

"Okay, see, now *that's* a gift! How the hell is talking to animals ever going to help me?"

She snickered. "I honestly couldn't tell you."

"This sucks." I sat back with a pout. "Drink the blood of a thousand-year-old vampire who was probably bursting at the seams with power, and this is my reward."

"Hey, just be grateful that you didn't lose your

mind or grow addicted to ancient blood."

Yeah, I was definitely thankful for that. The stories Vlad had told me were alarming. Scenario wise, this certainly wasn't the worst case. But it wasn't great either.

"Do you have your second gift yet?" I asked.

"That usually presents around the five-hundred-year mark, which is why Vlad's still developing his foresight."

I nodded. Another incredibly useful gift. One that would become invaluable the stronger it got.

"He told you about his vision?" I asked, even though I already knew the answer, seeing as I'd overheard their conversation.

Camilla grew quiet but eventually said, "He told me he dreamed of your death."

What a mood killer.

Camilla sighed. "Don't let his vision derail you. Right now, there are so many things up in the air. Vlad won't let anything happen to you."

"Yeah," I whispered.

The problem was that something bad had already happened. Michel had found us, and the queen was waiting for an update. We'd come to Perish hoping everything would blow over. Except, instead, it'd exploded. Right in our freaking faces.

CHAPTER NINETEEN

My fingers drummed against the kitchen table as I sat—more like hovered—near the window, staring out into the night. Vlad might have gone out to buy more blood, but something had certainly delayed his return. I knew better than to fret. He was a big boy, after all. I honestly doubted there was anything in this world that could truly harm him. But thanks to Michel's arrival, I was on edge, my every nerve shot.

In the back of my mind, this clock kept tick, tick, ticking away, counting down to the inevitable. Too bad I had no idea *what* the inevitable was. Right now, I just felt this overwhelming sense of dread. As though tomorrow night would determine the rest of my life. Crazy, right? Surely Michel didn't hold that much power over me, and yet every inch of me screamed that he did. That tomorrow night was it. The final curtain call.

Much like Camilla said, we had two choices here—or rather, *I* had two choices here. Either we let this play out or we take action. But which was the right one? Neither path ended well, as far as I could tell. If we let this play out and answered all Michel's questions honestly, chances were I'd end up dead. If we took action—"eliminated" the threat —the queen would find out, respond, and lo and behold, I'd end up dead. What fun, a lose-lose scenario.

Of course, there was a third option, one Camilla hadn't mentioned, but one I was leaning heavily toward as the night progressed. I could run. Stay one step ahead of the queen and her inquisitors. Except that way lay dragons. One, I'd never get to live my own life. I'd lose my vlog, Vlad, my friends, everything that mattered to me. Two, the queen would eventually find me, which would *once again* lead to my death.

With a deep groan, I leaned forward and rested my forehead against the cool tabletop. "When all paths lead to your demise, how do you choose?" I forced out a breath and watched as it fogged up the table. The answer came to me quickly because it was the only one that made sense. "You choose the one that harms the fewest number of people."

At the end of the day, it didn't matter what happened to me. But I refused to see Vlad, Camilla, or even Lucy hurt *because* of me.

Knowing that, I broke my three options down even farther, and even came up with a fourth.

Number one: We lied and told Michel absolutely nothing. That as far as we knew, Petrik was alive and well, and murdering more women somewhere across the country. But, eventually, the queen would learn the truth, and hunt us down. Secrets like that never stayed hidden for long.

Number two: We took action and eliminated Michel, thereby placing Vlad in danger as well. The queen certainly wouldn't look the other way if he helped me kill an inquisitor. Plus, was I really a murderer? It was one thing to defend yourself, but another to actively plot someone's death. Not to mention, the queen would obliterate us. Killing an inquisitor was pretty much a declaration of war, and I had a feeling she would win.

Number three: I ran. And spent the rest of eternity running because running meant guilty. This path only delayed my death, as far as I could see, even with my lack of foresight. Yes, it delayed the inevitable, but what kind of life would I live without Vlad anyway? And if he ran with me, the queen would surely blacklist him as well. No, I couldn't ruin his life as well as mine.

Number four: I told the truth about everything and threw myself at Michel's and the queen's mercy. This path only affected me. Vlad literally had nothing to do with Petrik's death. He hadn't even been there. I'd have to adapt my story, though, because if I told the queen that a werewolf killed her sire, I could only imagine the horrific fallout. They'd likely want to know how I'd killed an ancient vampire, but I was confident I could make something up.

Honestly, scenario number four was looking like the only good one. There was an infinitesimal chance that the queen would see innocence and send me packing.

Luckily for me, my phone rang *again* before I could make my final choice. I dug it out of my back pocket and stared at Lucy's name. We had plans to meet tomorrow, but with Michel here, that changed everything. I refused to even introduce her to the inquisitor. Refused to let him tell the queen about my relationship with a human. If I could keep her safe, I would. Which meant this might also be the last time we spoke. What with my impending doom and all that.

So, I took the call.

"Anna?" Lucy's voice carried across the line. "You there?"

I didn't immediately respond. I wasn't often hit with depression but when I was, it tended to hit hard.

"Anna? Hello?"

"Hey."

"There you are. I just wanted to check in, see how your visit with your dad went and make sure we're still on for tomorrow night."

Right. She wanted us to be there when she told Sam about her bloodline so we could analyze his reaction. Well, that certainly didn't work for me anymore.

"Um, listen, tomorrow isn't good for me. You mind if we reschedule?"

"Reschedule? Why? What's going on?"

I honestly didn't know how much to reveal. If I told Lucy about Michel, she'd march here and firmly implant herself into the situation. Her loyalty had always astounded me. But now wasn't the time for that. Now was the time to look after herself. No matter what happened tomorrow, I didn't see a happy ending for me. I couldn't outright tell Lucy that. I'd have to redirect her somehow.

"Some stuff came up. Nothing serious, so don't worry." *Liar, liar, pants on fire.* "But we don't have time for visits tomorrow, and Sam shouldn't come over anyway. You know how vampires are about werewolves."

Silence stretched through the phone.

"Anna, what's going on?"

"It's nothing, honestly. Just some vampire political nonsense. But hey, I've been thinking about your situation, and I wonder if it might be a good idea to go meet this alpha father of yours."

"What?" she screeched.

A sad smile played at my mouth. I should have known that would distract her from *my* problems.

"You've got to be kidding me, right? You can't possibly think I want to meet that asshole!"

Whoa, asshole. Strong language from her. "Did you learn more about him?"

"Yeah, I spoke with my parents tonight and got the whole story out of my mom. It's not a pretty one. Apparently, werewolves are known for seeking out people they believe have strong genes in order to create the strongest offspring."

"How the heck do they know who has strong genes?"

"It's some sort of sense they have. You know, like how in the wild, animals can tell who's strong and who's weak?"

Okay, that actually creeped me out a little bit. "So, he 'sensed' your mother's strong genes and impregnated her, hoping for a strong werewolf baby?"

Lucy grunted under her breath. "That's pretty much the gist of it. Then I was born, and he gave it six months to see if I showed any signs of lycanthropy—that's what they call it by the way. When I didn't, he packed his bags and off he went, I assume to find some other woman to knock up."

"A real charmer then."

Lucy hummed her agreement. "He means nothing to me. But now I'm worried that Sam is doing the same thing."

My stomach turned. What if he was? What if it was like some natural predisposition of werewolves? "Did your father ever tell your mother that she was his mate?"

"Yeah, so here's the thing. Mates among werewolves doesn't actually mean the same thing as vampires. I dug into that one a little too. My mom said, for vampires, mate is just another word for soulmate. But among werewolves, it's exactly like in the wild, when animals mate. Sam isn't telling me I'm his soulmate. He's telling me that he wants to fuck me."

Oh, shit. No, I didn't believe that. I'd seen the way Sam acted around Lucy. He was cuckoo for cocoa puffs over her. He didn't say much, but I could see it in his eyes *and* smell it in his pheromones. Of course, pheromones were usually just a physical response to attraction.

Damn it, what if I had it wrong this whole time?

"What are you going to do?" I asked.

"Well, I'm not going to sleep with him, that's for sure! Not if he's just looking for a broodmare."

I winced. "I really don't think Sam is like that."

"Why not? My sperm donor was."

"But maybe it's not a universal rule. Maybe your sperm donor is like every other deadbeat dad out there. Maybe Sam is looking for a relationship and a wife and..." I exhaled. "Lucy, you aren't going to learn any of these answers until you ask him. I think you need to stop drilling other people and just rip off the Band-Aid. Ask him directly—and explicitly—what he wants from you."

"I was kind of hoping you and Vlad could help me with that."

That wasn't a direction I wanted this conversation to take, so I steered her away. "Ask him, okay? Talk to him. Vlad and I can have this conversation with him any time. Don't you want to give him the chance to tell you the truth first? Don't start a relationship with someone assuming they're going to lie. And don't let your mother's situation color your opinion of Sam. He's good people. I truly don't think he'd lie to you just so he can knock you up."

Lucy released a shaky breath. "Anna, I'm... scared."

My chest swelled with emotion, and I rubbed it, hoping to loosen the pressure. "I know, sweetie. Love is a scary thing. I was frightened when I realized I was falling for Vlad. Listen to me," I said, still rubbing my chest. "Love is the scariest thing out there. Because you're giving your all to someone else and hoping they won't destroy you. That kind of vulnerability is absolutely terrifying. It's also beautiful. It's hard to take that first step but think of all the steps you get to take together afterward. If Sam is *the one* for you, you'll never regret taking that risk. But being too afraid to try, that'll haunt you. Do what you need to get all the information beforehand, but never base your decision off fear. Promise me you'll take the leap if he gives you the right answers. Okay?"

Lucy hesitated. "Anna, what's wrong?"

"Nothing's wrong." I knuckled away a tear before it could fall. I had this no crying rule because vampires cried blood tears, and I thought they were hideous. But mostly, I just didn't want her to hear me sobbing over the phone. If I gave in to them, Lucy would come running. I needed to stay strong.

"Hey, go to Mississippi," I told her. "I really think you should find your sperm donor and ask him why. Ask him how he could abandon you and your mom. Find out what he's really like."

"Why? He's not my father."

"No, and he never will be. But it might help resolve these issues with Sam. Maybe you'll see they're nothing alike." And it might get her out of Louisiana when the shit hit the fan. "Ask Sam to go with you."

"I still haven't told him about any of this," she admitted.

"Well, no time like the present. If you expect him to be honest and upfront with you, then he deserves the same. He should know there's werewolf blood running through your veins."

"Except, I'm human."

"Well, maybe it'll still change things for him. Best to be open about it, right? Then no one can call you a liar later on down the road."

And the award for the biggest hypocrite goes to... Here I was telling Lucy not to be a coward and to be honest with those she loves, and I was hiding a massive secret from her. I only hoped that one day she understood.

"I can't believe you want me to go to Mississippi," she said, laughing. "I think my mom would freak out if I told her that. Oh, speaking of, how'd the visit go with your dad?"

Grateful for the change in topic, I gave a light laugh. "About as great as you'd expect. He ignored me the entire night while Christina kept trying to make a move on Vlad."

"What a cow!" Lucy scoffed under her breath. "She steals your dad, practically bleeds him dry of all his money, then goes after Vlad? She's lucky you didn't rip out her throat."

"Oh, girl, I was tempted. The night finally ended on an explosive note when I told my dad off for being a shithead. You know, after all these years of imagining what I would say to him, it didn't feel as good as I'd hoped. I just felt crappy after."

"Yeah, that's generally how I understand these things go down. How'd he react?"

"He didn't. The man is the worst. But I knew that going in, you know. At least you got a great dad out of this whole mess with your mom and sperm donor."

"Yeah, I'm definitely lucky there. My dad's awesome."

I nodded.

"Are you still going to see Caleb tomorrow?"

"No. I'll have to text my mom with a cancellation. She'll scold me, I'm sure, but honestly, anything is better than seeing my brother. I know exactly how that would go down anyway. He'll call me a stain on the family name, I'll probably punch him in the nose, and that'll be that. Might as well save us the tears and frustration."

Lucy chuckled. "Your brother's an idiot."

"Yep."

"But I heard he's got himself a new girlfriend."

I blinked. "Where'd you hear that?"

"I've been chatting with a few girls from high school."

People I absolutely refused to talk to now. The

second Vlad turned me, and the photos hit the internet, a reporter had come sniffing around town here about me, they'd all given up the goods. Most had claimed to be my "best friend," and told the reporter we were like "sisters." When really, they were people I scarcely remembered.

"You have fun with that?" I asked.

Lucy exploded with laughter. "It's just hilarious, hearing about their lives and how simple they are compared to ours. It's actually kind of a relief to hear about their work or boyfriend troubles."

"Simple lives for simple people."

"Pfft. That might have been us if we hadn't gone to New Orleans."

I chose not to comment on that. Seemed like that direction lay a fight and seeing as how this might be the last time she and I spoke, I didn't want to taint this conversation with bad memories.

"Okay, well, if we aren't seeing each other tomorrow, then I assume we'll see you Saturday?"

"Probably. I'll let you know more after tomorrow night." After Michel lay down his verdict and decided my fate. "Worst-case scenario, we'll see you back in New Orleans."

"Okay..." Lucy hedged. "Are you sure everything's alright?"

"You bet."

Before I could say anything more, the front door opened, and Vlad stepped inside.

"Hey, Luce, I gotta go, 'kay?"

"Oh, okay. Text me tomorrow."

"Will do. Good luck with Sam. And Luce?"

"Yeah?"

"Remember what I said. Promise me you'll take the leap, okay?"

"Okay," she whispered. "You're scaring me."

"Nothing to be scared of. Just doing my job as the best friend to make sure you live your best life."

"Anna..."

"Night, Luce."

"Night," she murmured.

I ended the call, then set my phone down on the table and turned to Vlad. His gaze caught mine before he crouched to remove his shoes. When he straightened, I rose from my seat and came to stand before him, my hands tucked behind my back. I needed to make this right with him. But more importantly, I needed to tell him I'd made my decision and help him come to grips with it.

Unfortunately, we didn't have enough time left tonight to get into it all. Which meant deciding which conversation was more important, the vlog or my decision regarding Michel. I knew the answer without a doubt. Vlad meant more to me than anything else. He had to know how sorry I was for lying to him. I would do anything to prove it to him.

So, with a shy smile, I stepped forward and took his hands. "Can we talk?"

Vlad nodded without hesitation, his fingers squeezing mine. Relief rounded my shoulders. I would fix this problem. And then... then I'd tell him I'd decided how to proceed with Michel.

I only hoped he let me do it.

CHAPTER TWENTY

I LED Vlad into the living room, then glanced at the clock. Three in the morning. Ugh. Damn witching hour. As a connoisseur of nighttime, I could honestly say that nothing good happened around three a.m., almost like it was cursed. If something bad was going to happen, it would be now.

"Listen..." I sat on the couch and pulled Vlad down next to me. "I'm so sorry I didn't tell you about the vlog. I don't have a good explanation for you. I was just... scared. Nervous, I guess. I just..." I drew a deep breath. "I didn't tell you when Lucy and I first started working on it because I was afraid it would tank. And I didn't want you to see me fail. Then it started gaining popularity, and I started worrying about whether it would last. That happens sometimes. People hit it big for one video, and then there's no follow through. When there was follow through, I freaked out over *how* to tell you since by then, I'd waited so long." I sighed and raked my fingers through my hair. "There was this little voice in my head, telling me I didn't deserve any of this, that I was going to screw everything up, so by keeping it quiet, I felt safer in that little bubble. I'm not explaining this right. I know I should have just told you right away. And—"

"Anna."

I choked back the rest of my rambly tirade and met Vlad's gaze. As far as apologies went, this one pretty much sucked camel face. I could see the disappointment in his expression, in the grim set of his lips and narrowed eyes.

"I just... I'm sorry," I muttered.

Vlad sighed, then wrapped his arms around my waist and pulled me against him, tucking my head beneath his chin. "Stop talking."

Relief loosened my poor, tense muscles. I hated when people were mad at me, but with Vlad, that feeling quadrupled. There was a weight on my shoulders I couldn't shake off, and a heaviness in my chest that refused to abate. I never wanted to fight with him again—an impossible dream, I know, considering couples fight. But if we could go the next hundred years without another spat, I'd be a happy vampy.

"I realized while I was out that you have nothing to apologize for. We've both kept secrets from one another recently. Relationships require work. And while I would have appreciated a bit more honesty regarding your employment status, that wasn't the reason for my anger. I'm upset because the revitalization of your vlog has only further endangered your life. The queen will use this against you. Had you told me about it, I could have pointed that out."

I snuggled deeper into Vlad's chest and closed my eyes. The feel of his arms tightening around me was one I knew I would remember for the rest of my life. "I never thought they would use my vlog against me. To me, I saw it as a mark of freedom, a return to what makes me, *me*. And I think I was worried you wouldn't let me do it."

"Anna. I'm not your father. I have no say over what you may or may not do. You are an adult and your own person. But as *my* person, I only ask that you be open and honest with me. Never fear opening up to me. I have no desire to make your life more difficult. I only wish to share it with you."

Gah. Why was this man so good with speeches?

"If we're going to survive eternity together, we mustn't hide things from one another. We need to trust each other. I love you, Anna. I want to spend my life with you, for however long that might be. I only hope you want the same."

"Of course," I whispered. "You know I love you."

Vlad pressed a gentle kiss against the top of my head, then shifted his weight, unwrapping me from the warmth he'd cocooned me in. "Good. Because while I was contemplating all this, I realized I have a question I'd like to ask you."

Oh boy. If he was moving on from this topic, then that meant I needed to tell him about my decision. I really didn't want to. I knew it would ruin the moment. But with the sun approaching, and Michel's impending return tomorrow night, I couldn't delay the conversation any longer. Especially considering everything Vlad and I had just discussed.

He slipped a hand into his pants pocket and began rooting around for something. I rose off Vlad and scooted over to the next cushion to give him—and myself—some space. He seemed to be holding something shiny, but just as he began pulling it out, the words I'd been mulling over for the last few hours came spewing out.

"I want to tell Michel the truth."

Vlad froze, his hand still resting in his pocket. His expression tightened and his lips flattened, all signs that I'd pissed him off. He withdrew his hand—now empty—and stared at me. "I must have misheard."

I sucked my bottom lip into my mouth and shook my head. "Just hear me out, okay? I've gone through all our choices over and over. And I think our best-case scenario is me telling Michel that Petrik's dead and telling him I'm responsible for it all."

His eyes hardened. "I would love to hear your reasoning."

Yup. He was pissed.

I cleared my throat, then folded my hands together and placed them in my lap. I needed to explain this correctly. "The way I see it, we have four options." I held up a single digit. "We lie. We tell Michel we have absolutely no idea what happened to Petrik." I flicked up a second finger. "We kill Michel." My third finger rose. "We run." And a fourth. "Or we tell the truth and hope he and the queen show me mercy."

Vlad's expression darkened.

"The first option isn't ideal. Michel is a trained inquisitor and a vampire. It seems safe to assume he'll know the instant we start lying. A change in our pupils, a change in our scent. Or he'll just look at me and know, because honestly, I'm a terrible liar. Or, one day the truth will be discovered, and we'll pay the price then. Either way, a price is paid. Likely resulting in our deaths."

Vlad's lips thinned.

I forced myself to swallow and keep talking. "The second option is likely our worst. If we so much as touch a hair on the inquisitor's head, the queen will eat us for breakfast. From what I understand, killing Michel would be a declaration of war. And she has a hell of a lot more vampires on her side.

"Running is doable, but not ideal. Running suggests we're guilty of something and gives the queen every right to hunt us down and kill us. If we choose this path, we forfeit our lives, our reputations, our friends, everything. I can't imagine we'd enjoy that lifestyle.

"Which leaves telling the truth. I tell Michel that Petrik attacked me, and I was forced to protect myself. Hopefully, he'll understand, and he and the queen will move on with their lives."

A tic throbbed near Vlad's temple. Oh shit, he

was incredibly pissed. We might not have known one another for a long time, but I knew a great deal about him, including that he grew quiet when angry. Downright silent meant he was livid.

"Vlad." I scootched closer and took his hands, rubbing my thumb over his knuckles. "Coming clean is the best solution for everyone. It clears you and everyone else of any suspicion. Hell, you weren't even there. But it might also wipe the slate clean for me. Meaning no more hiding. No more worrying about the queen. No more living with a sword over my head. I have to believe the queen isn't the sort to kill someone for defending herself, regardless of her relationship with Petrik. We even have the files that show he murdered thirty-four women before me. Her relationship with the president is tenuous at best. That's something she wouldn't want getting out."

"Blackmail?" Harsh laughter burst past Vlad's lips. He shook his hands free of mine and carded them through his hair. "That's your plan? To blackmail the queen?"

"No, of course not. I just mean... there's hope."

He descended back into silence, his cold eyes locked on me as though they could unlock the secrets to my brain. Hell, I wished they could. I was trying to sound confident and determined, but inside, I was shaking like a terrified little pup. This plan involved putting my life in the hands of people I didn't trust.

When he didn't speak, I blew out a forced breath and cupped the back of my neck. I didn't know what else to do. The other three options sucked. I didn't see Vlad enjoying a life on the run. Hell, neither did I for that matter. What else could we do?

"Vlad—"

Before I could utter another word, he grabbed me by the shoulders, pulled me close, then crushed my mouth beneath his. Surprise widened my eyes for a fraction of a second before they fluttered closed, and I sank into the kiss. Now this, I understood. He didn't know how to respond without showing his true fears, so instead, he reacted. Showing me physically what he couldn't say with words.

He pushed me down on the couch, then rose above me, his hands bracing his weight on either side of my head. His kiss was devastatingly tender and heartbreakingly emotional. Almost as though he knew this would be the last time we could be together. I refused to accept that. Michel would return tomorrow night, and I would tell him exactly what happened, but I hoped they wouldn't kill me for it. Self-defense was a real thing, and it absolutely applied in this situation. But vampires functioned differently from humans, and we lived by the queen's rule. There wouldn't be an appeal process if I didn't like her judgement. There would just be a swift death. But I had to trust, for both Vlad's and my sake, that they would believe me.

Vlad's fingers slipped beneath my shirt and guided it over my head. He lowered his head to my lace-covered breasts and took my left nipple into his mouth, his tongue teasing through the rough material. I gasped and arched my back against him, reveling in the warmth of his mouth against the chill of the air and wet material.

He moved to my other nipple, his hands cupping and grasping as he went. I lifted my hips and eased down my own pants before reaching for his shirt. I slowly popped each button open, then slid his shirt off and let it fall to the ground. His pants were next and added to the growing pile of discarded clothing next to the couch.

Vlad's mouth skimmed my stomach as he headed south, his lips caressing my flesh. His fingers grazed my sides, then gripped my thighs. I didn't make a sound as he spread my legs, but I sure as hell quivered when his lips brushed my clit. The anticipation was almost more than I could bear. I was well-versed in his wicked talents and knew all the damage that sinful mouth of his could cause. I wasn't prepared when he unleashed himself on me, his mouth and tongue working in tandem to whip me into a lusty blaze. The man was a damn artist when it came to pleasing me. He knew exactly how and where to lick and stroke. I felt the orgasm building like a wildfire, every touch stoking those flames higher and higher until finally I erupted. Only then did he add his fingers to the equation, preparing me for the main event. When my second orgasm struck, he climbed between my legs and thrust within me.

I cried out, my head digging into the cushions as I rode the pleasure train.

"Vlad," I whispered.

"I swear, you'll be the death of me," he murmured, his movements barely pausing as he gazed down at me. "I can't bear to lose you."

"You won't," I said, realizing we were continuing our previous conversation. "I'm not going anywhere. I'm not going to let them kill me." I gasped and arched my back as a wave of pleasure crashed into me.

Vlad repositioned himself, gripping the armrest of the couch as he quickened his pace.

My eyes slammed shut as I succumbed to this beautiful torture.

"Anna..." My name came out sounding more like a whispered prayer.

"Vlad." I cupped his cheeks. "Look at me."

His eyes flashed open and caught mine. For a brief moment, I could see the pain and fear within. It broke my heart to see it, knowing I'd caused it.

"I won't let them kill me." I vowed. "If they try, we'll run. We'll fight. We'll do whatever it takes."

He nodded an instant before his eyes squeezed shut and his head dipped, his tips of his hair brushing my throat. "Bite me."

"What?" I rasped, convinced I'd misheard him.

With his next thrust, he lifted his head and stared at me. "Bite. Me."

"Are you sure?"

"Yes," he said on the edge of a groan. "I want your teeth buried in my throat right now."

I nodded, my mouth practically quivering with anticipation. I understood his need. Even though I had faith we'd survive tomorrow, that fear lingered. And what was a little ancient blood between lovers when the threat of death lingered over us?

Vlad slowed his movements, giving me a chance to thread my fingers through his hair and angle his head. The sight of his bare throat nearly undid me and sent me spiraling over the edge, knowing I'd soon be burying my fangs in it.

The moment they pierced his flesh, a massive rush of pleasure spread through me. Vlad grunted and resumed his bruising pace, driving into me with more force than normal. But I didn't complain. I loved the feel of him between my legs and the sound of us coming together. I bit a little harder, then gasped when Vlad found the perfect spot and brought me to climax. The feel of me tightening around him seemed to be all it took to send him spiraling out of control. He shuddered above me, groaning as he finished. He rode out his own orgasm, his body convulsing alongside mine, before he finally collapsed on top of me.

I slowly extracted my fangs and ran my tongue over them, reveling in his delectable taste. Then I wrapped my arms around him and held him against me. I never wanted to forget this moment, or what we meant to each other. No matter what, tomorrow would come and a verdict would be decided, but deep down, I believed we'd win our happily ever after.

Because we damn well deserved it.

CHAPTER
TWENTY-ONE

I WOKE with a sense of impending doom, which really didn't help matters. I needed to be fun and upbeat, confident that I would walk away from tonight with nary a scratch. It was a necessary façade, not only for my sake, but Vlad's as well. I sent Camilla a text early this morning before succumbing to the sun with my plan laid out, and I could only imagine her response. Camilla believed me to be stupid pretty much all the time, so I didn't see the point in trying to convince her otherwise. All that mattered was convincing Michel that I was no threat to the queen. And that meant playing a part.

So, with a deep breath, I palmed my coffin lid back and sat up. I had a few hours to kill before Vlad woke, and I intended on using that time to go over my story until I had it memorized. Not that I needed reminding. My time with Petrik was essentially branded into my brain, but I wanted to make sure I could recall every last detail without a hint of hesitation.

I took my time showering, reveling in the hot water and steam, then stood in my closet and meticulously picked out an appropriate outfit. I needed something casual, but clean. Something that suggested innocent and peaceful. But I also needed something I could possibly fight or run in. Strange, the life I led now. This wasn't something I would ever have had to think about when human. I'd always chosen my outfits based on my daily mood, not whether or not I would have to fight for my life.

I ended up opting for a pair of relaxed fit jeans—because who the hell could run in skinnies?—and a loose, flowy blouse. No heels today, for sure. I didn't own sneakers, but I did own one pair of knee-high flat boots. They weren't cushioned for running, but at least they weren't six inches tall. For a final touch, I added a pastel-colored cardigan. Because nothing said calm and peaceful like pastels.

Then I stood in front of the tall, thin mirror and studied my outfit. It'd taken a while, but I'd acclimated to the sight of my clothes hovering midair, with no body to ground the reflection. I sure did miss my reflection, though. A hundred years ago or so, Vlad had sat for a portrait because he'd forgotten what he looked like. I definitely understood that. Thankfully, I had tons of photos from before I became a vamp to remind me. But staring in the blank mirror at nothing more than clothing hit me right in the feels. Moments like these were the ones that reminded me of exactly what I'd become.

Those memories were what I needed right now.

I closed my eyes and sent myself back three months to the night I met Vlad. But more specifically, to the night Petrik brutally attacked me. I hated remembering this night. The visceral fear and the sense of helplessness weren't my idea of a good time. But I needed that tonight. I needed to tremble when Michel questioned me about Petrik, I needed to cry while recalling that moment when I knew without doubt, I was going to die. I needed to detail everything so Michel felt what I did. The terror when the sun touched me in his crypt, the scent of my burning flesh, right down to the moment I drank his blood to save my own life.

The only thing I couldn't confess was Sam's involvement. I refused to include the werewolves in this. Sam had saved my life, and he'd imparted upon me a secret even vampires didn't know—a weapon that could take down a thousand-year-old vamp. Had I known of Michel's arrival, I might have asked Sam to make me one, but I swore to myself now, if I survived this, I would whittle as many hawthorn stakes as possible and soak them in holy water and monksblood.

"You look beautiful."

My head snapped up at the sound of Vlad's voice. So lost in my memories and thoughts, I hadn't noticed the sun's descent or heard him wake. Not a great start to the night. I needed to be on top of my game here. Needed my senses primed. Because if Michel tried anything, I couldn't be caught unaware.

I turned to face Vlad with a soft smile and said, "Thank you."

Then I laughed at the sight of him. While I'd chosen every piece of clothing with painstakingly deep thought, Vlad had thrown on the same outfit as normal. Black shirt, black shoes, even black socks. I swear, the man didn't realize there were other colors out there. Or maybe he wanted to make a different statement than me. Maybe he wanted to silently threaten and intimidate Michel. A show of force in case Michel took the direction I desperately hoped he didn't.

"What?" Vlad asked.

I shook my head. No point teasing him about his outfit. Especially considering nothing could be done about it now. If Vlad was awake, then Michel soon would be too. He hadn't given me an arrival time, but I assumed we'd be hearing from him soon.

"Camilla is on her way to Perish," Vlad said, when I didn't answer his question. "Have you checked your phone?"

"No. Why?" I hadn't wanted to waste any time on social media, so it'd seemed best to avoid my phone altogether. I was an expert procrastinator when it came to social media.

"It would seem she doesn't agree with your plan and wants to be here. Unfortunately, I doubt she'll make it before Michel arrives."

"Ah." Might have been nice to have Little Miss Battle Strategy on our side, but the timing just didn't work.

"Are you sure this is the path you want to take?" Vlad closed the distance between us and enveloped me in his arms. I took the comfort he offered before I pulled myself together and stepped back.

"I really believe this is the only way to put an end to this. I'm tired of living with this fear hanging over me."

"I understand."

I lifted a brow. "You do?"

"Well, no." A soft chuckle slipped past his lips. "I respect your decision. But I want you to know, I will stand by you no matter what. Should you change your mind and decide to run tonight, I will be there with you as well."

"Can't get enough of me, huh?"

"Never." He leaned in and stole an ardent kiss. "You are mine, and I am yours. Whether that means living on the run for the next five hundred years or dying together in a glorious battle."

"You would think battle is glorious," I teased.

"There's a beauty to it."

"Well, let's avoid all bloodshed, shall we?"

"Of course." He dipped his head and brushed his lips along my throat. "Have we time...?"

I shivered with anticipation, then reached around and grabbed his ass. Because it was a fine ass, and it deserved to be cupped all night long. But someone chose that moment to ring our doorbell.

Despair tightened my chest, and my hands moved to grab Vlad's arms. Fear spiked the air, the scent triggering every instinct I had to run.

"Shh," Vlad whispered, tucking my hair behind

my ears. "It's a delivery. I ordered us some blood. We need to be at full strength tonight."

I almost burst into relieved tears right then and there. Maybe I wasn't as ready for this as I'd thought. But that didn't change anything.

We descended the stairs together, and Vlad opened the door. He took the delivery, paid, then closed the door and handed me a bottle. "Drink. This and the blood I gave you last night, should be enough to help you tonight."

My eyes widened. "Is *that* why you asked me to drink from you last night? To give me a power boost?"

He had the audacity to look unabashed. Even went so far as to *wink* at me. I nearly fainted on the spot. Vlad winks were deadly. "And other reasons, I assure you."

I upended the bottle and drained it in a series of quick swallows. Sadly, I couldn't take the time to enjoy it because we had a bit of a deadline. And from the sounds of it, that deadline was fast approaching, seeing as how a car had just pulled up in our driveway.

After swallowing the last bit, I slipped into the kitchen and discarded the bottle in the recycling bin. "He's here."

Vlad's hand found mine, and he pulled me close. "Remember, whatever you decide, I'm with you. If you tell the truth, then answer his questions thoroughly and honestly. Don't allow him to sway the conversation in any way that might imply guilt on your behalf. And do not allow him to confuse you. You've truly done nothing wrong." He swept my hair back, then lowered and pressed a kiss at the crook of my throat.

We embraced for a brief moment, then I squared my shoulders and faced the door. After three months, the time had finally come to handle this situation. Perhaps I should have done so sooner, but fear had a funny way of controlling someone.

"You ready for this?" I asked Vlad, while listening to the sound of Michel's approach.

Vlad hooked a finger beneath my chin and lifted my head, staring deeply into my eyes as though committing me to memory. Then he leaned in and brushed the sweetest, gentlest kiss against my mouth.

Only when we parted did he step back and nod. "Now, I am."

CHAPTER
TWENTY-TWO

"Please, have a seat." Vlad gestured to the couch.

I eyed Michel as he passed, scanning him for any lumps or bumps that might suggest he was armed. Truthfully, I couldn't see anything. And his outfit could have hidden any number of weapons. Guns concealed within his jacket, or knives strapped to his legs. Not that either would do any good. He could shoot us full of lead and stab us as much as he wanted, we wouldn't die. No, I needed to be on the lookout for stakes or swords. He carried a messenger bag, but I highly doubted he'd be pulling either of those out of there.

Then again, I really didn't want to put anything past him.

Michel seated himself on the couch and pulled an iPad out of his bag. He unlocked the screen, then opened a digital notepad. Next came a portable keyboard, which he quickly connected to the tablet. Guess some vampires kept up to date with modern technology.

I glanced at Vlad and lifted a brow, but he only rolled his eyes. Vlad hardly ever used his cell phone and saw no need for computers and tablets, an opinion he'd maintained even after Lucy and I outfitted his house in modern technology. Stubborn old man, Vlad.

"The queen and I have a few questions for you tonight, Anna, if that's all right. Hopefully, we'll be able to clear up this matter rather quickly and allow the rest of us to return to our night."

Even I could hear the false sincerity in his voice. I hoped I lied better than that, at least. And it seemed I wasn't the only one who noticed, seeing how Vlad had curled a lip up over his fangs.

Michel lifted his head and eyed me, as though waiting for my response. His fingers hovered over the keyboard, apparently keen to take notes. Twenty bucks said he was even recording my voice on his iPad.

This was it then. The moment of truth. Time to put up or shut up. I squared my shoulders and met his stare head-on, proving to myself and everyone in the room that he didn't frighten me. Michel was merely the queen's lackey. Yes, he might have a scary inquisitor title, but of the three of us, I put the odds in Vlad's and my favor against his.

"No," I finally said.

Michel's brow rose. "Pardon?"

"No more questions, no more demands, no more veiled accusations."

"Miss Perish—"

I held up a hand. "You're going to sit there and listen, and I'm going to talk."

"Oh?" He leaned back against the couch with the keyboard tucked into his lap. "I'm eager to hear what you have to say."

"Are you? Really?"

His smarmy expression faltered for a moment. "I'm not sure I understand your question."

"Never mind."

I glanced at Vlad, and once he gave me a reassuring nod, I grabbed the nearest chair and dragged it across the living room floor. I sat and rested my elbows against my knees, contemplating where to begin. I'd told this story countless times, but never for the queen's ears.

"The most important thing you need to know is that Petrik attacked me," I said, starting at the beginning. "I didn't even see his face until seconds before he struck. There was no connection between us, no relationship. I'd never seen him before that night. He grabbed me, dragged me out of the club, threw me up against a fence, and drained me."

I stared brazenly at Michel, hoping for a hint of emotion, something to suggest he might be on my side. But the man sat as still as stone, and just as cold.

"He left me in the alley to die. I have no doubts about that. Had Vlad not found me, I wouldn't be here right now. Petrik meant to kill me."

"You can't know that for sure—"

"He murdered thirty-four other women," I stated, my voice rising above Michel's. I wasn't in the mood to hear someone defend the bastard. "Thirty-four. And maybe that means nothing to you guys, seeing as you're vampires, but that means something to me. Yes, I'm also a vampire, but that doesn't make me a monster. Thirty-four women dead, because of him. So don't come at me with your excuses. Why would he intend for me to live when he killed every other victim? He was a serial killer, plain and simple, and you guys did nothing to stop it."

"Anna," Vlad warned, his hand falling on my shoulder.

I sucked in a shuddering breath and calmed my mind. He was right. I needed to remain composed. I couldn't give them any reason to believe that I was a danger. Once my temper cooled, I lifted a hand and placed it atop Vlad's, giving it a gentle squeeze.

"Vlad found me and turned me. He felt it might be considered bad PR if the human authorities found a woman murdered by a vampire while the queen was in the middle of arranging a peace treaty. Bad press and all that."

Something flashed in Michel's eyes then. Approval, perhaps? That shouldn't surprise me. These people didn't give a lick about me. Everything was about their damn public image.

"After I turned, we thought the matter was closed. But Petrik began harassing me. He trespassed on Vlad's land to taunt me, and a few nights later, he showed up at The Vampire Lounge and threatened both me and Vlad."

"Yes, we have a report here." Michel scrolled through something on his iPad. "A testimony from one Rainn Tremblay, a human employed with The

Vampire Lounge. She claims that Petrik and Vlad were speaking when things grew heated. You joined the conversation and threatened Petrik. You were quoted as saying you have human friends who would be willing to set Petrik on fire during the day."

My chest constricted. Rainn seriously heard that? And ratted me out for it? "I wasn't threatening him, I was reminding him that I might not be as helpless as he believed."

Michel hummed a nonverbal response and continued typing. "Please continue."

"Look, I don't know what you guys think happened, but whatever it is, that isn't what went down. I might have threatened Petrik, but that was as far as it went for me." Not quite true. Vlad and I concocted a plan to kill the bastard before he could kill me, but they really didn't need to know that. "That morning, he had one of Vlad's allies lure me onto a balcony so he could abduct me. When I woke up, I found myself locked in a fucking cement crypt full of windows. And the rising sun was shining through them. Tell me how that's okay. How I'm to blame for that. The bastard tried to burn me alive, but it's my fault, right? I egged him on?"

Vlad's fingers tightened on my shoulder, silently reminding me to calm myself. I sucked in another forced breath and centered my thoughts. I didn't realize how badly this still triggered me.

"Is there anyone who can confirm these events?"

Silence crashed through the room. Vlad's hand continued gripping my shoulder. But I think it was to help steady himself. They were literally asking me to provide proof that Petrik had abducted me.

I ground my teeth together and staved off a sudden rush of fury.

This was the moment where it all came to me in perfect clarity.

Michel and the queen had absolutely no intentions of clearing me for this "crime." They wanted me as their scapegoat. They wanted to chain me up and drag me in front of the masses for everyone to see. Again, all as a PR stunt. To show the humans we had a justice system and means of punishing misbehaving vampires.

"You have got to be kidding me." I hissed. "You want a witness? To my attempted murder?"

"If you can provide one, it would greatly help your cause."

My hands curled into tight fists and only the press of my nails against my palms kept me from lashing out at this asshole. "Sorry," I bit out through my teeth. "The only witness was Eli, because he betrayed me, and he's dead now."

Michel's mouth thinned. "Yes, we received reports of his grisly death as well."

"But his death doesn't concern you, right?" I asked sarcastically. "Just the one that means something to the queen."

"Careful, Anna," Michel warned.

Careful, my ass. They were literally setting me up to take the fall here. To go down as the first vampire charged with murder. Prior to the queen's treaty with the humans, disputes between vampires often ended bloody, such as Vlad's and Eli's. The queen hardly ever involved herself. But because Petrik was dead, and he mattered to the queen, special actions were being taken.

"Well, I'm sorry, but I don't have a witness to confirm my statement. You'll have to take my word that Petrik abducted me."

Another annoying little hum fell past Michel's lips. I was beginning to hate that sound.

"So, you claim he locked you in a crypt with the rising sun. How did you survive that? You wouldn't have been a month old at this time, correct? Newborn vampires can't withstand the sun."

"Believe me, I couldn't. I was burning alive,

about to become a roasted marshmallow when I managed to defend myself." Okay, so that was a lie. The truth consisted more of Sam and Lucy rushing in to save the day, but I refused to drag them into this. "Petrik grew cocky, and I took advantage of that. I attacked him and was able to save myself."

"And how did you manage that?"

This was where things grew dicey. I had to outright lie here, in order to keep Sam's involvement secret.

"Petrik had a blade on him. Once he got close enough to me, I managed to steal it from him. It surprised him, and before he could react, I cut off his head."

Michel's head snapped up, his mouth a perfect O-shape. I saw it in his eyes, the triumph he was about to lord over me. "Are you confessing to murdering Petrik?"

"Anna..." Vlad whispered.

I swallowed and considered my next words. I needed to tread carefully. "No, I didn't murder Petrik. Murder suggests premeditation. What part of he abducted me and tried to burn me alive don't you understand? If I hadn't defended myself, I would have burned to death. I did what I had to in order to save myself. And it haunts me to this day." Also not true. I was glad the asshole was dead.

"Walk me through this again—"

I sighed and shook my head. "Have you ever been burned by the sun, Michel?"

His brows creased. "Well, no, but—"

"Then there's no place for buts here. Tell me what you would have done. If someone locked you in a room with every intention of watching you burn to death. What would you have done?"

"That's irrelevant."

"It's perfectly relevant!" I shouted. "You're acting as though I shouldn't have defended myself. Are you seriously suggesting I should have just rolled over and let the sun kill me? Is that what you would have done? Are you that cowardly?"

"Anna," Vlad snapped.

"No. This is ridiculous." I shot up from my chair and waved my arm at Michel. "They're setting me up to fail this little inquisition of theirs. They want to find me guilty so they can use me as an example for all other vampires."

"I assure you—"

"You can't assure me of shit," I snarled at Michel. "Answer me. Right now. What would you have done?"

"Petrik was a thousand years old," Michel argued.

"And? Does his age mean I should have sacrificed my life for his? Did you forget the part where he was a serial killer? Where he'd murdered thirty-four other women—"

"Human women," Michel stated.

Boom. And that was the truth right there. They didn't give a shit about Petrik's victims because they weren't vampires.

"Human, vampire, who the hell cares?" I demanded. "Or are you suggesting that human lives don't matter compared to vampires? Bet the president would love to hear that. A serial killer is a serial killer. But all you care about is that he was the queen's sire. So the fuck what? Maybe she should have kept a better eye on him then."

"Are you suggesting the queen should have babysat her sire?"

I rolled my eyes. "Don't put words in my mouth."

"She is the monarch of our people and is tasked with so much more—"

"Yeah, yeah." I waved a dismissive hand, my anger still bubbling in my veins.

Michel grunted and tapped his iPad screen. "You said the sun burned you and that you were locked in the cement cellar with the rising sun. After you killed Petrik, how did you escape? How did you avoid the sun and survive?"

"Once I was out of danger, I drank Petrik's blood to heal myself and then avoided the sun's rays until nightfall—"

"Wait, what?" Michel's head snapped up, his face purely aghast. "You did what?"

Oh shit. See, this was the problem with lying! It always got you in trouble in one way or another. I was so focused on keeping Lucy and Sam out of it that I'd forgotten not to mention the whole blood drinking thing.

"Say that again?" Michel pushed. "You said you drank Petrik's blood?"

I swallowed but didn't utter a sound. Somehow, I knew speaking would make this worse.

"Miss Perish," Michel pressed. "Did you or did you not drink Petrik's blood?"

Fear zipped through my veins and lifted the hairs on my arms. I snuck Vlad a glance to find him withdrawn and paler than normal. He stared at me with such a sorrowful expression that I knew I'd screwed up. Bad.

I wrung my hands and turned back to Michel. "I-

I had to. The sun had fried my legs, I needed to heal so I could move and keep out of the rays."

"You're confirming then that you drank his blood?"

It was almost like he needed me to say the words. "I—yes, I drank his blood."

I didn't even see Michel move. One moment, he was seated on my couch, his keyboard in hand, the next, he had me thrust up against the wall with a machete pressed against my throat.

Holy shit. A fucking machete! Where the hell had that come from? And how had he moved so fast? He had to be old to move like liquid silver. But how old? Older than Vlad? Were we actually at the disadvantage here?

"Thank you for your candor," Michel hissed in my face.

"Get your hands off her!" Vlad shouted.

My gaze rose over Michel's shoulder, and I spotted Vlad hovering behind him, about to attack.

Michel seemed aware of it too. He tightened his grip on me and pressed the cold blade harder into my flesh, drawing blood. "Don't. Move."

Vlad froze, fury alight in his eyes. I could read the desperation in his face, knew he wanted to rip Michel to shreds, but couldn't. Not without beheading me. So, this was it then. The vision Vlad had been having. The shadows haunting him.

"Anna Perish, I find you guilty of the murder of Petrik Kamen," Michel announced in a cold voice. "The queen authorized me to deal with you in any manner I saw fit. You are a danger to my queen and our people. I hereby declare your death as recompense for Petrik."

"What?" I sputtered, my fingers opening and closing into fists to keep me from lashing out. If I so much as twitched, that blade would cut clean through to the wall behind me.

"What the fuck are you doing?" Vlad snarled, his voice thick with restrained violence. "If you kill her, I assure you, I will rip you apart with my fucking bare hands."

My bottom lip trembled. I'd never heard Vlad curse before. Somehow, that frightened me more than the machete at my throat.

"Silence," Michel barked. "I suggest you remove yourself from this situation right now, Vlad. You don't want to see this."

A deep and threatening growl rose from Vlad's lips. He sounded animalistic, almost feral.

"I will not ask you again," Michel said, his head slightly turning toward Vlad.

I whimpered when the blade pushed deeper. The feel of cold steel lodged in my flesh wasn't something I ever wanted to feel again. It took every ounce of willpower I possessed not to claw at Michel. *Don't move,* I told myself over and over. *Don't fucking move.*

"We appear to be a stalemate here," Vlad uttered in a deeply aggressive voice. "Believe me when I tell you I will make you regret it if you kill her."

"She is a danger to the queen and to our people!" Michel shouted. "How can you not see that?"

"She did nothing wrong!" Vlad yelled.

"She drank the blood of an ancient vampire! You know our laws. That cannot be forgiven."

Terror infused my body and held me frozen against the wall. Vlad and I had never discussed this outcome. And with how fast everything had taken this turn, I'd never given thought to Michel's age or strength. Maybe he was older than Vlad. Maybe Vlad would lose a fight between them.

"Vlad..." I whispered. "J-Just go."

His livid gaze shot to mine. "Like hell."

Okay, okay. Maybe I could diffuse this situation somehow. Maybe I could change Michel's mind. Maybe I could save everyone's life here.

"How?" I whispered. "How am I dangerous? I

drank his blood two months ago with no negative effects. There's no threat here."

"*You* are the threat," Michel snapped, his one hand pressing harder in my chest, trapping me against the wall like a pinned butterfly. "I see through your lies. You pretend to be innocent, but you're an insolent child who cares nothing for the rules."

"I-I'm a nobody," I stammered.

"A nobody with millions of human acolytes."

Acolytes was a terrifying word. "You make me sound like some cult leader."

"Are you not?" he retaliated. "Your followers fawn over you. They believe every word that falls out of that bewitching mouth of yours."

Bewitching?

"One word from you, and the humans might rise up against us. We are woefully outnumbered. So I can't allow that. I can't allow your manipulative words to bring harm to our queen. She's been our sovereign for nearly three hundred years. And she will reign for three hundred more. Long after you are gone."

Holy shit. There was so much to unpack here, I didn't even know where to begin. "So, this is all about Genevieve then?" *Keep talking. Keep distracting him.*

Michel's eyes flashed with rage. "You will address her properly."

Actually, I wouldn't. She wasn't *my* queen, but it really didn't feel wise to point that out right now. Not while one of her inquisitors was literally trying to murder me.

"What's this really about?" I rasped. "Me drinking Petrik's blood, my vlog, or your natural dislike of me?"

"All of it!" Michel shouted in my face.

He pressed the blade a little deeper. I gasped and pressed myself deeper into the wall, trying to gain an inch of freedom. Pain burned through my throat, but I couldn't focus on that right now. I needed to turn this conversation in a more pleasant direction. Needed to calm everyone down before someone did something stupid—like behead me.

Vlad stepped closer, and Michel responded with another press that had me crying out.

"I truly recommend you leave," Michel said to him. "And before you get any ideas, know that I have a dozen inquisitors stationed throughout this neighborhood. You may kill me after I dispose of Miss Perish, but my inquisitors will kill you before you can escape. Think this through, Vlad. Are you ready to die for her?"

"Unequivocally," Vlad snarled.

No, no, no. I couldn't let that happen. No one was dying here tonight. Least of all, Vlad. "You're seriously going to go through all this trouble for your queen?" I babbled.

"I would do anything for my queen," Michel crowed, lifting his chin as though offended I'd dare doubt his commitment.

I'd heard Marie Antoinette had cast a similar spell on her people when human. She'd somehow commanded a loyalty from her most dedicated people, enough so that one of them had been willing to die in her stead. Maybe that power had carried over into her undeath, given her the power to command such loyalty from her people. If that was the case, doubtful I'd be able to break Mikey's fealty. To him, Genevieve was the sun and the moon.

"Let's think this through. You kill me, then what?"

"Stop stalling," he snapped. "And I will only ask you once more, Vlad, out of respect for you. Leave."

Every nerve in my body came alive, and I panted for unneeded breath to center my thoughts and focus on anything but the pain. Funny, the things panic did to you. The way it warped your thoughts, and made you feel almost human again. Alive. Vulnerable. Emotions I didn't appreciate right now. I couldn't lose myself to mindless terror—no, I needed to remain focused.

"You planned this," Vlad suddenly growled.

Michel's body twitched in response. He didn't deny the accusation.

"I did no such thing. Miss Perish herself confessed to murdering Petrik and drinking his blood. Even if we ignored her so-called vlog, in which she told millions of humans how to kill us, there remains the fact that she's sampled ancient blood."

"But that was months ago!" I shouted again, desperate to drive the point home. "If something was going to happen, it would have already."

"You expect me to believe you aren't also drinking Vlad's blood? You two are lovers, are you not?"

His question startled me into silence.

"I thought so," Michel said. "You are far too dangerous to let live."

I felt it then, the moment his unwavering conviction won this battle. Michel's body shifted against mine, his weight leaning into the blade. I cried out and lifted my eyes to Vlad's. If this was to be my last moment on this earth, I wanted to only see him. Not the crazed lunatic at my throat. I wanted to go surrounded by sweet memories and loving moments.

I opened my mouth to tell Vlad I loved him, but before I could so much as utter a sound, Vlad lunged.

CHAPTER TWENTY-THREE

Holy shit. My life flashed before my eyes.

And all I saw was Vlad. He *was* my life.

Fuck, I hope I didn't die here tonight.

A gust of air whipped by my face, and I squeezed my eyes shut so tightly my face screwed into a horrible knot. But there was no fresh pain at my throat, no agony as my head detached from my body, nothing but literally sweet *nothing*.

I slitted a single eye and found myself standing alone against the wall. The machete was gone from my throat, and Michel missing. For a moment, I had to wonder if I truly *had* died, when the disturbing sound of two animals fighting drew my attention.

My head snapped to the side, and I barely caught sight of Vlad before he charged Michel like a freaking bull. I'd never seen him like this before. So livid and violent. He was always so composed in my presence, calm and gentlemanly. But this situation didn't call for any of those behaviors. I knew of his darker side—I'd seen it stuck on a stick in our front yard back in New Orleans. Lucy had told me the whole story. How he'd ripped Eli's head clean off, then walked away like it meant nothing to him.

But it was different this time. Michel was armed, and I knew from experience that blade was wicked sharp.

Chaos descended the instant the two crashed together. I felt my eternity with Vlad growing shorter and shorter every time he deftly dodged Michel's swings.

I felt so useless just standing there, watching. But what else could I do? Their movements were so fast, *too* fast. Camilla had trained me to fight, but she hadn't shown me anything like this. It made me realize how much further she and I had to go before I could hold my own. The two were literally clawing at each other's throats and faces in a brutal brawl.

In a series of movements I could scarcely follow, Vlad shoved Michel's arm aside, knocking the machete out of the way, then dealt a series of blows that sent Michel staggering backward into the wall. Vlad struck again, but Michel dodged, and Vlad's fist caved through the wall. While distracted, Michel retaliated, swinging out with his machete.

I almost screamed at the sight of that damn blade closing in on Vlad. I rushed forward, determined to help, but Vlad wrenched free of the wall, grabbed Michel's arm, then bent and twisted until it snapped in half.

Michel hardly grunted.

I skidded to a stop and stared at him. What the fuck? How could he *not* feel a broken arm? Or did he just not care?

Vlad latched onto Michel's damaged arm and forced it backward, then grabbed his fingers and snapped them one by one until the blade slipped free. It clattered to the floor, but neither made a move for it. Doing so would break focus and allow the other to sweep in for the kill. Fighting a vampire wasn't the same as fighting a human. Humans had weaknesses that could be exploited, whereas vampires only had to worry about decapitation. Everything else would heal.

I needed to be the one to retrieve the blade. Neither had so much as glanced at me. It would give me the chance to gain control of the situation and help Vlad. With the machete in hand, I only needed one single second and a clean line of sight.

I bounced on the balls of my feet, waiting for the perfect moment to dive in. This certainly wasn't how I'd seen tonight ending, but there wasn't any other option now. Michel had thrust us down this path, and I didn't see this fight finishing without a death. I just needed to make sure it was Michel's and not Vlad's, or mine.

I tore my gaze from the machete in time to catch Michel taking control of the fight. He had Vlad's arms pinned to his sides, his fangs bared as he aimed for Vlad's throat. But before I could so much as cry out a warning, Vlad snapped his head back and smashed it into Michel's face. Blood erupted from his newly busted nose and gushed down his face.

This was getting bad. So very bad.

I needed that machete.

I needed to end this fight.

Then Vlad and I needed to get the hell out of here before the other inquisitors came a-knocking. That was our only option now. This had gone way too far for any other solution.

Michel staggered back from Vlad, his hands instinctively cupping his nose. He hadn't cared about his broken arm, but it was hard to ignore a smashed face. I jumped at the opportunity, tucked low, and dove between the two men. The instant my fingers instinctively curled around the hilt, I snatched the blade out from between them.

I scrambled back to my feet, about to see how else I could help, when the sudden sound of shattering glass rent the night. My head whipped up just in time to catch Vlad sailing through the living room window.

"Oh shit," I whispered.

This was the very last thing we needed, and outside was the absolute last place we wanted to be. Michel's warning about the inquisitors came rushing back to me, and I peered into the darkness, watching as shadows suddenly descended like locusts. We had to move quickly now. Once they got their hands on Vlad, we were done for. I couldn't allow that to happen.

Having completely forgotten about me, Michel climbed through the broken window and stalked toward Vlad. His hands were fisted at his sides, even though his arm hung awkwardly. I had to give him credit for playing through the pain. Unfortunately, I could read the intentions in his body. Camilla had taught me how to analyze an attacker's body language, and I could see it now, clear as day. He was like a walking viper, coiled to strike, and the scent of his fury riding the air only confirmed my assumptions. Without a doubt, Vlad wouldn't survive this fight. Not with a dozen inquisitors barreling our way, not with Michel leading the charge.

I knew exactly what I needed to do to level our playing field. I needed to turn the attention away from Vlad. Keep him safe. Because at the end of the day, that was all that mattered. I could live with myself dying—in a manner of speaking—but I knew I wouldn't survive Vlad's death. And I couldn't let him take the fall for me. No way in hell.

So I repositioned my grip on the machete, then launched myself through the window after Michel.

I could practically hear Camilla's voice in my head, shouting at me to survey my surroundings, map out an exit strategy, *then* attack. But I didn't have time for any of that. Not tonight. Not with Michel bearing down on Vlad.

Michel's position gave me the upper hand. He wasn't facing me and couldn't see my approach. I needed to be quick and quiet. If I so much as tipped him off, he could block my attack and turn the blade on me. Camilla had shown me that move once. Except, this wasn't like my training sessions, and we weren't in a controlled environment. This was terrifyingly real, especially the part where Vlad's life depended on me.

Tightening my grip, I made my decision. The inquisitors were only seconds away. And Vlad's life hung in the balance. With a determined breath, I rushed forward and tackled Michel from behind.

"Anna!" Vlad shouted, struggling to his feet.

I didn't let his voice distract me, nor did I hesitate. Camilla would have been proud. I lifted the machete, placed it against the back of Michel's neck, and *pressed*.

I heard the cut. Felt the blade slice through bone and sinew. Watched his head detach from his body and roll across the yard. Smelled the blood as it poured onto the grass.

My stomach turned.

Before I could climb off Michel, someone grabbed my shoulders and wrenched me back. Unfortunately, they weren't familiar hands.

"Get off of her!" Vlad shouted.

It was good advice because I could feel the heat rising in my throat. I'd never killed someone before. Petrik had died because of me, but I hadn't actually been the one to do it.

I couldn't say that anymore.

This would haunt me forever.

Knowing I'd stolen someone's life.

Deep down, I knew it'd been an untenable situation. Him or us. He hadn't given us a choice, but that didn't make this pill any easier to swallow. For all I knew, he had little vamp babies and a vamp wife out there somewhere waiting for him to come home.

But he never would.

Someone forced me onto my knees in the grass and wrenched my arms behind my back. I was too shocked to focus on them. Too stunned to do anything other than stare at the beheaded corpse sprawled in my front yard. His blood looked black in the darkness, seeping through the soil, creeping toward my knees.

"Whoa!" came an unfamiliar, high-pitched voice. "Did you see that?! She cut that guy's head clear off! Did you see it, did you?"

"Duh! I'm standing right here! Of course I saw it!"

The odd voices cleared the fog, and I lifted my head. My surroundings came roaring back to me. There was so much yelling, screaming, crying. My neighbors, I realized. Except the voices hadn't come from them.

Because of course not.

"When that other dude came through the window, I thought damn, he's done for!"

"I know!" the second voice commented. *"Me too!"*

I followed the sound, then groaned at the sight of two squirrels standing in a nearby tree, clinging to the branches, their tails and whiskers twitching with excitement as they recounted the fight to each other.

"And that blade. Wicked, right?"

"So wicked. Don't go near it."

"Why would I go near it? I'm not stupid!" A slight pause. "Think she's okay? The girl who cut off that dude's head? She doesn't look okay. Does she look okay?"

"I'm fine," came my own thought before I could stop it.

"Whoa! Did you hear that? Was that her?"

"Yeah, that was her! She can talk to us! Hey, hey lady! Can you hear us? If you can hear us, just know you kicked ass! That dude had it comin', you know?"

I groaned and closed my eyes. I *really* didn't need to be talking to squirrels right now. Not when my life was falling apart around me. But at least now we knew for sure that I could communicate with animals, for as much good as that did me.

"Anna Perish!" someone shouted, clicking their

fingers in my face. Yeah, maybe I'd let the squirrels distract me a little.

I jerked and glanced back at the unfolding mess. Vlad knelt in the grass across from me. Glass particles shimmered in his hair, but he looked otherwise unharmed. Thank goodness.

An awkward silence fell over us as the other inquisitors inspected the gruesome scene. There was blood everywhere. The machete, the grass, me... everywhere. Decapitation was a messy business.

God, I was going to throw up.

I caught Vlad's gaze again and held it, all while forcing myself to swallow. He lifted a questioning brow, and I nodded, reassuring him wordlessly that I was fine. My neck had already healed thanks to the infusion of Vlad's blood early this morning and the bottled blood this evening.

But just like Michel had said, there were a dozen inquisitors surrounding us. Damn. This situation had gone from bad to worse in the blink of an eye.

"Anna Perish." Someone clicked their fingers in my face yet again. Made me wanna bite it off. "You are hereby under arrest for the murder of Michel Aubert and Petrik Kamen."

Great. Why not just add Eli into the mix then? Go for a hat trick while we were at it.

"Ohhhh, damn. That sucks. They arresting her?" the stupid squirrel asked.

"Yeah, definitely arresting her. She did kill a dude!"

"Thought you said he deserved it?"

"Well, he did... I think."

"Shut up," I snapped in my head.

The inquisitor remained completely oblivious to the noise in my head. "You will be detained and transported to England, where you will stand trial. Do you understand?"

Wait, *what*? Transported to England? What the *fuck* was going on? Michel hadn't mentioned *any* of that.

"Do you understand?" the new inquisitor demanded.

I didn't understand anything right now. I simply stared at him and blinked. Unfortunately, with Michel, I really didn't think I could claim innocence. Twelve inquisitors had witnessed me kill him.

"What about Vlad?" I asked.

The inquisitor gave my cheeks a sharp slap. "You are under arrest for murder. Tell me you understand."

All I could do was nod, even though my brain was little more than a jumbled mess of thoughts.

"He was going to kill me," I mumbled.

"He totally was going to kill her," one of the squirrels confirmed. "I saw everything."

Somehow, I doubted a court would allow a squirrel's testimony.

"You seem fine." The inquisitor sneered as he slapped a pair of reinforced cuffs around my wrists. "Load Ms. Perish and Mr. Vasek for transport. The queen will want to see to them personally."

The queen. England. Trial. Murder.

Oh fuck.

THEY LOADED us none too gently into a massive van. Except this vehicle had been rigged specifically with vampires in mind. One of the inquisitors shoved me down, chained me to a bench, then pressed a button that activated floor to ceiling stakes. I gasped and squeezed my eyes shut, praying that nothing nudged me into one, like the driver purposely speeding over any bumps or potholes.

Vlad climbed into the van next, and my body relaxed at the sight of him. For a moment, I'd worried they would load him in a different van. He sat on the bench across from me, his gaze locked on the inquisitor handling him. Even I could see the rage within. Vlad was definitely plotting their deaths. Surprisingly, I was perfectly fine with that.

Once he'd chained Vlad, the inquisitor sneered, then slapped the button next to Vlad's head, activating his own personal wall of stakes. "Enjoy your ride."

Vlad didn't respond, and the inquisitor retreated, slamming the door shut behind him.

Finally, we were alone.

I shivered and glanced at Vlad. "So, this is romantic."

His mouth quirked. Glad to see he hadn't lost his sense of humor throughout all this.

"Um, you don't by chance know how to pick handcuffs, do you?" I asked.

"No."

Yeah, I kinda figured that'd be the case. It wasn't a skill in my repertoire either.

The sound of voices faded as the driver fired up the van and pulled away from our house. "I gotta say, this is not my idea of a fun time."

"Nor mine," Vlad said. "Are you okay?"

"I'm fine, I promise. What about you? Are you okay?"

"Not in the least," he growled.

"Are you hurt?"

"No. He was going to kill you."

That was for damn sure. I still felt the cold steel of the blade cutting into my throat, and I suspected that wasn't something that was going to go away soon.

"I'm so sorry that I dragged you into this," I whispered.

"You haven't dragged me into anything, Anna. What don't you understand? I would die for you."

"Right. About that." I shot him a tentative smile. "I'd really like if you could stick around to actually spend eternity with me."

Vlad met my gaze, then smiled grimly. "I'll tell you what. When people stop trying to kill you, I'll stop risking my life to save you."

"Aww, such a romantic," I teased, hoping to lighten the situation a little. I didn't want to think about our coming days. They seemed like they were going to be pretty bleak.

The van hit a pothole, and I gasped, squeezing my eyes shut. This entire vehicle was a death trap. Twenty bucks said they wanted to stake us before reaching the airport. Would probably make this trip a little easier for them.

"Do you see any way out of here?" I asked.

"Not unless we can free our hands."

Hands that were currently chained behind our backs and to the benches. Not to mention, the obscene number of stakes pointed at us. I had a feeling that if we so much as twitched, the driver could likely hit a button that would release every single one of them, effectively turning us into stake cushions.

"Well, this sucks," I announced.

"Indeed."

Vlad stretched out one of his legs and touched my foot with his. I melted inwardly. Would he never stop charming me? I hoped not.

"I think I can improve matters a little bit though," he said.

"Really? Can you get out of your chains? Shift into your bat form?"

"Not in the least. These cuffs are enchanted to keep vampires from being able to shift. I'm not going anywhere anytime soon. And neither are you." He chuckled quietly. "So since we're both stuck here, there's something I've been meaning to ask you, and now seems as good a time as any." He glanced around the van. "What's more romantic than a van full of stakes and chains?"

"A lot of things," I joked.

"Yes, well, our lives don't seem conducive to flowers and picnics."

"Couldn't hurt to try," I said, laughing. "But hey, I'm flexible."

Vlad caught my eye and winked. "Yes, you are."

"Tease."

"I can't reach into my pocket at the moment," he said. "But that doesn't mean I can't ask my question. Anna, you know I love you. More than I ever thought capable. You breathed life back into me and made me remember what it means to feel."

Holy shit. Was this... was he...? Here? Now?

"I've lived an incredibly long time. And no one has inspired me the way you do. No one has stirred within me the things that you do." He laughed quietly. "No one has brought out the worst in me like you do."

"Vlad—"

"Hush. Let me finish."

"Here?"

"Yes, here," he huffed. "Who knows what awaits us in England, and I refuse to miss this opportunity."

Holy guacamole, he was really doing this, right here, right now, when our lives were an absolute shit show.

"Anna Marie Perish"—I was going to kill my

mother for revealing my middle name—"you already know I intend to spend all of eternity with you, so this is more of a formality, but one I eagerly await to hear your answer to. Marry me. Be with me through the good and the bad, the ups and the downs. Love me like I love you."

Oh, I hated him right now. Because the jerk had gone and made me cry, and I couldn't wipe my tears away, not with my stupid hands chained behind my back.

"I—I can't believe you chose this moment to propose," I laughed weakly.

"I enjoy keeping you on your toes," he retorted. "I highly doubt you anticipated this."

"Of course I didn't! No one proposes after they've been arrested and chained up."

"I'm a unique soul."

I burst out laughing. "You can say that again."

"I await your reply," he commented, as though this was just any other day for him.

Meanwhile, my damn chest had grown so tight, I had to wonder if it was about to explode. "I fucking love you, you know that?"

"I had an inkling."

"Are you sure you want to marry me? I seem to attract a lot of trouble."

He stared me in the eye and said, "Unequivocally," reminding me of the answer he'd given Michel before the fight. How the hell did I get so lucky as to find this man?

I laughed quietly, astounded by this turn of events. "Of course I'll marry you, you fool."

An easy smile chased across his face, as though nothing about this fazed him. Not me. My head was spinning. Engaged to Vlad. Dracula. The Count. The legend.

Somehow, he'd managed to turn the worst night of my life into the best. And that was saying something, considering I'd been arrested for murder.

Here was hoping we survived this somehow.

Because I desperately wanted to marry this man.

EPILOGUE

Oh boy, where do I even begin?

I know you probably hate me right now, ending my story here, but honestly, this seems like the best spot for now. Things are certainly grim. Grimmer than grim. They're downright dismal. When I was a little girl and imagined my life, this was *not* the direction I saw it taking.

I don't know what the coming days have in store for us, but I can't imagine they'll be good.

So, here I am again, caught in this mess because someone else tried to kill me. Why does this keep happening? And how the hell are we going to get out of it?

Ever feel like you're the butt of some huge cosmic joke? Like everyone else in the world is in on it, and you're the last one, running to catch up? That's how I feel right now. This *has* to be a joke. They can't actually intend to ship us to England to stand trial for murder.

Yeah, I'm definitely the butt of the joke.

I suppose there's some sort of irony here. That everything I've been avoiding is coming to pass. Makes a girl wonder just what sort of control she has over her life.

Vlad believes we were fated to meet—his dreams told him so. Does that mean this was all preordained? I became a vampire only to meet the love of my life, then be executed less than a year later? There's gotta be some irony there, because half a year ago, humans didn't even know vampires existed.

Now look at me, chained to a vehicle stuffed with stakes. Like, there's literally one resting six inches from my chest. It'll be a miracle if Vlad and I even make it to England alive.

I pray Camilla and Lucy are safe. Knowing they're out there somewhere gives me a sense of calm. I have hope they'll find us. They wouldn't abandon us to these jerkoffs.

But there's also this little voice in my head telling me they don't know where we are. Vlad and I will likely be in another country before they even learn about all this.

I can't think like that.

Happy thoughts, Anna. Happy thoughts. That's the only way we're getting out of this. Because if I let the darkness in for even a second, I might lose myself. And I can't let that happen. I have to stay strong.

Because there has to be something of me left to marry Vlad.

MARRYING DRACULA SNEAK PEEK

I HUM-A-LUM-LUMMED A SILLY SONG. For the unlife of me, I couldn't remember the words, only the melody. I knew it was a Disney song from Snow White, something about wishing for the one I love to come find me, but that was all I remembered. Oh well. The lyrics didn't really matter. I preferred to make them up anyway, if only to piss off my captive audience.

"I'm wishing... I'm wishing..." I sang, horrendously off-key. My mother had always said my voice could peel the skin off an onion—whatever the hell that meant. "For these guards of mine..." My fingers tapped to my imaginary beat. "To fuck off... to fuck off... today... today."

A long, drawn-out sigh came from outside my prison cell.

"I'm hoping… I'm hoping…" I continued, raising my voice an octave. "And I'm dreaming of… the ways that… the ways that… they'll die… they'll die."

I continued humming all while purposely dropping some idle threats and chipper F-bombs along the way. When I grew bored with that annoying song, I quickly dug into my mental library for something I *knew* would piss off Tweedle Dee and Tweedle Dum out there.

"This is the song that never ends," I belted out, tapping my toes against the cement wall. "Yes, it goes on and on, *my friends!*" I shouted the last two words so loud, my voice went hoarse, and the sound echoed through the prison. "Some people started singing it, not knowing what it was—"

"Shut the bloody 'ell up!" One of my guards barked. He whirled to face me and slapped his sword against the metal bars. "Fucking nutter. Can we kill 'er yet?"

A small smile pulled on my lips.

"Just ignore her," the other guard commented, his tone practically limp with boredom.

Considering I'd been abusing them with nonsense like this for six months, I had to give the guy credit. He was steadfast and calm. In all our time together, I couldn't remember a single time he'd raised his voice or cursed at me. That didn't make him a friend, though. I'd overheard his private conversations detailing how he'd love to drain me, just to shut me up. Between the two of them, he concerned me the most. He didn't lose himself to anger like the other one. That made him far more frightening and unpredictable.

"What'll it be next, boys?" I asked, running my hands through my slick, greasy hair. Gross, right? Well, not my fault. The queen was the one who refused to let me leave my cell. Considering vampires didn't require potty breaks, she seemed to feel showers were equally unnecessary. "Beyonce? Or maybe a little Britney Spears? How about I serenade you with a little Toxic? Or maybe Criminal? I feel like I could really pull that one off."

"If you open yer trap one more time—"

"Oh, come on!" I retorted. Tweedle Dee's threats didn't frighten me. I'd learned early on that neither of the Tweedles had permission to enter my cell. And I'd been listening to them for nearly two hundred days now—yes, I kept count. "Who doesn't like music? Or did you prefer the Disney songs?" I twirled a lock of grimy hair around my finger. "I mean, I *am* a Disney princess, after all. Locked away in a tower, singing songs, guarded by two brutes... Did you know Rapunzel lived in a tower? I'm blond, so I guess I could be her. What do you think? Of course, we could just dye my hair black, then I'd be Snow White. She talked to animals, you know. Hmm, maybe I have more in common with her, what with the whole evil queen thing—"

"For the love of everything unholy, shut yer fuckin' trap!" Tweedle Dee shouted. "I swear, if you utter another word, I'm gonna—"

I sat up and spun to face him with what I called my "innocent eyes." Mostly, it just involved me batting my eyelashes. "You're gonna what? Talk me to death? You and I both know the queen forbade you from touching me."

Fury blazed in his dark eyes, and a promise lurked in those depths. One that involved my death. I admit, it amused me. I pushed Tweedle Dee's buttons so much, the vamp had lost all semblance of humanity. Wonder if there was a trophy for pissing someone off so much, they actually wanted to kill you.

"Accidents are known to happen, ya get me?"

"Ooo." I mock-shivered. "You've got me shaking in my boots."

He bared his teeth. "Keep this up, and..."

Laughter slipped past my lips. I'd learned early on how to ruffle their feathers, so I rose to my socked feet and skipped playfully across my cell, all the while singing aloud.

Tweedle Dee's face mottled, and his knuckles bleached when his grip tightened around the sword hilt. I pretended not to notice and instead began performing the Phantom of the Opera musical. I'd never seen the actual Broadway show, but I'd watched the movie starring Gerald Butler—because who hadn't?—so I had something to work with. It wasn't until I reached the second chorus of Think of Me when I heard a familiar squeak. I continued singing, slowly moving into Angel of Music, but my gaze swung to the side of the room where a small, albeit familiar, beast cowered in the shadows.

"Ignore her already," Tweedle Dum commented, his words hanging on the edge of a heavy sigh. "She'll lose interest if you stop reacting."

I quirked an ear and listened to their conversation, all while belting out the Phantom's part in a bass register I sorely lacked.

Tweedle Dee mumbled some crass curse and turned his back to me. He sheathed his sword, then fisted and unfisted his hands at his sides. I'd definitely pricked someone's nerves and wasn't ashamed to admit it. In fact, I felt a small swell of pride. My antics were childish, but hey, they kept me sane. Not that my guards understood that. They thought me well and truly mad, which was exactly what I wanted.

I slowly crept back toward my bed, now belting out the main theme song, and sat on the steel edge. I lowered my hand and rubbed my fingers together, silently summoning the small animal.

Weasley scurried over to me, careful to keep hidden in the shadows, and bumped her soft head against my palm. Tweedle Dee and Dum seemed determined to ignore me, so they didn't notice the arrival of my little friend. Weasley was a common weasel. Nothing fancy about her, other than her cutie patootie face that I desperately wanted to smoosh between my palms. I couldn't, though. It was very important that her presence remain a secret, considering she was my spy.

The tower dungeons were infested with rats, so I'd spent my first month here practicing communicating with animals. But rats were *not* my favorite. Too twitchy and demanding and... well, gross. Just thinking about them gave me the shivers.

But Weasley? She'd sought me out during my

second month of incarceration. How the heck she'd found her way into the dungeons, I had absolutely no idea. But I'd welcomed her comforting, furry face. I had absolutely nothing to offer her, but she didn't seem to mind. A gentle soul, this one. She genuinely enjoyed helping me, and I appreciated that quality like no other.

I drew my hand back to perform an air piano solo, one that had Tweedle Dee cringing.

"Are you okay?" I asked Weasley.

Six months ago, before the inquisitors had stuffed me and Vlad into a plane and shipped us across the Atlantic, I'd discovered I had the ability to communicate with animals. Luckily for me, I'd also learned I didn't need to speak out loud for them to hear me. It wasn't a particularly powerful gift, like shifting or telekinesis, but right now, it was the only thing I had working for me.

"Weasley good!" she chirped in my head. *"Weasley happy to see Anna!"*

"And Anna is happy to see Weasley. Alright, fill me in on everything, Snicker Doodle."

The sound of her humorous snuffling filled my mind and I grinned, even as I continued serenading my guards. She loved her nickname, one I'd given her during a low point in my incarceration. Something to cheer me up.

Learning to mind-speak with animals while talking—or in this case, singing—aloud had taken *so much* effort. To this day, I still couldn't believe what I'd accomplished in my time here.

"Queenie has summoned you! Her men come now. I bite one?"

I had to choke back a laugh, one I disguised as a cough. *"No, no biting. They can't find out about you."*

"Boo. Queenie mean. Don't like."

"You and me both, girlfriend. What does the queen want?"

"Don't know. Only heard her men coming, so came to see you."

I scritched her little head and listened to the sound of her contended purr. *"Guess we'll just wait and see what she wants then. How's Vlad?"*

"Sir Battikins?"

Another laugh rose in my throat. I almost regretted telling her about Lucy and Vlad and the nickname Lucy had given him. Keyword, *almost*. There was something entirely too adorable—and comical—about listening to my weasel-friend call Vlad, *Sir Battikins*.

"He not okay."

Her words sparked fear in my chest. I rubbed the aching spot and stopped singing.

Tweedle Dum shot me a quick glance over his shoulder, but he clearly saw nothing out of the ordinary, because he faced forward again immediately after.

My throat thanked me for finally shutting the hell up. Sometimes these games of mine exhausted me, but they were important. I had to do whatever it took to keep the guards focused on *anything* other than me and my animal friends. If they even so much as suspected us, I'd lose everything. Including my one way of checking on Vlad.

"Tell me," I whispered in my head.

"He miss you. Every time I visit, he darker. Angrier. A black aura around him."

Well, that certainly didn't sound good. I wished I had a way of communicating with him, but since he couldn't speak with animals, there wasn't much I could do. This was the extent of my one and only power. I could hold conversations with them, but Vlad couldn't. And my animal friends couldn't make a spectacle of themselves, otherwise Vlad's guards would immediately notice.

"Any news regarding him?"

Weasley trilled in my head, and her whiskers tickled my palm. *"Queenie only interested in you. Battikins safe for now."*

I considered our situation. There had to be something I could do to show him I was fine and hopefully perk him up. These past six months had been harrowing to say the least, and lonely as all fuck, but we were in this together. I just needed him to hold on.

The inquisitors had taken everything from us when they loaded us into the van, but I stared down at my shirt. My shirt cuffs had once had buttons, back before imprisonment. Now, all that remained was one tiny brown button hanging on by a loose thread. Grinning, I plucked it off and held it in my hand. It was only a button, and yet the thought of communicating with Vlad in *some* fashion bolstered my mood.

I *missed* Vlad. The agony of being separated from him was unlike anything I'd ever experienced before—including death. Right now, I would do anything to see or speak to him, both of which I knew were impossible. For now, this would suffice.

"Okay, Weasley. Can you take this to Vlad? Don't let the guards see you. Stick to the shadows. Just sneak up to him and give him this button."

Weasley's nose touched my fingers, and her little grabby paws snatched the prize from my hands. *"For Anna, I do anything."*

Her loyalty brought tears to my eyes. I quickly blinked them back, though. Sadly, we vampires cried blood tears, and if the guards so much as caught a whiff of that, they'd know something was up. Thankfully, they remained completely unaware of Weasley's scent, but considering the stench of my cell, that didn't surprise me. Blood wasn't the same, though. Much like sharks, vampires were excited by the scent. No need to incite the Tweedles more than I already had.

"What about queenie?" Weasley asked. *"Her men come soon. They take you."*

Fear tightened my throat, but I tried not to show it. "I'll be fine. You wouldn't be able to come with me, anyway. Stay with Vlad if you can. But remember—"

"Stay hidden, yes. Weasley know."

I smiled and stroked her side, reveling in the feel of her clean fur. Strange, the state I'd been reduced to. Filthier than an animal. I tried not to think about it, though. Tried not to think about the condition of my hair and clothes. At least the filth clinging to me was nothing more than dirt and grime, and I no longer had any biological urges. I couldn't imagine the condition I'd be in if I still had to obey a bladder.

"Weasley?"

She stilled against my hand, her head cocked to the side.

"If you can find some way to touch him, even if all you can do is brush your nose against him, please do it. I think he'll understand it's coming from me."

Weasley chittered in my head, then she touched her nose to my palm and backed away.

I rolled my head and stared out the cell bars. The Tweedles stood with their backs to me, their ears primed, but their eyes facing forward.

"Go," I told her.

"I come when you're back. We see each other again..."

ACKNOWLEDGMENTS

As always, I would like to start by thanking everyone who made Loving Dracula possible. Everyone who cheered me on and encouraged me, or just made themselves available on some zoom calls to help me push through when I got stuck.

Loving Dracula had its challenging moments! Parts that made me ready to burn it all down and start again. But around the halfway mark, the story really started to take shape. Of course, that led to massive revisions of the first half, which is stressful when under a deadline. But it strengthened the story overall, and helped me fall in love with Anna and Drac all over again.

Which means it's time for the thank yous!

My wonderful editor, Missy Borucki, who always has fantastic ideas on how to improve a story. The funny squirrels at the end? All her, guys. And it was genius.

My incredibly talented cover artist, Molly Burton, who can take an email as vague as "Um, like book one, but different colors" and design something truly beautiful.

Elizabeth Grover and Jori Buchanan for proofreading and finding all those little mistakes that get missed.

And of course, my critique group for acting as a soundboard and helping me get this book into fighting shape.

Thanks to everyone who helped turn Loving Dracula into a novel! Now it's time to get back to work with more Anna and Drac, in Marrying Dracula.

ABOUT THE AUTHOR

Kinsley Adams is a thirty-something-year-old author who stopped counting when she turned twenty-five. When she isn't writing uproariously hilarious romantic comedies, she's raising her womb-gremlin with the hopes that he might one day become the world's first Supreme Leader (and yes, *Debbie*, that's a Star Wars joke). You can find her online at kinsleyadams.com

If you enjoyed this book, please leave a review! Your support and feedback are greatly appreciated. And be sure to sign up for Kinsley's newsletter at kinsleyadams.com/newsletter for updates on new releases, sales, and more!

ALSO BY KINSLEY ADAMS

DATING MONSTER MAIN SERIES

DATING DRACULA

LOVING DRACULA

MARRYING DRACULA

WOOING THE WOLFMAN

MATING THE WOLFMAN

WEDDING THE WOLFMAN

SMITTEN WITH THE VAMPIRE KING

HOOKED ON THE VAMPIRE KING

HITCHED ON THE VAMPIRE KING

DATING MONSTERS SIDE STORIES

WHEN VLAD MET ANNA

MR. & MRS. DRACULA

MONSTERS & CHOCOLATE

www.ingramcontent.com/pod-product-compliance
Lightning Source LLC
Chambersburg PA
CBHW020250030726
47499CB00001B/133
9781989308486